FOR DOREEN ROBERTS, NANA
(1907 – 1995)

whose incredible stories of escape
taught me the importance of freedom.

A Special Signed Hardback Edition of

RISE

limited to just 50 numbered copies

Kim Lakin-Smith

This is number: 26

Kim Lakin-Smith

NewCon Press
England

First published in November 2019 by NewCon Press,
41 Wheatsheaf Road, Alconbury Weston, Cambs, PE28 4LF

NCP206 (limited edition hardback)
NCP207 (softback)

10 9 8 7 6 5 4 3 2 1

ISBN:

978-1-912950-31-7 (hardback)
978-1-912950-32-4 (softback)

Cover by Daniele Serra

Text edited by Ian Whates
Book interior layout by Storm Constantine

PART ONE

ONE

The sky was on fire when Kali Titian first set foot inside a gunner. One moment the sun beat down, sweat soaking the collar of her uniform and tickling her back, the next she passed through the doorway into a cool, dimly lit corridor smelling of iodine and leather. Chief of Staff, Secretary De Agnes, walked ahead. De Agnes, with his small smug eyes and intent way of peering at her like a doctor conducting a medical, was a bore and overly patriotic even for Kali's taste.

"Naturally, I have briefed the guard on board about your presence," the man was saying over a shoulder.

"I wish you hadn't done that." Kali couldn't hide her contempt. De Agnes had irritated her ever since he arrived at the academy earlier that morning and insisted on inspecting her shared quarters before they left. "I will request a private room for you," he had told her, eying her superior officer with derision. Kali had despised his interference and been quick to tell him so. As now, De Agnes had stared blankly at her.

"It's protocol," he said, a snap in his voice. "And it saves on explaining why you have a foot up on your fellow recruits."

"You're trying to make me feel guilty for the privilege."

"Not in the least." De Agnes glanced back as they walked. His small eyes were almost black in the low-lit corridor. "The Youth Guard are your father's favourite assets, closely followed by National Guard recruits. It isn't a great surprise that he should choose to reward you for excelling at the academy. It also helps that you are a close relative!"

"I certainly have my father's best interests at heart," said Kali with a small flare of her nostrils. "Specifically, his desire that I extend myself beyond the expectations of the average recruit. That is the true reason I am here today."

"I believe that *I* am the reason you are here." De Agnes forced a tight smile. "Captain Hanan is my brother-in-law. As a special favour, I asked him to accommodate you."

"And I have accommodated him. This is not my first invitation to board an active gunner."

Kali liked the way De Agnes fell silent and walked a little faster. She hoped she'd left an overriding impression, preferably one of deep dislike.

Half an hour later, De Agnes had disembarked, and Kali was belted to a riser stool behind the navigation station and semi-circle of data operatives, finally left to her own devices. The bridge was self-sealed; no windows gave out onto the battlespace. Instead, the screen walls swarmed with spectroimages of the vast battleships belonging to the United Dominions alongside hundreds of thousands of smaller, attendant craft.

Kali pictured the gunner's exterior rings in blurring revolution around the central hub, the steel strips of warheads shooting off the craft and punching through the thin atmosphere. Having only recently embarked on mesospheric conditioning training, she struggled with the extreme shifts in momentum. Her brain felt as if it was being pushed to the very back of her skull as the motion of the ship gave off a cloying hum. She had the disconcerting sense of being entirely separate from her body; were she to stand, Kali knew she would topple off balance.

In contrast, the crew kicked into a balletic flow of motion. Hands worked the banks of gel patches. Eyes swept over screens. Voices called out feed codes and affirmatives. As one syncopated organism, crew and gunner navigated the heaving battlefield of the mesosphere.

Kali shifted her attention to the captain. The man was young and slick, with numerous pins of valour crowding his lapels. His riser stool was set into a circular track in the middle of the bridge, allowing him to control the vein frame of the gunner's stem – a central trunk of alloid bio cells powering the ship. Nearby, a pair of dalma plates sat locked into their twin ports, moving and syncing data around the ship like a peripheral nerve interface. Despite her disorientation, Kali felt a tingling sense of awe. She had studied her father's development of dalma plates and data flow gel technology at the academy, but to see it in action was breath-taking! The plates, which resembled large rectangular stones, sandwiched together, their intricate pattern schemes lighting up as the gel coursed through them. It brought about such an exhilarating mix of emotions and physicality – nausea, wonder, pride, alarm...

Her breath was snatched away as a tremendous grinding noise reverberated through the bridge and the entire hull bucked. One moment, Captain Hanan was in synergy with the stem, the next it was spasming. Kali clung tightly to the sides of her stool as the bridge lifted on its axis and descended in a series of violent drops. Pitching in her harness, she lost all awareness of which way was up. Flushed with adrenaline, she tried to get a grip on her body as her mind screamed *I don't want to die like this! Not as an observer. Not when I'm a parasite on board!* To overcome the instinctual panic, she forced herself to imagine she was back on manoeuvres, just another recruit practicing wargames. Breathing in, breathing out, breathing in, breathing out. *Refocus*, she told herself. *Make your father proud.*

She forced her eyes wide open and centred them on the activities of the crew. One man was unhooking his harness and running in zigzags as he made his way over to the captain; she recognised the green cell icon of her own unit, the bioengineers, stitched to the man's sleeve. He was soon elbows deep in the stem, searching for the source of the breach.

Her focus was distracted by the weapons unit of the guard as they worked to earn the sliced atom badges on their sleeves. The ever-shifting canvas of the walls lit up as enemy craft returned fire or flew out of range. Kali wanted so very badly to dash over and launch every weapon in the gunner's arsenal – anything to obliterate their attackers and make sure she kept on living. Instead, she stayed bolted to her stool. Back soaked with sweat.

Mind struggling to focus.

The ship gave another great shudder as it apparently took a second impact and the whole hull revolved again a rapid three sixty, crew continuing to work the navigation desk as they strained in their harnesses. Kali struggled to hold onto the contents of her stomach until the great motion rings and the black exoskeleton of the hull stabilised and the bridge stilled.

"Corporal Titian!"

It took Kali a moment to realise she was being addressed by the captain.

"Get over here and act as my Second! My engineer's out of action."

Kali forced her mind to sharpen. The senior bio-engineer was bleeding profusely from a head wound as the medics hauled him onto a riser stretcher; it took her a moment to work out that he must have been wounded during the manic rotations of the ship. She met the captain's eyes – they had a grit to them – and she remembered her father's words: 'Get to know the scale of the ship you one day hope to captain,' as he stood, blocking out the sun, valour pins shining on his spotless epaulets.

She undid her harness with clumsy hands and, using the backs of the occupied riser stools as handholds, she made her way over.

Captain Hanan shook the buckles of a long harness belt that fastened into the same channel as his mobile riser stool. "Hook yourself up, Corporal! I don't want to lose another engineer if my ship starts bucking again."

Kali did as commanded. Once she was buckled in, the tether allowed her to lean back on her heels and examine the stem, floor to ceiling. Functioning as the gunner's energy capacitor, the stem was fat as a baobab trunk and protected by a slick membrane of gel – that pale green bio-constituent fusing algoid fuel and alloy fibre for conduction. Just visible beneath its gel skin, the vein frame pulsed with an arterial beat.

Kali swung around to the far side. A section of the stem had lost its slickness and was bulging slightly, coloured purple like a bruise.

"Stem's blocked! A faecal thrombosis."

The captain rolled around in his riser stool to arrive alongside her.

"Cause?"

"Anaphylactic build-up of waste deposits. I need a tool roll…"

Captain Hanan was already handing her a kit and Kali squatted down to undo the roll. She selected the two-bore scalpel. There wasn't time to glove up.

Resting a hand on the bruised stem – firm to the touch, it reminded Kali of her grandmother's favourite boa snake – she lent in and pressed the tip of the scalpel to the bulge.

"This will get messy."

Captain Hanan's face was rigid. 'Kill my ship and I'll have you shot, no matter who your father is,' he seemed to say without words.

It was an empty threat. Kali could strangle the man with her bare hands and not a soul aboard would dare stop her.

For now, she focused on the bloated stem and made a deep incision. Gel gushed from the wound, a dark green bile instead of the usual soft emerald colour. Kali returned the scalpel to the roll, reached between the veins and flesh folds she had exposed and manoeuvred the inner tendons apart as if threading her hand between harp strings.

"Pass me the suck syringe – no, not the mini. I need the wide-gate." She took the instrument from the captain. He had asked her to be his Second, but, in truth, that role now fell to him.

Slamming the wide-gate syringe into the clot, Kali heard a bilious slap of air as the needle pierced the thickened gel. She yanked the plunger free and forced her hands around the mass. The clot felt dense and resinous – a direct result of the blast to the lower levels shocking the system. A gunner's metabolism would usually turn off the damaged parts of itself like tourniqueted limbs until it came safely down to land. Rarely, the damage was precise enough to aggravate the bio materials and cause damage at a cellular and mechanical level. Bio-engineering was a modern science and Kali was still in training. She knew enough, though, to ease the clot carefully from between the web of sinews and past the vein frame. It released in a rush of bile and flesh threads. She tossed the mass aside.

"I need the wound mesh." She took the adhesive strip from the captain and slid it into place; seconds later, the mesh had imprinted over the gash.

Kali lent back from the newly coursing stem. At her feet, the slop of surgery soaked her boots.

"Well done, Corporal." Behind the captain's cool gaze, Kali caught a flicker of relief. "Now, unhook and get yourself to the viewing level." Captain Hanan pointed up. "I'll give you a moment to get seated before we light up the skies."

A minute later and Kali was strapped into a riser stool a level up from the bridge, on the viewing platform. In front of her, a wall of toughened glass-sheet gave out onto the heavens. Above, the black shine of outer space, all around, the wild blue of the mesosphere. Hard ahead lay a battleship of the United Dominions on the defensive. Sentinel craft packed around its sides while the gunner poured down a torrent of firepower.

Kali pressed her hands to the glass, feeling her breath rise high in her chest as she watched the gargantuan show of strength by her father's fleet. Moments later, the battleship splintered apart, sprites of fire shooting across its hull. The might of her father's fleet reflected in her eyes.

TWO

A Decade Later

Sometimes, when the wind dropped, and the city was unusually quiet, Mohab would listen to the sounds of battle taking place high above. Seated on the narrow balcony outside his suite of rooms at Nilreb Universium, Mohab would stare up at the night sky with its tracery of stars and he would see flashfire and, occasionally, the ghost of a gunner. Nothing rained down; the sifter satellites atomised the debris. He couldn't help wondering though; *how much damage can a sky take before it falls?*

Tonight, though, it was his mind on fire. "I will keep my head down," he had told the universium's dean earlier that day. Professor Michaele was a good man – one of those rare citizens who did not recoil in his presence nowadays. Michaele was Bleek, but he also taught classes on ethnic displacement and assimilation, and wrote, at least theoretically, of a route to peace.

However, that afternoon the dean's hands had appeared uncharacteristically nervous and stroked the downy hair at the back of his head as if self-soothing. "The universium cannot sustain this level of interrogation, Mohab," he had said, somewhat mournfully. "Already, we are forced to redact so much, to censor our symposiums and research. We have pitifully few students as it is! Everyone's too busy waging war." Michaela blinked rapidly. "Our Vary students have all been sent away or restricted to their home districts. You, Mohab, are our final fugitive."

Mohab had not liked that title. "Hardly a fugitive! The universium has been my home for five years. I have cooked for you, Professor, in my rooms. We laughed over spine pig steak and yams. You showed me the notes for your next paper."

Desperation scraped the inside of his throat. "Remember, you talked about your love for Vary diction? Our south westerly colloquialisms – how my mother used to say 'bide the riverbed' whenever she thought we were in danger."

"I remember. I still intend to write that tract. But you, Mohab, you have not my privilege of birth. You are the last Vary in residence here and I fear for your safety."

"Fear for me more if you throw me out! The Vary slums are riddled with lungrot. All but my father were lost to it. You know this, professor."

"And I know your father is the single most important man to your people."

"A choice that was his to make and I have no part of!" The injustice gnawed at Mohab. Pain and loss floated up to the surface. He pictured his dying mother's face, eerily beautiful in its fragility, and he recalled the damp wheezing of his young sisters before the terrible silence.

Another emotion niggled at him. It had the shape of anger, but the sharp corners of guilt. "I just want to keep my head down and stay," he said, knowing his time had run out.

He left the professor's office with a handshake and a promise of one last month of lodgings. "To give you time to make alternative arrangements"; the dean had given him that much.

But in the hours since, Mohab had found himself incapable of action. He didn't want to leave the universium. He didn't even want to acknowledge he was Vary any more. Instead, he stayed out on his balcony, sipping cherry wine and watching the sky flash as if the moon and Mama Sunstar crossed swords up in the heavens.

The sudden insistent smack of a fist against the door forced Mohab from his stupor. Agitated, he called out, "I am sleeping. Go away!" and then, when the noise persisted, "Okay, okay. I'm coming! Quiet now. Quiet."

Turning up the fire lamps as he went, Mohab crossed the sitting room to the hallway. He paused at the door, listening to muffled voices he didn't recognise on the far side.

"Open up!" said a voice out loud. "Open up for the National Guard, Mohab Tredora."

Fear jolted Mohab's every nerve and he was forced to double over, clamp a hand to his mouth and do his best to fight the nausea. Momentarily, he considered escaping over the balcony railings. He could lower himself down to the balcony below and so on for seven floors until he reached the ground... Only, he also knew with absolute certainty that the guards would hunt him down and execute him on the spot.

Instead, he did the only thing he could. He reached out with a trembling hand. Thinking of his mother and his father, he thumbed the gel patch to roll the door aside and let the monsters in.

THREE

"Wrists."

Kali reached out her arms as the guard grabbed the next pair of cuffs on the chain running the length of the wagon. He snapped them around her wrists and she shuddered as the internal plungers rested snugly against the pulse points.

Turning her head to one side, Kali tried not to think about the consequences of those lethal 'nicks' being activated. The bio gel which was the life force for so much of her father's new technology had also been harnessed as a weapon; pulse stimuli could solidify the gel inside each nick into a cutting edge, designed to slice the wearer's veins. The guards wore master key versions of the wrist cuffs. One brush of a finger could activate a solitary nick or all those within a five-metre radius; Kali knew the hardware inside out.

Her neighbour showed his big teeth. "What you staring at?"

"No talking!" The guard put a hand to his belt where a beater stick was holstered.

Kali tried to ignore the male and all the other prisoners manacled to either side of her and opposite.

"Name?" The guard stared out from beneath his visor. His eyes were the chalky green of the thermal baths in Geno; 'well-bred,' her grandmother would have whispered cynically by her ear. His breath was perfumed with schnapps.

"Lieutenant Kali Titian of the ninth Geno Battalion," Kali said without inflection.

"Welcome aboard, Lieutenant. I presume this is your first time travelling in a livestock bay, but there aren't enough haulage wagons running to transport you separately from the Vary. The ground is breached by fifty-two new splinter zones between here and Nilreb. You may not know that, given your recent

16

incarceration at the courts." His gaze skimmed her throat, collarbones, and down. "Out here, we've baked bone-dry." He slipped a finger into the front of her vest and skimmed left to right, his rough fingernail grazing each nipple. "Not enough release for all that hot swollen air. Eventually it busts through."

Kali stayed motionless and tried to disconnect from her own body. 'My father will personally tear out your spine', she might have said once. Except, her superior ranking would have made it unthinkable for a subordinate guard to even behave in such a way. Today, though, shoehorned into that stinking can of Vary livestock, the rules were very different.

"560-59 secured!" hollered another guard from the far end of the gangway.

The man left off groping and secured Kali's nicks to the bolt bar at her back. Turning on his heel, he marched down the gangway between the shackled prisoners and joined his fellow guard at the airlock. Through the gloom, Kali saw him thumb a gel-patch on the wall. A synthesised voice listed off the cargo.

"593 Vary, 1 Bleek. Engaging engines."

The guards shut themselves safely away behind the airlock.

Back in the haulage wagon, the lights dimmed, and Kali tried to rest against a narrow perch. Her guard stared in as the porthole misted with slow gas escaping vents in the floor.

Kali held out as long as she could. But at last she was forced to gulp for breath and the gas filled her airways like syrup. It was a nauseating sensation, designed to keep her precariously pitched between consciousness and blackout. All around her, prisoners dozed and ricocheted off each other's shoulders as the wagon's huge wheels set in motion. Kali's view seesawed between the bolted roof and the marsh glow along the gangway. The wrist-nicks pulsed in time with her heartbeat.

The Nedmac Delta covered an area 72,000 clicks north of the city of Geno. Rifts formed daily, the lava bubbling up in red rivulets that cooled to form unstable folds of basalt. The haulage wagons wove in and out the creases, dirtying the air with their blue-black smoke and gripe of sandy engines. Inside the livestock bay, the slow gas stabilised the temperatures of the occupants. Kali nodded in her cradle. Chained either side, Vary snored or murmured. Time stretched, the wheels long since retracted to allow the car smoother passage through the plateaux's crosswinds. Every so often, the levy-ports buffeted on contact with an air pocket. Mostly though, the caravan might have sped over water.

It was evening before the guards returned. Coming to as the slow gas feed cut off and the atmosphere clarified, Kali screwed up her eyes against the flood of artificial light. The closer she came to consciousness, the worse the nausea became. Everywhere she looked, Vary emptied the contents of their stomach onto the grid-floor.

She was still drowsy when a blast of water struck her in the face, forcing her to gasp against the sting of it. The guards advanced down the gangway, hoses looped over their shoulders as they washed the vomit into gutters under the prisoners' perches.

"Ironic they have to throw up their last good meal!" she heard one remark. The kid looked like a recruit; Kali could smell the zeal.

"Uh-huh." Kali's guard stopped in front of her. He grabbed hold of her chin, turning her face side-to-side. "You didn't throw up, Lieutenant? Takes a strong stomach to rise above slow gas."

The other guard laughed. "What do you expect? Given her origins."

"I think my compatriot means that as a compliment, Lieutenant." The officer grabbed a fistful of hair and pulled her head back. Kali blinked against a torch shone in her eyes.

"I'm my own strength. My origins have nothing to do with it," she said into the light.

"Is that what you said in court too?" sneered the younger guard.

Kali's guard shifted the torch to the other man's face. He nodded down the gangway. "Far end of the wagon. There's a clutch of Vary suffering from lungrot. Oldest is a shitter. Get along there and help out."

Whether the new guard felt the snub or not, he didn't react, just pulled out his beater and expanded its baton in one sharp swipe, then strode away.

Kali's guard chuckled under his breath as he scanned her data on his gel set and moved down the line.

Left behind, Kali blinked rapidly in an effort to clear her eyes. Struggling to swallow, she licked her lips for any residual water from her hosing down. The taste was grit and sweat.

A sudden tremendous grinding noise rolled towards her from the far end of the wagon. Kali braced herself. The huge chained wheels were descending in preparation for braking; she recognised the hiss of pneumatics and waves of vibrations from her time piloting personnel wagons. Next moment, the wheels touched down and locked, and the wagon filled with the colossal roar of braking and the back-burn of engines.

Finally, the noise eased off. The guards let go of the handgrips in the roof space over the gangway and continued hosing down the prisoners.

Geno. A sprawling citadel carved out of the basalt after the great Skyfall five hundred years earlier. In recent times, the inky sands of the Rudein Desert had been blasted into glass-sheet. Now, the ancient caves were lost behind the reflective manmade towers, pressing skyward like crystalline Bravais lattices.

Kali knew she and the rest were not destined for the city. Emerging from the depths of the haulage wagon into the searing sunlight, she looked for the skyline of Geno but saw only miles of ash and sand. She had been raised by a grandmother behind Geno's obsidian walls, her father forgoing his parental duties in favour of state politics at Capital Hall in Nilreb or diplomatic duties abroad. Between the ages of sixteen and twenty-six, she had fallen in line with her father's expectations. Then she started thinking for herself.

All the same, Kali wondered how her father would react if he could see her now, manacled and forced to stumble forward with the rest. Would he grieve for the child she once was? Or would he nod grimly and say, "Here you are, then. You got what you wanted."

"Want me to trample you underfoot?" The prisoner behind her laughed. "Then again, that's more your style, Lieutenant."

She glanced back. It was the male who had travelled beside her. His fat teeth were uncomfortably near.

"I said no talking, you Vary bastard!"

Forced to go with the flow of the herd, Kali was propelled into the prisoners in front as the guard who had dealt with her forced his way through, beater readied. Whether it was the effect of the slow gas or being led as part of the chain gang, she flinched when the beater slammed into the Vary male.

The prisoner clutched his side. The second blow produced a snap of bone and a strangled cry.

'You are a fool!' she wanted to shout. 'Showing spirit will only make them beat you harder!' Instead, she steeled herself as the beater plunged into the soft parts of the male – the belly, a cheek, the genitalia.

"Do you want him dead?" she said instinctively. Her years as a Lieutenant did not wash away as cleanly as a floor full of vomit.

The beater was under her chin in seconds, forcing her head back. Familiar now, the stench of schnapps on her guard's breath. He flecked her face with spit. "Kill him, quarter him, roast him on a stick, it's my choice! Perhaps you'd like to tell me otherwise, *Lieutenant*?" Her title – once a weapon – was now a slur. The guard laughed, showing the small neat teeth of the Bleek – a sharp contrast to the Vary's molar-filled jaws.

Despite the cold shine to the man's eyes, Kali wasn't afraid. "I have no opinion on the matter."

The beater strained at her throat. "Yet in spite of your

circumstances, in spite of your time as a decorated member of the guard, in spite of your father, you speak." The man leaned in. "You are as low as Vary, lower if there were such a thing. Your betrayal has cut your people to the bone."

Forced to her tiptoes, Kali focused on the boundless sky and tried to tune out the pain. *If I were to die straight away, it would be a blessing. Anything to avoid the horrors of what is to come!*

The guard stepped back and she collapsed to her knees, dragging in aching lungful's of air. Her world turned red as her focus oscillated between the bare ground and the punished male. His face was bloody and swollen.

"Lieutenant Titian." This voice was new. Quietly intense. Like a whisper from a lover.

She scrabbled around on her knees to face a fresh batch of guards. Amongst them was Micha Joltu, formerly a high-ranking official at the Imperial Courts, now Camp Commandant Superintendent. Blinking away the dizziness, Kali recognised him from her father's dinner parties. "You held my hand once. I was nine. You showed me a magic trick." She pressed a hand to her throat, choking with the effort of speaking.

Joltu nodded. "You were desperate to tell me about all the swallows you had shot earlier that day. Brimming over with pride to have slaughtered so many." His eyes shifted to the guard intent on violence. "There is a mind we may yet use in the Speaker's son. Don't be so quick to break his body. That's an order." He stared down at the injured male before turning his back on the scene. "Get these prisoners processed."

The guards encouraged the crowd to move on. Kali stole a glance at the male who had been beaten. Blood, blacker than her own, stained the dusty ground.

"Goodbye," she said. Because no one else would.

FOUR

The city was filmy with heat. Grizmare Titian did not want to be taking high tea up on the roof garden of the Red Orchid hotel. She wanted to be seated behind smoked glass-sheet, at home preferably, a generous glass of sour gin in one hand, the other smoothing the luxuriant fur of Josphire, her favourite maw cat. Instead, here she was, pushing puffs of flower grass around a plate and drinking something sparkling and minty. A few feet away, the roof garden's famous fountain kept up its infuriating racket, the candy-green water cascading over the featureless black figures like the flow of nations it was designed to represent. That the fountain was still intact was ludicrous! How long had it been since relations between Bleekland and its neighbours soured? Ten, eleven years? Grizmare scowled at the fountain and willed it silent. At the very least, she would leave a message for her son and have the thing dismantled before her next visit!

"I have got around to reading High Judge Titian's novel, *Our Holy Nation*." Mrs Harriot Zoorbiah nodded in self-approval. Her hair was a mass of tight white curls and pale-yellow ribbons; a ridiculous choice for a widow of almost ninety, thought Grizmare. "It is quite a remarkable tract," Harriot went on. "A bible for our times."

That was the final straw! "Do stop your gibbering, Harriot! If the Sisters of Gothendore hear you talking like that, they'll have you crucified before you can even think to call on that daughter of yours playing politics at Capital Hall!"

"I am merely suggesting there is a spiritual quality to the book. I am enthralled by the principles which underpin it. The strengthening of our national ideology, the Clean Breed plan…"

Grizmare maintained her hard stare and Harriot gave up her defence. She waved a lace fan in front of her pink face, trying to waft away attention.

"Clearly my son inspires. Just look at all this!" Grizmare threw out an arm to suggest not just the elite roof terrace, but the soaring black towers of Geno. "He works tirelessly to resurrect this great nation from the dust, to free us from the yolk of national debt. But even my son cannot control the ground beneath our feet! There is something futile about his efforts. As if our downfall is preordained."

"And you advise Harriot to watch her mouth...?" Morantha, Countessa De'Shone of Varbardige, leaned in, the beading of her exquisite shawl twinkling in the sunlight. "If a father can sanction his daughter being condemned to life – and, yes, inevitably, death – in one of those hideous Vary camps, then how will he chastise his own mother if she speaks out of turn? I know you don't like the idea of your son as a living god, but, face up to it, Grizmare, he's the equivalent."

Morantha had a way of cutting to the heart of a situation, Grizmare gave the woman that much! All this hero-worshipping was precisely why she tended to hide her feelings about her son. She had given him life, raised him in an orthodox neighbourhood, sold her ancestral linens to fund his studies at the Nilreb Conservatoire for Modern Architecture, and watched him build an empire from a steel will and glass-sheet. But the instant he threw it all away for politics and warmongering, she knew that he was lost to her.

"I don't know why you insist on dining in this insufferable heat, Morantha!" Tugging at her stiff collar, Grizmare wondered why she had settled on such an uncomfortable outfit. Even now, seated here with Harriot and the countessa – both women of social standing and matriarchs of their own political dynasties – she still felt like that young mother, piecing together conservatoire fees from the scraps of her past.

Morantha sat up stiffly. Hers were still the purest, crystal-green eyes Grizmare had ever seen, even if the jet-black hair was dyed now and the skin papery. "The Red Orchid remains the best restaurant in Geno. Do you read the datastacks? It is very hard to get hold of desert otter meat now. I dine here because the quality of the food is outstanding."

"The rest of these parasites have a different motivation." Grizmare arched her pencilled brows as she took in their fellow diners – high ranking National Guard, a good many fellow octogenarians draped in finery and self-importance, and a handful of brats with trust funds and palaces. "Everyone likes to boast how easy it was to get a table. Mostly, they want to rub shoulders with me on the off-chance the man himself might put in an appearance."

"You are terribly sure of your own importance today, Grizmare." Harriot was apparently still sore after being chastised for her patriotism. She pushed her plate away and patted her curls. "High Judge Titian has washed his hands of Kali. Morantha and I thought it would do you good to show your face at the old haunts. Remind folk exactly who you are."

"And who am I, Harriot?"

"The mother of High Judge Titian, of course."

"Nothing more?"

"What more is there?"

Grizmare drained her glass and grimaced. "If I have so much power, how come I'm being forced to drink this... piss?" She caught her companions' mock shock and revelled in it. "I rather like to think I was someone long before I squeezed the High Judge from between my thighs." She unhooked her cane from the back of her chair and, leaning heavily on the handle, got to her feet. "I cannot abide this wretched heat any longer. I have shown my face and now I am ready to return to my empty nest, having been abandoned for the crime of being irrelevant to that self-same son this nation is so intent on worshipping! It is how I like it. I do not need this grotesque display of worth, or these turgid flaps of desert vole or rat or whatever it is they're serving." She jabbed her cane towards the fountain. "I certainly don't need that infernal din."

"Stay, Grizmare." Harriot's plea was half-hearted.

Morantha gave a limp wave. "Go then. You are in danger of putting out the sun with your ill mood. I will call on you in a day or so, when you are not being subjected to daylight and hopefully better company." A smile formed on the countessa's cosmetically fattened lips.

Grizmare gave a curt nod. Turning her back on the two women, she set off for the elevator to street level and her waiting driver, the taps of her cane counting out the steps.

FIVE

Abbandon. Home of the wretched.

Kali knew the statistics. Five thousand Vary tucked away from the rest of Bleekland, protecting the country from their inherent leeching. Walking through the gate, her throat bruised from the pressure of the beater, she felt awash with the fear of the Vary. Mothers clutched children to them, repulsive with their long arms and blockish teeth. The males trudged alongside, as if it took every trace of self-preservation to persuade their feet to carry them. Guards pulled on smoke sticks, relayed news from the outside, and made liberal use of their beaters.

As if watching a government data reel, Kali took in that the camp was enclosed by two high fences of slice-wire; if the wrist nicks failed for any reason, there was the backup of the patrols between the fences and guards' towers either side of the gate. More than enough manpower to contain the Vary! Even now, shuffling forward with the rest, she couldn't help but feel an instinctual, perverse burst of pride.

They passed a giant sink hole where the sounds of sledgehammers reverberated through the air. The camp had a basalt quarry which supplied the stone-wool production at an onsite factory; given her past connections, Kali had been privy to the camp's schematics when it was designed. She understood the value of stone-wool as thermal insulation for tyre components, construction materials, and the mesospheric craft her father was relying on to help him win the war. The ground might be splintering beneath their feet, but in the skies it was a level battleground.

Further along stood a large stable block, smelling of gorse grass and sweetly vegetative manure. Kali heard the *hoo-hoo* of razingstock and the clap-clop of the spread hooves that helped them navigate sand and dusty ground. The complex ropes of the animals' bridles and other tack hung off nails on the outside of the stable wall. A row of sand-sledges suggested the razingstock worked the quarry.

The sight reminded Kali of her childhood home in Geno – a grand glasshouse with a desert garden which had taken so much watering. At the far end, her grandmother's zoo housed a miniature oryx, a family of desert otters, pock pigs, tiger dogs, several rare species of maw cat and a large aviary filled with cactus wrens, megapodes and parakeets. As a girl, Kali had suspected the creatures tended to die, cooped up in the heat as they were. Or perhaps she had just underestimated their brief lifespans.

Judging by the position of the sun and the faint ghosting of the moon, Kali put it at mid-afternoon. Her thighs ached from the strain of perching inside the haulage wagon while the tingling in her arms told her that the nicks at her wrists were that bit too tight. She was thirsty – so very thirsty – and needed to pee. She also knew with absolute certainty that there was no use complaining. The urine felt hot and achy inside her. Voices came to her in waves. "Varber iubită, Louanne, Louanne." *Enchanted beloved, Leanne, Leanne.* A Vary song which her grandmother had sung on occasion, her excuse being, "You don't have to be friends with a man to hum his music." Kali always thought it the most ridiculous contradiction.

A second group of Vary moved towards them, singing the old songs. Kali found the sound strangely comforting. Had her grandmother's convolutions rubbed off on her? If so, she hoped to channel even a tenth of the woman's strength for what lay ahead!

The two groups passed one another, the newcomers staring at the camp prisoners with wild desperation. She wondered what scared them more – seeing their fellow Vary so emaciated or realising that it was possible to look that way and still be alive?

Kali clutched her belly on instinct, feeling for the small fold of fat there. While conditions in the labour camps were not discussed openly in polite society, there were always rumours of her father's true intent, which was to work and starve the Vary into extinction. How long until she was just a slip of skin?

At last, they were herded inside a large hall at the municipal offices. The weakest Vary were picked off and steered back outside the moment they arrived. Kali remained bunched in with the rest. Her eyes stung with sweat and fatigue.

Every wall was billboarded with propaganda. 'Beware Thy Neighbour!' declared one poster and showed a pair of Bleek housewives on one side of a wall and a repellent Vary crone listening in the other side. Another announced, 'Do Not Shirk From Work – Keep The Blood Pure', a clear and pointed reference to the sluggish ways of the parasitic Vary. Both sentiments were as familiar to Kali as breathing and she still felt a kinship with the principles. Her world had been so regimented even before she joined the National Guard, so direct in terms of who belonged where and why. She missed the simplicity.

"Females to the right. Males, stay where you are. Children, to delousing!" said a Gothendore sister, wearing the black habit of her order and oozing condemnation.

The family groups proved the most difficult to part. Beaters were used liberally along with threats to fire wrist nicks on the spot, for individuals and the entire group as one. Eventually the females were forcibly moved on, leaving the children behind, wide-eyed and trembling. More of the Sisterhood materialised, as if from the walls. They steered the children out the room with tight efficiency. As for the males, Kali saw the grease over their eyes and wondered what it was like for Vary to balance their innate savagery with this most fundamental of affections?

The Commandant Superintendent addressed the remainder. "You will register with the clerks. Give your name, address, age, and occupation. You will surrender all personal possessions. You will speak only when spoken to. At all times, punishment will be swift and administered with force. After your medicals, an existing prisoner will lead you to the barracks. Tomorrow you will be assigned duties appropriate to your previous employment." He held out his hands to indicate tables running either side of the room. Behind sat rows of clerks, the data code of their gel frames pulsing.

The Vary queued up in front of the clerks. Kali found it eerie – the steady trudge of males in line, the stifling of coughs behind hands. Vary tested her patience; she wanted to shake each one by the shoulders and shout, "Why did I fight for you? You are nothing more than they say you are!" At the same time, she saw the un-cried tears in their eyes and it was as if their souls were trying to wade through sludge. Then she felt shaken anew, because she was thinking in terms of Vary possessing souls. The idea made her flinch and dig her fingernails into her palms.

It was her turn to step up to the table.

"Name." The clerk stared at the gel frame.

"Kali Titian."

The woman looked up. "Titles," she said rather sourly.

"Lourdes Marquis VanGuard the Third. State Daughter of the High Judge of the Bleek Nation. Excommunicated 7.1.5059."

Kali gave her personal information as it was requested. She was a bio engineer and First Lieutenant in the National Guard. She had six years of active duty, followed by a post dedicated to home security at Capital Hall in Nilreb. Her betrayal of the information she had been entrusted to protect resulted in a lengthy trial at the Imperial Courts. For the crimes of espionage, treachery against her people, and pollution of the datastacks, she had been sentenced to life imprisonment at the labour camp, Abbandon.

The clerk imputed the information with tight taps of her fingers. Kali kept her nails cutting into her palms. The pain gave her something to focus on.

Mohab came swimming up to the surface through an ocean of pain. Voices bled in and out.

"He should not have been beaten so hard."

"My apologies, Commandant General. The guards were forced to keep this one in line. If action had not been taken, the entire herd might have played up."

Mohab became aware of pressure at his neck. The toe of a boot, lifting his head.

"How easy it would be to let him die here in the dust!" A deep breath. "But he is the Speaker's son and I will not make a martyr out of him."

The boot pulled away and Mohab's head hit the ground.

six

Groff was in the Wash Hall when the call came down the line. Overhead, the ducts belched out clouds of sulphurous steam. Condensation formed on the men's skin; they scrubbed themselves with fistfuls of ragweed, desperate to wash off the stink. Fire lamps spattered and gave off an eerie crimson glow. The shadows of the men stretched high over the walls.

"I've only just got naked..." Groff hurried to ball the ragweed and scrub his underarms. He worked the plant matter at his neck, the crack of his backside and around.

"Groff. Get out here now!" The loud clunk of a makeshift beater sounded against the pipes.

Groff tossed the ragweed aside and ran through the sluice, the dirty water stinging his raw skin.

"I am dressing now!" He struggled into the coarse pyjamas of the prison uniform. The neon brand of a Perversionest glowed on his left cheek.

Hurrying along the corridor, he found the block chief leaning against the doorframe, makeshift beater in hand.

"Hey Suckgap. Looking as handsome as ever."

Suckgap had become Groff's new nickname ever since he came up against two blockers – those prisoners, like the block chief, who acted as unpaid thugs on behalf of the National Guard, and who would have sold out their mothers for the chance to bunk up separately from the majority. He had lived. His two front teeth had been lost.

Groff cocked his head. "Can't all be a lady killer like you, Block Chief."

The larger prisoner gave Groff's cheek a hard poke with the tip of his beater. "Got a funny on you, Suckgap? Aren't you the comedian? Now cut the shit and get to the infirmary. Order of the Commandant Superintendent."

"The Superintendent?" Groff's eyes widened with panic. He grabbed his boots, and with a nod to the block chief, started for the external door.

"Suckgap!"

Groff turned around slowly. In Abbandon, the wrong response cost people their lives.

"Put your fucking boots on."

"Yes, Block Chief." He struggled with the worn leather, pulling on one lace too hard so that it broke off in his hand. Tucking the remains of the lace down the side of his boot, he made it to the exit and hurried away.

A former razingstock shed, the infirmary was cramped and hot, with back windows looking over the firing range. Groff suspected far too many Vary had lain in their sickbeds watching the retribution of the guards on those who failed to keep up or didn't obey orders quickly enough. Rather than fire a man's nicks and make him bleed out on the spot, it was more convenient to have him fall into the curved guttering out on the firing range. Once he was dead and drained, another prisoner would lift the body onto the next passing cart to the furnaces and hose down the mess. A pragmatic solution which kept the firing of rock shot to a minimum, helping to keep the camp calm and a method in place for larger culls.

The firing range was empty. The sky beyond was purple and yellow. Dusk was setting in.

"Eventide, Groff." A Gothendore sister looked up as he entered the ward. She soaped her hands in a washbowl, rinsing off blood.

"Eventide." Groff pressed his tongue to the gap between his teeth.

"It has been quite the hectic day." Drying her hands, the sister eyed him. "Where have you been, Groff? We've had three expire from lungrot and one die in childbirth. The infant was stillborn, cord wrapped around its throat like a monkey tail."

"I was in the wash hall. Before that I was sent to the factory to act as a Second for one of the engineers in the loading bay." Groff scratched at his hairline. He had a headache. After a while, the clamour of the machines had worked away at his nerves.

"The block chief sent you to the factory?"

Groff was distracted by the cry of the patient in the nearest bed.

"Sister! Sister, please help me!"

The patient's lower body was hidden beneath a thin blanket. Where his chest was exposed, it looked as if his ribs were attempting to work their way out.

The sister didn't flinch, just kept up her hard stare while Groff admitted that the block chief had sent him to the factory. In part, he had been grateful. He needed relief from the suffering he witnessed in the infirmary now and then.

"Fucking blockers! If I had my way, I'd pop all their nicks and volunteer to scrub the bastards' blood from the ground myself." She spat onto the floor. "Who knew there could be such an abomination as a Vary with power? The hell hag Demonia herself must have a hand in it."

Groff didn't know what to say. Mostly, he was left alone by the blockers, but they were violent men who terrorised their own kind even more successfully than the guards – had to or else risk being stripped of their status and returned to the barracks. Fed to the same dogs they had kicked earlier.

He plucked at the hem of his vest. "I don't know much about the block chief and his men. As for Demonia, I don't know much about her either."

"Don't know much about anything, Groff!" The sister grimaced inside the stiff folds of her wimple. "If I didn't know better, I'd say you were simple. Probably better off that way." She snorted. "Maybe the blockers feel sorry for you."

"I don't think anyone is safe from bad men." Groff looked at the floor. "Except the sisters, of course. Your Lord Gothendore smiles down on you."

"And punishes those with whom he is displeased." The sister

nodded curtly towards one of the low beds. It was occupied by a
man – what was left of him, at least. His face was swollen like a
spoiled rind fruit while the bones of his arms and shoulders sat at
awkward, ragdoll angles. It amazed Groff that tiny *pop-pops* of
breath still escaped the bloodied lips.

He gave a low whistle. "Poor bastard probably won't last the
night."

Already in the process of walking away, the sister said over a
shoulder, "He'd better, Groff. The Commandant General wants
him alive and it's your job to keep him so."

Perhaps the Vary males were still in medical, naked as piglets
while their weight and height was recorded by the sisters. Or
perhaps they were already fed and watered and tucked up in beds
in the barracks. Kali wasn't sure why, but a tender part of her
hoped the males were sleeping. She envied them that temporary
darkening of the mind.

Separated off from the rest, she was led across a wide-open
space that served as an assembly yard and in through the door of
a glass-sheet accommodation dome. She felt a disorientating rush
of familiarity as the baking ground gave way to heat-regulated
tiles and the glaring sun was exchanged for shade. Architected in
her father's modern style, the dome was arranged in a spiralling
corridor with rooms feeding off. She could smell fresh coffee and
spiced meat cooking. Fire lamps spattered on the walls while
laughter reached her ears. Such a foreign sound now! Down the
spiralling corridor, she was ushered into a large oval office. The
guard left the room, closing a set of tall white doors at his back.

Kali waited opposite a highly polished wetwood desk. Eddies
of cool air escaped the ceiling vents, chilling her shaved head. For
the first time since leaving her cell back at the courts, she was
alone. The fact was strangely unsettling, as if the layers of numb
resignation she had built around her might dissolve and she
would be left raw and exposed. But then the double doors
opened and closed again briskly, and she sensed herself under

scrutiny once more.

"How was your journey?" The Commandant Superintendent shook off his jacket and hung it over the back of his chair. He went to a side table and poured a glass of wine from a decanter. Taking a seat behind his desk, he eyed her over his glass.

Kali stared back across the desk. "The slow gas made the Vary sick."

"And you? Did it make you sick, Lieutenant?"

"No," she said, and with measured emphasis, "I am no longer a lieutenant."

"Because you rescinded on your vow of loyalty to the Bleek nation. Because you spread poison through the government metadata. Because you infected our infrastructure with your lies." He took another sip from his glass.

"Yes." *What more was there to say?* She had hacked her father's data farm and stood back to watch the syntax crumble.

Joltu relaxed into his chair. "Why did you attempt to corrupt the datastacks?"

Kali fell back on her court testimony. "I did not consider it an act of corruption. I wanted the working man in this country to step back and consider what we hope to achieve with our segregation of the Vary."

"You are a Vary sympathiser."

"I do not see myself that way."

"You believe their incarceration is necessary?"

"Their incarceration, no, their deportation, yes. Back to their homeland of Raestan, or any other country where they are welcome. They weigh us down. Bleekland must be allowed to thrive. But..." She drew breath; it still hurt her to betray her father's secrets. "There must be recognition of our linked past. We cannot simply seek to erase the connections between our people, no matter how much High Judge Titian may order it."

"How curious you are, Lieutenant."

"How so?" She rubbed at her forearms, just above the nicks. The skin was tender.

"I believe your manifesto called for the acknowledgment of a debt and the decriminalisation of the Vary assault on our national resources."

"I do not consider it an assault. I consider it the inevitable outcome of the Vary presence in this country. They eat, drink, breed and die within these borders." Kali felt her blood rise at the idea – a familiar response to the pestilence. But there was also the nagging need to move against the violence of her father's Pure Breed solution. She had an urge to sink her fingernails into the skin at her wrists, but the metal nicks were in the way.

"You also proposed the need for official escorts to ensure the Vary's safe passage into neutral states. As if the National Guard are sitting about with their feet up."

"How is your wine, Commandant Superintendent?"

The mask of congeniality slipped. The man was instantly on his feet. Coming around to her side of the desk, he grabbed Kali around the throat with one hand. She was tall and athletically built, but he was larger. Forced to her tiptoes, Kali struggled for breath.

Joltu brought his face close. He smelt of wine and smokesticks. His fingers bruised her trachea, even as his voice stayed soft. "I sit and drink my wine because the day is almost at an end and the swine are in their sties. I cannot slit all of their throats without being ordered to, and so I watch them die, diseased and wasted. I am not without pity, Lieutenant. My men and I abide the malnutrition and decay under our noses. Every day I ask myself, when will these swine finally *die*? It gnaws at the part of me that was a child and hated to see suffering. I long to be rid of the Vary too, Lieutenant. Long to be rid."

Joltu breathed heavily. The hands left her throat and Kali doubled over, wheezing for a second time that day. Any indignation she might have felt was overpowered by an internal voice which told her she deserved this treatment. "I am... proud of my... heritage," she told the Commandant Superintendent between gulps for air. "Nobody's blood is purer."

"Which makes the betrayal all the more acute." Joltu dragged a hand across his lips. For a moment, Kali thought that he might strike her. Instead, he returned to his chair behind the desk and sat down heavily.

She soldiered on. "The point I'm making is that I had no desire to betray my own people. I just believe there is a better way to deal with the Vary."

"Deal with? You mean, a better way to treat them."

"If you see it that way."

Joltu stretched back in his chair, fingers locked behind his head. Kali felt a strange coupling of sensuality and brutishness in the man. The constraint in his voice was at odd with his spread legs and physicality.

"Teach me, Lieutenant. How should I see it?"

"I could not persuade a jury of my good intentions. I doubt you are any different."

"I may be very different, Lieutenant. Despite appearances."

He was sneering at her now, Kali was sure of it.

"A copy of my testimony is in the public records."

"I have it here, in fact." Joltu rocked forward and swivelled his gel frame towards her. The load-code was encrypted. He punched in a passkey and the data clarified to reveal a document headed with the insignia of the High Judiciary – a howl hawk with claws wrapped around a scroll and a dagger, representing Bleek mastery over knowledge and defence. It was the convolution of that message into censorship and Vary genocide which had motivated Kali's rebellion.

"This says you 'sought to expose an underbelly of murderous psychopathy in the National Guard'. And – your words again – 'Awaken the Bleek nation to the exploitative and financially exhaustive housing of the Vary in labour camps while provoking fresh debate on the cleansing methods at interpersonal, municipal and state level. Also, to acknowledge a technological debt…' The rest is redacted." Joltu narrowed his eyes. "Quite the fan of words. Grand concepts too. What did Daddy think to your revolt?"

Kali lifted her chin. "My father was disappointed in me. The same way he was disappointed when his wolf hound soiled the study rug with its dirty paws. In that case, my father led the dog outside and shot it between the eyes. Some would argue I got off lightly."

Joltu didn't look like he believed her. Or did the idea of a father soliciting his own child's public punishment sit uncomfortably with the Commandant Superintendent?

"Well, Lieutenant Titian. Regardless of how you arrived here, my job is to treat you no differently to the rest. Except, you are different, aren't you?" He brought his wine to his mouth, breath misting the glass. "I despise your presence in this camp. If I deal with you kindly, I'll be accused of coddling a traitor. If I abuse you, what's to say your father may not decide to come for his princess once he thinks the lesson has been learnt? What then, if you return a broken woman?"

"Then my father will delight in the fact."

"And will he?" Joltu maintained eye contact. "Break you, I mean."

Kali didn't answer, and the Commandant Superintendent gave a snort and shook his head. He tapped the gel frame and her case history vanished. "You have been assigned duties in the Construction and Bio-engineering department of the factory. We may as well make use of your brain while it is still lively. Your nights will be spent in the barracks with the Vary males. I suspect you may survive longer that way. A Bleek Lieutenant responsible for the forcible deportation of hundreds of Vary young may not fare well in the company of the womenfolk. The men may yet find a use for you." His tone had an edge.

"I'll take whatever treatment is due to me," Kali said, newly fearful of the words.

"Will you?" Joltu searched her face. Apparently, he didn't find what he was looking for. Getting to his feet and striding over to the doors, he threw them open and signalled a passing guard.

SEVEN

Kali knew death; she had grown up in the shadow of her mother's. She also understood that, sometimes, death was essential for the greater good. The first time she'd tested the theory, she was seven years old. Her father had just returned to Geno from Nilreb, having been recently appointed to the role of advisor-in-chief in a cabinet reshuffle and this was one of his rare home visits. He was still capable of tugging off his own boots at that point. Still happy to bounce her on his knee.

"So, your grandmother tells me old Jimney died."

"Granny loved that maw cat more than you love me. She fed it bits of razingstock jerky. Stroked its nasty fur where the scabs grew. Old Jimney bit me once." Kali showed off the tiny worm of a scar on her left index finger.

"The cat is dead now. Aren't you sad?"

Kali shook her head vigorously. "It was made fat by Granny feeding it all that jerky. Jerky is my favourite." She sucked the tips of her fingers. "It smells like you."

"I smell like jerky?" Her father raised his eyebrows in mock alarm. But then a new thought must have struck him, and he lost his playful edge. "I am like this country, once handsome and well fed, now suckled dry." He swaddled her tight in his arms, one ear pressed against the chest so that she could hear his muffled breathing.

Her father released her and he looked so serious that Kali thought he must have hated old Jimney as much as she did. She decided to push her luck.

"But you will tell Granny not to feed the jerky to her cats?"

Her father gave her a reassuring squeeze. "I will insist Granny stops immediately or I will have her throat cut." He did a good impression by sticking his tongue out a corner of his mouth

39

and splaying the fingers of one hand near his neck to represent squirting blood. Kali enjoyed the joke and laughed a great deal.

But she still hadn't answered her father's question. "The dead cat? Granny said it was her oldest, so you must have known the thing all your life. Granny even shed a tear, and who knew she had any liquid left to squeeze from her body. But you are unaffected?"

"Things die. They're old or sick or greedy."

"Greedy?"

"Like old Jimney."

Her father held her gaze. "Kali, did you kill old Jimney? I know how much you enjoy shooting garden sparrows from your bedroom window."

Kali didn't know how she felt about her father's suspicions. Did he like the idea of her doing away with the ugly cat – in which case she should confess? Or was he disappointed in her savagery? She thought a moment, and in the end settled on a version of the truth.

"I caught Jimney with his nose in that bag of bobbit poison in the gardener's shed. Next day he was dead."

"Greedy," her father affirmed. He stared past her to where the wall of smoked glass-sheet gave out over her grandmother's glorious garden; taking stock of her reflection, Kali thought that she looked like another maw cat, curled up on his lap.

Her father pressed his knuckles to his lips and sighed. "You are right, Kali. Greed is a form of death. It happened to this country before you were born. The greedy bankers promised to pay back debt that became almost insurmountable after the great Skyfall. The greedy politicians wanted to stay friends with the other countries draining us of geothermic energy and water from the hot springs until our land was dry and desolate. And then, of course, there were Vary. Incapable of any valid contribution, they swarmed our land, devouring everything in their path. They are the epitome of greed."

Kali wiggled on her father's lap. "Granny says Vary keep pots full of grease which they use to cook their dumplings, and it is using this same oil which keeps up the stink."

"And your granny would know, having abided that foul boy next door all these years." Her father made a hack sound in the back of his throat.

"Boy?" Kali sat up in confusion. "The only person who lives next door is Mister Thatchett, and he's old. Ugly too."

"And he's Vary."

Kali clutched to her father. "How do you know? His teeth are all gone!"

"The hands." High Judge Titian flexed his fingers. "Next time you see Mister Thatchett, look at the hands. Look for the fingers being slightly longer than normal, and how the knuckles stick out. The nails too. They are slightly thicker and tend to flake."

This was new information for Kali. She went back to sucking her fingers, but her father slipped her off his knee. Even at that tender age, she understood his mind had turned elsewhere.

"To bed now, Kali. I will see you again the next time I am in Geno."

Kali wanted to cling on to her father's leg and beg him to stay. But she knew it would be pointless. There was a whole other city that her father called home, and so many demands on his time. As her grandmother would complain, "Your papa is masterminding Bleekland's resurrection from the ashes. At least that is what he is always telling me."

She leaned forward and kissed his hand. "Goodnight, Papa."

Her father didn't reply, just stayed staring out onto the garden, a deep groove running down the length of his forehead and between his eyes.

Years later, Kali stood at the entrance to the male barracks, the familiar stench of death in her nostrils, and wondered what had happened to that man who bounced her on his knee and told her fairy stories.

The Vary stayed in the shadows of two rows of crowded

bunks with a narrow gangway between. As if realising there would be no attack on the Bleek bitch with them around to witness it, the blockers sloped off, kicking at the dusty ground and spitting aside wads of contraband tobacco.

"They leave the door open at night?" Kali heard her voice catch. She had ordered armies, but the Vary on mass were unknown to her. What diseases did they carry? The stench of so many in close quarters was nauseating.

She heard murmurs. One of the number said, "To aid air flow", and another, "Where is a man to run to?"

A man? Kali was confused for a moment. She did not think of Vary in terms of men and women, only males and females. But she understood the sentiment. What use was there in escaping through the door when blockers lay in wait and guards who could activate every wrist nick on the spot, not to mention a double fence of slice-wire and the black desert beyond?

She cleared her throat. "I am to be housed here. My name is..."

"Lieutenant Kali Titian. Yeah, we know." A male strode towards her, long arms dangling as he walked. Kali had the measure of him in an instant; a bruiser – most likely an ex dust hauler. The job tended to attract physical types, being filthy, exhausting work that attempted to fight back Mother Nature on the streets of the cities but paid well.

Now that they were starting to speak up, the Vary crawled down from their bunks and stood in huddles, easing the kinks from their necks. In close quarters, Kali saw how inexorably thin they were. Skin clung to their bones like wet silk. Would they have the strength to kill her? If they rushed her as one, she would not be able to fight them off.

It appeared that her death sentence was to be carried out by one individual. The bruiser grew up out of himself and spread his arms. "What do you make of your new home, Lieutenant? Not quite what a State Daughter is used to."

"It is not. Labour camps were originally intended to house

EIGHT

Mohab dreamt of beasts rising from the fire pits in the north, their golden wings coruscating under sunlight. The beasts unleashed a torrent of sound – high pitched cries and yelps, low mews which hurt the soul, and, now and then, the snap of an order to "Be quiet!" Rising through the sludge, he tried to claw his way back below consciousness but couldn't keep a grip. His eyes flickered open.

"Thank fuck you're alive!" A figure leaned over him, backlit by a guttering fire lamp.

Mohab blinked. His throat was red raw. He tried to swallow and broke into a coughing fit.

"Steady now. I set your ribs with green paste, injected it myself and while I'm a trained nurse… Well, it's not an exact science." The man showed a gappy smile.

"Not sure you should have bothered." Batting the man's hands aside, Mohab struggled to sit up. He found himself in a room lined with narrow beds, most of which were occupied. A number of ghostly figures drifted around the ward; Mohab recognised the black habit of the Gothendore Sisterhood. As a student, he had taken a summer job as a gardener at The Holy instance of St Marie in west Nilreb and seen for himself how the tended to attract those with a violent predisposition. In place of prayers, he had witnessed a barrage of spite against the poor. In place of caring, he had witnessed cruelty towards the old and failing. He was grateful his unconscious body had been in the hands of this strange man with the gap-toothed smile.

"Not like I had a choice," his personal nurse was muttering. "could have steered you towards a happy grave, I would have. The Commandant General himself demanded that I keep you

So here you are with the rest of us miserable souls.

criminals. Their recent use is not something I sanction."

"Spoke out about it too from what we hear." The bruiser jerked his head towards the others.

"I did."

"And now are brought here, same as the rest of us. Only –" His eyes narrowed. There was a nasty twist to his mouth. "You aren't the same, are you, Lieutenant? Headed up a guard battalion since you were old enough to piss in a pot, I shouldn't wonder." A finger elongated and pressed into Kali's shoulder. "We pricked your conscience at last, did we, Lieutenant? Question is, how many Vary did you round up or execute in the years before?"

"Five-hundred and ninety-two." Kali didn't blink.

A gasp rolled back through the barracks.

"Five-hundred and ninety-two arrested?" The bruiser's hand dropped to his side. Even he balked at the idea of touching her.

"Five-hundred and ninety-two executed. Not by my hand. It is a task for lower ranking officers. But authorised by me during official raids."

The bruiser's eyes became glassy. It was a strange display of hurt or hatred, or both, thought Kali. As if the male was overriding his stunted capacity for emotion.

"You don't get to rewrite history just because you say a few pretty words about Vary and upset your daddy…"

"That's exactly what she gets to do." The voice was weak but had a force to it that reminded Kali of her father's. Whoever it was that spoke had a settling effect on the Vary. They crept back into their niches.

Narrowing her eyes, Kali peered into the darkness and made out a solitary low cot tucked under a razingstock manger. A trembling hand signalled her over.

"You'll go see the Speaker if you want to survive the night." The bruiser stepped between her and the exit, a pointless move but Kali understood power play, even in their pathetic circumstances.

She approached the elderly male on the cot. His hair was very fine and his fat teeth were all missing, like her grandmother's neighbour, Mister Thatchett, all that time ago.

"I didn't think a father could treat a daughter so," said the man in a coarse whisper. "The message you distributed across the datastacks was hardly treacherous to the Bleek; it simply advocated gentler means of our removal. I do not understand the severity of your crime. And now you are put among us as punishment, the people you have spent so long trying to destroy."

"I was raised to follow orders. It takes time to grow an opinion." Kali felt awkward standing over the male. Warily, she crouched down so that they were on the same level.

The male held up a finger and choked into a rag. He patted his chest. "Did he say goodbye?"

"Are you still referring to my father?" Despite the chill from the open door, Kali felt her cheeks grow hot. "He is the most excellent of men, a strategist and a patriot. I never expected him to support me through the trial."

"And yet you published your affidavit anyway."

"He has his politics and I have mine."

"So you admit it was a political act?"

"Of course it was political! What kind of question is that?"

"You do not need to rile so easily, Lieutenant." The male gave a weak chuckle. "We still aggravate you. And by we –" He pointed towards the bunks. "I mean, Vary. You have no love for us. We are other to you. But there is something in your conscience which says we are alike enough in our use of speech and coherent thought to deserve better treatment."

Kali rubbed the heel of a hand against her forehead. She didn't find it easy speaking to this male. He looked like the beast he was. The words he used, though, they were elegant and organised. It was unsettling. He was exactly the kind of individual the authorities sought to weed out. That *she* had sought to weed out.

"You are the Speaker," she said in dawning recognition. "I've read your tracts."

She had also spent a great deal of her time in the Guard rooting out members of the Resistance, those Bleek men and women who risked their lives di pamphlets the Speaker had put his name to. The trans attempted to bridge the cultural divide, detailing financial input to the Bleekland economy, the cont Vary aesthetes to the country's arts programmes – Eustang Holt, famed for his neuro linguistic philos the soprano, Octavia Drethoan, who sang at High Ju inauguration before her imprisonment – as we specialisms in seismic mining, micro surgery, bo None of it had any effect. How could it? The Ble afford to be swayed by sentiment. They had invested High Judge Titian's ideal; to believe otherwise woul their actions towards the Vary were motivated darker than patriotism. Instead, those who dis words of rebellion were rounded up and execu labour camps like Abbandon to pay for their crim Speaker himself had been arrested too.

The man struggled to clear his throat. "Their is barbaric," he hissed. "*Your* treatment of us was

"It was." Kali recalled the scores who had d She tried to feel more, but the deaths were met the male's rheumy eyes questioned in a way tha What did he see? An ally? A monster?

"Find her bunk space, men, and leave her more at the hands of her own than ours. In will have victory." He chuckled hoarsely and the laughter turned to choking.

Kali heard each squeeze towards death lungs. She walked between the rows of males hut where she found space had been made f squalid bunks.

Welcome to Abbandon!"

Mohab looked down at his coarse pyjamas uniform. Blood had seeped through the knee of one trouser leg. His left eye felt swollen. A molar was missing; he prodded the gap with his tongue. It was hard to find a part of him that didn't hurt.

The nurse kept jabbering. "My name is Groff, and what can I tell you, Speaker's son? They made a mess of your face. Far as I can tell, the one who went for you had no intention of stopping. It was the Commandant Superintendent who intervened. I'm sorry, but it would appear you are meant to suffer more at the guards' hands before Mama Sunstar delivers you."

"I put no trust in the old mother." Mohab touched the criss-crosses of thread running the length of one cheek, surprised and afraid of the damage.

Groff nodded sagely. "Pain will dent a man's faith."

Mohab snorted. "I'll curse the Bleek to kingdom come, but I put no store in religious hocus-pocus. Power comes from words... or maybe that's my father speaking." His hand fell from his face. He watched the sisters drift between beds, mumbling incantations. "Maybe these witches have enchanted me."

"Sisters can be more terrifying than the guards." Groff chuckled softly. "Witches? I like that. The cackling kind who steal children from their beds." He might have said more, but their whispering had attracted the attention of one of the order.

The sister moved towards them in a ripple of blackness. "He's awake then? Groff, your nursing skills remain up to scratch."

"Not so much nursing as gluing him back together."

"Can he eat yet? The sooner he can eat, the sooner we can have him out of here."

"I can eat. Shit and fuck too if the mood takes me." Mohab's throat spasmed and he bent forward, choking and spitting phlegm into the bowl Groff provided.

"I'd expect nothing less of the Speaker's son." The sister folded her arms. A fly buzzed nearby and she slapped it out of the air. "Groff, get him black bread and a cup of sour. We had better fortify him given how the Commandant General has taken a particular interest in his health. I will take a sample of the dissenter's blood to keep on record."

The sister reached into a top pocket of her habit and produced a suck syringe. Mohab forced himself to stay still as the sister took hold of his arm. A pneumatic puff left a burn circle where the blood had been vacuumed. Mohab shuddered, which seemed to please the sister. She pocketed the suck syringe and blood core with a superior smile.

"You think a suck syringe is bad, you should see a pair of nicks activate." She knocked her nails against the metal band at his nearest wrist."

Turning on her heel, she left his side in a whisper of skirts and condemnation.

"Yes, I am not an imbecile, Tula. I know my son is very busy. The whole country knows High Judge Titian is fucking busy! All the same, I've been trying to speak to him for three weeks now. Am I to believe he has not one minute to spare for his own mother in all the hours he dedicates to everyone else?"

Grizmare heard the silence stretch across the gel line.

Just as her patience was about to snap, her son's personal secretary launched into the familiar platitudes – all about how important Grizmare's call was to High Judge Titian, how he talked about her often, and how strong she was in mind and body despite her advanced years.

"Tula, enough! I don't need your brownnosing. If my son has decided I am no longer worth his time, then at the very least, can I rely on you to deliver a message?"

"But of course, Madam Ti..."

"Tell High Judge Titian his mother says he's an asshole. That should get his attention. And when you've done that, tell him to do something about that ridiculous fountain on the roof of the Red Orchid hotel. It's an eyesore and I can't stand the noise!"

Grizmare swiped the connection out.

✗✗

Years earlier, Kali had played with a ball and racket on the forecourt of her grandmother's estate as a child, when she heard a raspy voice call out to her.

"Kali! Come over here, girl. Come, come!" Mister Thatchett, the neighbour, peered through the bars of the front gate like a beggar wanting coin.

Kali screwed up one eye and squinted over, wary and irritated by the interruption.

"Come, come. Your grandmother said you will help me out with my boxes, and now's as good a time as any."

Kali did not want to leave her ball game, especially not to help the creepy old man next door. "My father says you are Vary." She spat out the word *Vary*, like something unpalatable in her mouth.

"Then your father is a clever man for stating a fact."

"I'm not meant to talk to you." Her father's judgment against the old neighbour certainly suggested something to that effect.

"I'm only asking you to help me fill some boxes." Mister Thatchett pointed to his house, a neat block of white glass-sheet at the bottom of the driveway next door.

"My granny says I have to help?"

"She did."

Kali kicked the ball aside and threw down the racket. She really didn't want to go with the old man, but the idea of going against her Granny Grizmare's wishes was even less appealing.

Mister Thatchett's home turned out to be phenomenally warm. When Kali remarked on the fact, the old man told her it was on account of his parents being born in Raestan, the sub-tropical motherland. He showed off dark gums in place of teeth. "It's even warmer in Raestan than here. The heat can boil a man alive!" He gave a low chuckle as he led the way. "Mama Sunstar needs the odd bit of suffering now and again. It keeps her fires stoked."

Kali followed at his heels, up a flight of stairs and up more stairs, to a circular living room. At least half of the space was given over to large sealed boxes. The other half was full of open boxes alongside a small mountain of curios, books and clothes.

"Are you going away, Mister Thatchett?" Kali rather hoped so.

"Yes. And no. I'm fortunate to have an old colleague settled in Augland. I've decided to stay with him for a time. It would be nice to think there may come a time when I return." Mister Thatchett turned his rheumy eyes on her. They were the grey of chipped rock and had a black ring around each iris. "There are events taking place which suggest it would be unwise for me to stay. This" – he held out one of his big hands to the round room and its contents – "has been my home for several years. Geno? I was born here. But your father and his kind see things differently." He waved his hand to suggest it didn't matter. "Let the young stay young as long as possible. That's how I see it. No reason to fill your head with all the nonsense."

Kali wasn't sure she understood what the old man meant. She jutted her chin into the air. "My father is High Judge Titian."

"And judging by that grin of yours, you are proud of the fact." Mister Thatchett shuffled off to the back of the room and disappeared behind a wall of boxes. He started tossing items over the wall to Kali while talking. "My son, he tells me. Stay. Work it out. The trouble will pass. No need to exaggerate. No need to alter course."

He sent more objects over the wall and Kali made a game of catching them – a black and grey flag with a sun embroidered at the centre; purple cord with yellow fringing which she wrapped around her waist; and more embroidery on banners, handkerchiefs and gloves, even a pair of shoes.

Mister Thatchett emerged suddenly. He carried a large brown leather book under one arm. "My son is a big reader, but he does not see the signs of what is to come." Setting the book down on top of one of the closed boxes, he tapped his nose. "I've been here before, though. When Vary had to register on a separate data stream forty years ago. And before that, when we had our own churches, water channels, grocery stores, story screens, schools, doctors, nurses, surgeons... There was even a time we had to register to own animals. But, pish!" Again, Mister Thatchett gave a weak wave to suggest it didn't matter.

"I use the sanitation room for girls. Boys have their own room," Kali said knowledgably. "That's what happens because boys and girls have different bodies."

Mister Thatchett folded the flag. He handed it over. "Here. Don't unravel it. Just put it in on the bottom of that open box there." Turning his attention to the gloves, he searched around for pairs. "So, I am a boy and you are a girl, and that's why we are different."

"Yes." She nearly fell into the box as she reached to pack away the flag. Recovering, she watched Mister Thatchett thoughtfully. Wasn't it obvious there were other differences between them?

Mister Thatchett threw the balled pairs of gloves at her. "I suppose your father would have you go along with his doctor generals and declare some are human and some are not." He shook his head and pointed at the sash around her waist. "Take that off now. It's sacrilegious to wear it without having a commitment ceremony."

She undid the sash and folded it into as neat a square as she could manage. "Why have you got it?" she asked, and added the sash to the box.

"It has been mine since I was nine years old and said my vows to Mama Sunstar." The old man gave a sad smile. "Long time back. Before I lost my mother, same as you. My commitment ceremony was a good day. We ate sugar cream pie, all us youngsters, and we sat at long tables with our families and tied on our sashes, and ate and drank and sang the old songs." He cleared his throat and started to sing, and Kali was surprised to find she knew the words.

"Varber iubită, Louanne, Louanne." *Enchanted beloved, Leanne,*

Leanne.

"My granny likes to sing that song!"

Mister Thatchett chuckled. "Grizmare never did abide by the rules. Have you noticed that about her?"

Kali had, although she wouldn't have thought to put it into words. She just knew that her daddy liked to use that big cave of a voice of his in public, and that her grandmother would pull a face and grumble in the background.

"What's this?" Kali tried to lift the big book and 'oomphed' in defeat. The leather was cracked on the corners while the familiar sun image was pressed into the centre like the brands she had seen on the hides of the razingstock in her grandmother's stable.

"It is heavy." Mister Thatchett undid the clasp and opened the book, unleashing the smell of dust and aging paper. "This is the family book of the Thatchetts."

"What's inside?" Kali nosed closer.

"Stories, mostly." Mister Thatchett ran one long hoary finger down a fragile page.

From upside down, Kali saw spidery writing in dark red ink. Mister Thatchett turned the thin pages, several at a time, revealing more spidery writing and, occasionally, a picture taking up a whole page. The pictures reminded Kali of the stained-glass windows at the Church of St Chen where she spent a morning now and then – whenever her grandmother had one of her bouts of 'faith.'

"This book records the history of my family," said Mister Thatchett. Closing the book with a resolute thwomp, he did up the clasp and rested his age-spotted hand on the cover. "It is the stories which keep our blood connected. They remind us of where we came from, how we've changed over the centuries, and where we might be headed. Once upon a time, they were etched into stones. But the words had too much power that way. It is subtler, safer, to use paper, which can always be burned. The important thing is to preserve the words. They are our lifeline."

Kali had the feeling that she was supposed to be impressed. Children liked stories, didn't they? Except, she suspected that only Vary had secret books, with secret plans etched in blood-coloured ink.

Mister Thatchett packed away his book of dangerous stories. Then he leaned down to Kali. His strange smell filled her nostrils. She imagined his hands clawing, the nails growing out to points. His nose was fat, his skin thick and cracked at the edges of his mouth like the skin of his family bible.

"Going to help me put these boxes into the attic?" he said. Teeth all gone. Eyes bulging.

It was too much. All this difference living just next door! In that moment, Kali decided her granny was wrong. Wrong to sing songs which were not hers to sing. Wrong to offer up a granddaughter to help the swine. Her father knew the true measure of these strangers who lived amongst them but had their own food and smell and stories and religion and strange magic books.

"I don't help filthy Vary!" she cried out suddenly, and in case the old man made a grab for her, she ran. Ran and ran, down the sets of stairs and across the hallway of that big white house designed to boil a person alive as if the door to a giant oven were left open. *Get out*, screamed her mind.

Whatever curses she imagined Mister Thatchett throwing after her were lost to the noise of the front door slamming. Then she ran again, never once looking back.

NINE

A gunner came on occasion, vast and industrial, its friction discs whirring in constant, deafening rotation. Kali would hear the warcraft long before she saw it. The whisper of engines would hang in the air like the threat of a storm, building to a deep, reverberating hum as the colossal ship drew closer. The arrival of a gunner in the repair dock would send a wave of peculiar excitement through the prisoners. Once, they would have reacted on impulse and crowded around the blue-black skirts of the craft, poking at its diamantine crust. But there was no spontaneity in Abbandon, just a blaze of awe in tired eyes and quiet murmurs of fascination. The guards allowed it because they were busy admiring the warcraft too, and because there was a political point in the display of this superior Bleek technology. 'You are under our feet', said the colossal gunners.

A month had passed since Kali's arrival. She had lost weight rapidly and was forced to belt the rough pyjama bottoms with a length of stone-wool cord she stole from the factory floor. Still, she was fortunate. Titian's daughter did not starve along with the rest; Joltu saw to it that extra jerky and sod pudding was added to her rations. Kali understood. It didn't pay to abuse the offspring of Bleekland's High Judge, not when a father could rescind his punishment any day and hold others accountable for her treatment. But for the most part, her life went hand in hand with the Vary. She marched with the rest, slept in the same septic tank of foul breath and night terrors, and endured the guards' spit in her face. And like the rest, she watched the sky for gunners.

"It's a 9532. Latest model," she overheard a fellow machine worker tell his neighbour.

"I'll get a look when the next load comes from the quarry. The block chief doesn't like us sniffing around the repair dock."

The neighbour croaked against the back of a hand. Kali recognised the symptom of lungrot and tucked in closer to her station. The large spinner drove back and forth, teasing out the threads of stone-wool. Kali tried to lose herself to the hypnotic motion of the spindles knitting in and out of the weft. The heat off the furnaces swelled around her.

"What about you, Lieutenant? Got a glimpse yet?" The male who had initiated the conversation stared over. Acceptance was too strong a word for how the Vary felt about her. Tolerance was closer to the mark.

"I was raised on a gunner," she lied, adjusting the spindles as the molten wisps crisscrossed over one another. Life with her grandmother had often felt like she was aboard a warcraft.

The two males exchanged glances. "I am certain that the castle you grew up in has as much in common with a gunner as my arse does with soak-paper," said the second male, and both clucked their tongues and laughed.

Their humour didn't last. A pair of blockers had been harassing the production line and now they arrived behind Kali. One prodded her in the back with his makeshift beater. When she kept on working, they turned their attention to the Vary males. It would be difficult for the blockers to find fault. Her companions were good workers and Kali was glad of it. She had been put alongside a pair of females originally. Both had come at her with frantic eyes and gnashing teeth. Their nicks had activated instantaneously, their screams staying with her long after the blood had been washed away.

"How do you gentlemen like shacking up with Titian's daughter?" The blocker kept his hand on his makeshift beater, a length of knotted stone-wool cord soaked in tannin until it was stiff.

"Does she sing to make the hours go quicker?" The other knocked his companion's elbow and grinned. "A nice, uplifting anthem like 'Behold our Great Nation.'"

The Vary kept working. Inside the spinner cabinets, the burning flax hummed.

"What's the matter, gentlemen? Afraid to answer?" The blocker with the stiffened rope gave Kali another jab in the back. "Lieutenant can't burn your homes any more. Or break your children's bones."

Kali knew what the blockers were doing. It paid them to aggravate the Vary into action when they had orders to let her be. A rogue Vary who could be neutralised after the event was the perfect scapegoat to bring about her death. Except, to date, the Speaker in his filthy cot had more hold over his kind than the blockers. And she had grown used to them, these Vary with their dangling limbs and fat teeth. Their monstrousness was strangely less acute.

"I do not sing for them, but I can sing for you," she said quietly. "Do you prefer a ballad or a march?"

The blockers chewed on their tongues and came around to her station. The one with the cord weapon swished it against his thigh absentmindedly and leaned against the covered feed-shaft to her left. The other poked around her station with his makeshift beater, threatening to push gel patches at random.

"Or perhaps the song you mentioned earlier? I'm sure that is a favourite." Releasing the handles of the spinners, she put the machine in neutral and got up from her stool. Pressing a hand flat over her heart, she cleared her throat and sang out with the same voice she had used at church throughout her childhood.

> "All hail Gothendore, hoist our flag on high,
> A pure day of strength and faith and unity,
> Let the guard march, brave comrades all,
> All hail the True, the Just,
> This, our Great and Holy Nation."

She stopped after one verse. Around her, the machinery whirred in repetitive motion. No voices could be heard, only the imagined echo of hers in the steaming air. But then the male suffering from lungrot began coughing and the sound broke the silence.

"What's that, man? Speak up!" The blocker drove the hard rope against the man's thigh and the prisoner squeezed his eyes shut over tears.

"He didn't say anything." Kali would have stepped between the blockers and their victim if it would have done any good. As it was, the brutes had made up their minds to cause trouble and now the prisoner had coughed out of turn, they had their excuse. Kali stared into the male's wet eyes and knew the life there was to be stubbed out. She thought she caught a glimpse of relief, as if the male said without words, "At last. I am done."

The blockers set upon him. There were no guards in the vicinity to activate the nicks and that wasn't what the blockers wanted anyway. Creatures born of the gutter, there was pleasure to be found in violence – each punch to the male's gut, the crunch of the cosh to an eye socket. It wounded Kali's pride to see this stranger beaten in her place. She almost felt sorry for him.

"Stop it!" she cried in the voice that had commanded battalions. The stiff cord struck her in the face. Kali reeled backwards, feeling the pain whip-sharp across her cheek. Her foot caught on the feed-shaft and she fell, jarring her wrists on the floor as she tried to brace herself. A few feet away, the blockers kept up their assault on the prisoner. Kali heard his stifled moans and the slam of weapons against flesh. She strained to see the other worker. The male cowered by his stool, a hand pressed over his mouth to keep the fear in.

"Leave the man alone," she said thickly, for which she received a second thump of the rope. Her head ricocheted back, and when she looked at the ground again, she found herself focusing in on a square of white. Spidering out her hand, she pinched the object between a thumb and forefinger and brought it to her eye. It was a tooth. Kali ran her tongue around her mouth; there wasn't a gap.

She homed in on the Vary male, spread-eagled on the floor, the upper portion of his skull caved in. One of his front teeth was missing.

Later, when the blocker had gone and the body of the lungrot sufferer had been thrown into the furnaces, she managed to sit up and, holding the tooth up to the sunlight, asked herself why it looked so small and ordinary?

Grizmare sent the driver home. Truth be told, she wasn't sure that she even wanted to employ a driver any more. The past weeks had seen a sharp decline in her willingness to leave home. *What's out there for me*, she wondered? Amongst the black towers where the sky baked and the earth boiled. Better to stay in the shade of the temperature-controlled house her son had built for her. Cooped up in the darkness which reminded her of their cave home where his father died of lungrot and which had been replaced all too soon by something new and shiny.

Grizmare stroked the ornate walking cane that rested against her chair. Her son had gifted that to her as well, with the reassurance that its unusually light alloy was exceedingly strong, rather rare, and worth a small fortune. *Nothing wrong with my old one*, she had told him at the time. *Nonsense*, her son had told her, and demonstrated the worth of the new cane by using it to smash the old.

"Can I get you anything, Madam Titian? Lemon cider, perhaps."

Lizabeth, a Gothendore sister and Grizmare's paid companion, checked the hands of the water-clock taking up an entire wall, another of her son's extravagances in that time of draught. "It's not yet noon. I'm thinking we wait on cracking open a new bottle of sour gin a few minutes yet."

Grizmare snorted. "What exactly are we waiting *for*? And when I say we, I mean me. It's not as if you're about to touch a drop."

Lizabeth pulled her 'Are we going there again?' face, which always made her look younger. So much more of the girl she really was, Grizmare thought, and so much less of the nun.

"Not everyone in the order is corrupt, Madam Titian."

"Grizmare! I've told you a million times already. Use my name or I'll shit the sheets on purpose and you'll be the one left rolling up your sleeves to change them."

"*Grizmare.*" The woman stared out from her wimple, serene and irritatingly knowing. "Shall we start our rounds? As I understand it, the bill deer have developed mange and the anus glands of the Metadonian tiger dog need squeezing." Lizabeth lifted her chin a notch. Her green eyes sparkled. "That is one job I draw the line at."

Luckily for the nun, Grizmare had never been squeamish when it came to animals. As she informed Lizabeth when the girl first arrived, "Animals make sense. There is nothing affected or malicious about them, unless we have made them so. *We* are the assholes." Fifteen minutes later, as she sat on her milking stool in the pen of the muzzled tiger dog and attended its backend, she was grateful for the basicness of the task.

"Better than cooking myself alive on that damned rooftop," she muttered, wiping at the dog's backend. "Harriot really is quite the imbecile! Not that Morantha is much better. Both are puffed up with their self-importance. Liable to float away into the ether if they don't keep a grip on something."

"You okay there, Grizmare? Muttering away to yourself." Lizabeth stayed outside the pen rather than risk close quarters with the tiger dog.

"I'm okay." Grizmare threw the dirty rag past the woman's shoulder and struggled to her feet. "Can't say the same about the rest of those society lollygaggers!" She handed over the stool and hobbled up to the gate. The tiger dog followed her, recognising its master while still wild enough to bite the hand that feeds. Beneath the stripes, it was a densely boned, muscular creature with a jaw full of curved black teeth. Grizmare got the other side of the gate before leaning over to yank the muzzle away in one swift, well-practised movement.

"I thought you enjoyed seeing your friends?" Lizabeth poured a scoopful of blood pelts into the feed funnel. The tiger dog snapped and snarled at the emptying pipe, bolting down mouthfuls.

"You make me sound like a babe in kindergarten! The only reason I enjoy seeing either of those old hags Morantha and Harriot is to make their lives as miserable as mine is."

They moved on to Grizmare's favourite pets – a family of desert otters. While the young splashed about in the sand, the mating pair, Shy-lo, the male, and Boohoo, the female, peered out the entrance to their burrow and nosed the air.

"Boohoo! Come see the old gal!" said Grizmare, easing down onto the sand bank inside the large pen. The skylight was open, so she had Lizabeth set up the parasol which enabled the two of them to withstand the heat of the sun razoring down. Once they had settled, Boohoo came bouncing over, Shy-lo following, and soon the two adult otters were chitter-chattering as they crawled over Grizmare's lap.

"You can smell the worms in my pocket. This is false love. False love!" Grizmare was laughing.

"It's good to see you smile, Grizmare." Lizabeth nodded to the otters. "We should bring Shy-lo and Boohoo up to the house. Let you play with them awhile."

"Don't be ridiculous! They're animals, not aristocracy. We don't invite them to supper." Grizmare pushed the squirming otters off her lap and struggled to her feet, refusing Lizabeth's offered hand.

"I just meant if you are… lonely."

Lizabeth was taking time with her words; *doesn't want to hurt me*, thought Grizmare. *Well, tough!*

"I am lonely, yes, Lizabeth. My son has forgotten me and sent my granddaughter to certain slaughter."

"And how do you feel about that?"

Oh, Lizabeth! Not careful enough with those words. It was the kind of question a doctor might ask. Or a person who was fishing.

"I'm tired. Get the keeper to muck out the rest. I've had my fill."

"Of course, Grizmare. Shall I call for a riser chair or will you manage the walk back?"

Grizmare grabbed her ornate cane from where it rested against the wall and waggled it aggressively. "Call for a chair if you are tired, Lizabeth. Me? I'm not done with my own two feet just yet!"

TEN

The sweat between them had its own perfume – oakmoss at the foot of the damask tree in her grandmother's garden, the fetidness of stank bulb in the desert, and the death notes of sulphur at the Nedmark Traps. It was very different to the brew of Vary males in their tin can barracks. There was taste too, alien and sour as tongues touched. The sensations belonged to her old life, this crushing hand around her breast, the sound of a belt being unbuckled. She had gone to Joltu to plead for clemency in the workplace, arguing, "Why do you let the blockers break skulls at will? The factory is forced to train up Vary replacements constantly." Now they were rutting, she suspected her motivation was a lie. The soak of mouths and clutch of fingers – these were the reasons she had sought him out. If there was rage to be spent, it would be spent on him. She clawed the man's back, folding him up inside her like a secret.

It was strange and sour-tasting and empty, this fucking when her belly ached with hunger and lice infested her hair. At the same time, she didn't want it to stop. Here, there was peace from her harsh reality. It also reminded her of the baseness she had enjoyed as a free woman. She rocked fiercely against Joltu, drove his mouth to her breasts. He was no different to the others, just a pinprick of cold emotion.

His smear left between her thighs, she got dressed and waited to be dismissed. It was a more intimate imposition when Joltu started to talk. Pouring a glass of wine, he sat down behind the desk where her backside had so recently rested.

"Do you miss home, Lieutenant? By which, I don't mean your grandmother's estate. I mean life in the National Guard? The freedom it afforded you?"

Now the adrenaline of the sex was fading, Kali felt the weight of her fellow worker's death again. "I don't miss my part in the mistreatment of the Vary. I do miss the freedom to speak out."

"But wasn't speaking out what put you here?" Joltu didn't let up. "Do you feel that you let down your battalion? Your command was ironclad. Even as a child, you were committed to the cause. At every party, your father would produce you to recite his manifesto. 'To raise my voice as one pure son or daughter, to oppress those who would leech our holy nation.' You remember, of course."

Kali nodded. "I remember that my father wrote that manifesto, not Lord Gothendore or any other divinity. My father is an outstanding orator, an astonishing strategist, a national hero. But he is as fallible as any other man. We had a simple disagreement on policy."

"You betrayed him!" Joltu snapped, eyes blazing. He visibly calmed himself. "You betrayed us."

"Who do you mean by us? The National Guard? Bleekland? Does it not occur to you, Commandant Superintendent, that I was trying to repair our Bleekness? Since when do we murder infants, tear apart families, mutilate the old, punish the weak? Is that part of our holy manifesto? Or is it the posturing of one man at a time when we are debt-riddled and desperately need someone to blame? The Vary are our scapegoat. We are sacrificing their blood in an effort to fertilise the land, or appease whatever God is angry with us." She wiped spit from her lips. His warmth soaked the crotch of her coarse pyjama bottoms.

Joltu took a sip of wine. "I would never have pinned you for a romantic, Lieutenant."

"Romantic, no. Compassionate...? Well, I got there in the end."

"And ordered the deaths of Vary every step of the way."

"I saw a tooth today." Kali pictured the tooth in her palm and how she had thrown it aside, as if the truth might burn her.

"A tooth?" The Commandant Superintendent looked amused.

Kali shook her head; the tooth itself was irrelevant. Rubbing her temples, she did her best to explain. "I'm less and less certain that we are the divine. Every day I see Vary beaten and bled out by dent of their inferiority. But the more I live alongside them, the less vulgar they appear. Perhaps the differences between us are not so great."

"Perhaps." Joltu squinted across the desk. "But the great thing about putting faith in one man — in your father — is that our fellow Bleek don't have to question the morality of such acts. They are simply ridding Bleekland of a blight. The rest of the world might even thank us for it one day."

"Unless they succeed in their campaign against us. We are not indestructible."

Joltu snorted. "Tell that to your father." He drained the last of his wine and pointed to the door. "I will instruct the blockers to back off at the factory. The Vary do a good enough job of dying on their own. It makes sense to keep those that can working."

Kali nodded at the Commandant Superintendent. "Thank you."

"I don't give a fuck about your thanks, Lieutenant. I'm just interested in keeping the stone-wool quotas in line and burning as much coke in the furnaces as we do bodies. Coke produces a hotter flame." Joltu slid on his glasses and returned to his paperwork.

Kali straightened her jacket and left.

"Might want to finish that before we leave the ward. The block chief and his men will prise it from your cold dead hands otherwise." Groff offered a look of encouragement until the Speaker's son tore up the black bread and swallowed it down in chunks. He couldn't help a pang of resentment as the last bit was swallowed without any being offered.

"Good, good." He gave the bed a glance over. "You got everything?"

Mohab huffed. "Camp issue uniform, the socks my mother knitted for me two winters past, the boots I was arrested in. What else is there?"

"There is your health, Mohab. Your health!" Groff patted Mohab on the shoulder. "Not much to go on, I know. But look on the bright side. You get to escape these vampires." He nodded in the direction of the sisters negotiating the ward, sucker syringes in hand. "You get air in your lungs. And you get to see your papa!"

Mohab crossed his arms and stayed quiet.

Groff persevered. "You'll be glad to see your father, yes? He's older, a little doddery on his feet. But the voice is still strong."

"And do they beat him for it?"

Groff shrank under Mohab's gaze. "They do on occasion. But as with you, the more they despise a man, the keener they are to keep him alive and suffering." He shrugged. "It's a blessing and a curse."

Mohab stared at the ground a moment. He took a sharp intake of breath and nodded towards the door. "Lead the way then. It's about time I got the tour."

Sunset bled over the buildings. Leaving the infirmary behind, Mohab passed a range of offices Groff described as "The political buildings. Where the newbies get measured, weighed and processed." Further on was a glass-sheet dome. "Home to the guards." Groff kept his voice low. "Commandant Superintendent Joltu has his office inside."

The nurse's voice trailed off as a woman emerged from the dome. Mohab was surprised to recognise Lieutenant Kali Titian, wearing the coarse pyjamas uniform allotted to the Vary men. The women usually wore camp issue shifts; he had registered as much in the infirmary.

"Strange goings on." Groff shuffled on the spot.

"I don't think any of us believed the court indictment. And

yet here she is like the rest of us. Only, not quite like the rest. Sneaking out of the Commandant Superintendent's quarters. I don't think it's too hard to guess why."

"The High Judge's daughter and Joltu?" Groff sniffed and ran a finger under his nose. "More likely she's put in an appeal for clemency. And who can blame her? Forced to tuck up between the men in the stinking barracks."

"She sleeps in with the Vary? And her throat hasn't been slit?" Mohab watched the Lieutenant hurry away. He imagined her directing troops into the homes of the innocent, or heading up one of the grand marches through the streets of Geno or Nilreb. His heart hurt with loathing.

"She is safe because your father ordered it." With a tilt of his chin, Groff added, "We are not animals, Mohab. We may be caged and menaced for the pleasure of the masses, but we have worth. Your father taught us that much."

Mohab felt a hollow space beneath his ribs. "He's dying. My father." He looked over at Groff. "You're a nurse so you know that."

Groff concentrated on the flaming sky. "People say he has lungrot."

"He's also old, and the equivalent of a living saint. People don't want to imagine a time when he might not be here any more."

They walked along the fence where guards patrolled. Groff's voice brightened. "But now you are here the old man can pass on his speaker duties. A strong young voice, that's what the Vary need."

"Screw that!" said Mohab so resolutely that Groff physically jumped.

"But isn't that why you are here? To find a way to unite and overthrow the Bleek. To lead us underground so we can add our number to the ranks of the Resistance."

Mohab heard the longing, but it did nothing more than anger him. How dare these starving fools presume he would lead them in his father's place? What with the blood of his mother, the arrest of his father, and the death of his siblings from lungrot in the Vary slums, hadn't his family given enough?

"What are you doing here if not to save us?" Groff pleaded with his eyes.

"I was arrested the same as any other fucker. I didn't criticise the state or otherwise aggravate the status quo." Mohab pointed to the receding figure of Lieutenant Titian. "Titian's daughter did more to advocate the Vary cause. And still they condemn me to die in this hellhole." He clenched his hands. "Head down, mouth shut. That always worked for me."

"Until now."

Mohab stared at the vast silhouette of the factory and the threatening edge of the quarry. "Until now."

ELEVEN

"Do you miss her?"

Oh, but it was an impertinent question, thought Grizmare. A childish question, because how could she not?

"You really do ask the most ridiculous things, Lizabeth! Do you miss your family? They are in Nilreb, no?"

"Yes, I miss my family."

"So how do you expect me to feel about Kali's absence? Her being sent away is the single most devastating thing that has ever happened to me. And I hate my own son for his part in the whole wretched event."

There. She had said it. The unsayable. Grizmare was glad the fact was out, and confused as to why it should be the young nun who coaxed it from her and not her fellow matriarchs Harriot or Morantha. Or even High Judge Titian himself!

The young woman nodded thoughtfully. She was fixing Grizmare's second sour gin of the afternoon. "I was surprised by your daughter's actions. She was such a key figure in the National Guard." Pouring the lemony coloured liquor over the back of a tiny teaspoon, she took care to lay the sour gin directly on the surface of the ice and soda.

"I'm surprised you know the slightest thing about my granddaughter. You being a nun, I mean." Grizmare took the freshened glass. "I've always believed politics and religion should stay wholly separate. It's rather like sour gin, best in layers so neither one curdles."

"I wish the order was so innocent." Grizmare prayerfully interlaced her hands. She sat down and admired the garden through the glass. "I'm afraid it is one of the reasons that I went into private service rather than civil. The Mother Superiors take your son's laws as scripture. They have hardened the hearts of their orders, sent us out to Holy War. I opted for a different path."

"One which led you directly into the employee of High Judge Titian. Ha!" Grizmare screwed up her old eyes and laughed and laughed until the tears squeezed out.

"It led me to you as well." Lizabeth's gaze didn't wander from the garden. She got a small, nervous shake to her clasped hands.

Grizmare took a sip from her glass, hawkish in her intense way of studying the nun.

Lizabeth appeared to physically gather her wits again. She sat up straight and looked away from the garden. "But of course you miss your granddaughter, Grizmare. What a stupid thing for me to ask!" She smiled enigmatically and her well-bred eyes shone very green.

The gunner dominated the holding bay. Three huge steel arms pinned it mid-air, allowing workers access to the blue-black hull. With temperatures soaring out on the desert flats, the glass-sheet double doors were wide open.

Down in the bay, the air reeked of dust and glut oil. Kali didn't know how the air smelt up on the wire-cage balconies reserved for the guard who kept watch; even blockers were excluded from those lofty heights. All she knew was it felt good to have escaped the repetitive task of stringing stone-wool in the factory. Bleek were nothing if not manipulative of prisoners' skillsets, and while some Vary worked hard to keep their talents hidden, Kali's were a matter of public record. She understood the principals of the concentric friction rings and biological generators, had lived for it once upon a time! The sting of hunger could almost be forgotten before such grand design!

"Cease! Cease!" called down a guard from one of the wire-cage balconies.

The workers left off as a party of guards entered the hold, headed up by Joltu and with five of the Gothendore Sisterhood in tow.

"Guess it's time to bless the gunner before we break her open," whispered the Vary male who had been set on as Kali's assistant. He had a gappy smile and appeared more settled to his incarceration than most.

"I can't abide their hocus-pocus," she said under her breath.

"Titian's daughter rejecting her national religion? You are brave, Lieutenant." The male winked at her.

Kali didn't answer as the parade of officers and sisters passed close by. She homed in on the officers' faces – the shadow of stubble, moles on a cheek, cracked lips from the heat, a sweat stain at a shirt collar. The sisters stayed in the folds of their wimples.

Arriving at the gunner, Joltu ordered the prisoners to join hands in prayer while the sisters spoke their incantations. For the next few minutes, Lord Gothendore was beseeched, the sisters lifting their hands and forcing tears and wailing. After, they fell silent, rocking back and forth.

Joltu led the party out again. The order came to "Resume!" and work began again inside the hold.

Kali's new helper leaned in. "Hi. I am Groff." He shuffled his feet. "You don't need to introduce yourself. It's not like the camp is overrun with Bleek women forced to share our barracks." She didn't say anything and he went on unhindered. "You are a bio-engineer. It was your mother's profession too, by all accounts."

He joined her on a narrow platform and she started to crank the handle manually. The concertina lift stuttered into life and started to rise. "I take it you are my Second." She panted as she worked; the handle was stiff and took effort to turn. Looking up, she was newly fascinated by the pocked diamantine skin of the craft.

Groff snorted. "I'm not sure what I am, Lieutenant. In my old life, I was a nurse, specialising in paediatrics and minor maxillofacial procedures. Now I make do with injecting green paste with dirty needles. On occasion, I bring the dead back to life. Ah, don't look so cynical! The not-quite-dead then. Like the Speaker's son. The guards made a mess of him. He's walking now, though, and put to work at the quarry, poor bastard!" Groff took the screen plate she unbolted and handed down. He wiped a rag over the plate, cleaning off the dust kicked out by the giant rotator rings above.

"And is the Speaker's son looking to step into his father's shoes?" Kali focused on the hose and wires which had been protected by the plate. The bare cable was circumnavigated with positively charged ion bands.

"Doesn't look that way." Groff sounded sad. "I guess it can hurt a boy to grow up in his father's shadow. Mohab has lost plenty — a mother and sisters to lungrot. I guess we must understand his reticence."

Kali grunted. Lungrot made no distinction between rich and poor. Her mother had drowned in her own phlegm the same as the Speaker's family, and her father's father before that. The great Skyfall had released enough fine particles into the air to last a thousand years or longer.

"Maybe you could speak to Mohab?"

"What?" Kali glared down at her Second. The request was ludicrous!

Groff appeared entirely sincere. "You gave up your freedom for the Vary cause. You oppose our subordination."

"You seriously expect me to hold any sway over the behaviour of a rebel?" Kali smashed her hands in amongst the guts beneath the bolt plate. She spoke through gritted teeth. "You ask this of me, daughter of High Judge Titian, an ex-Lieutenant in the National Guard? You expect me to support dissent, to encourage talk of resistance? Who do you think I am? A Vary whore in Bleek skin? No matter what political agenda I have championed in the past, I am a Bleek nationalist, born and bred. I am no confidante and I am no sweet-talker."

She expected Groff to fall silent and instinctively lean away. Instead, he folded his arms and nodded slowly. "I'm asking too much, I know. It must be hard for you. Very hard." He cocked his head and squinted up at her. "Your people don't want you and you don't want us. As the Speaker tells it, 'Kali screams and her screams answer back'."

"The Speaker should keep his fucking mouth shut before I help him meet his maker."

"Ah, don't you worry, Lieutenant. The Speaker's end will come soon enough." With a sigh, Groff returned to polishing the bolt plate. He sang as he worked. "Varber iubită, Louanne, Loua…"

Kali's patience snapped. "Shut the fuck up!"

"No talking!" A beater dragged along the wire-mesh overhead.

Whispers died down all around the hull.

Kali went back to her wiring while Groff said under his breath, "If our songs affect you so, Lieutenant, you must learn to close your ears to them." He fell silent and Kali did her best to forget that he was there.

TWELVE

Grizmare leaned heavily on her cane as she walked. Her breath came in spurts, like the sprinkler valves on timers around the garden. It didn't help that she had been woken by a tremor that morning. One moment she was a desert otter, running from a chef's blade, the next she was blinking awake to find her bed shaking. And now, hours later, she was stiff and cranky with a pain between her eyes.

"Being old is shit!" she said aloud. Bones cracking. Hips sore. "Shit as Demonia's own dung. Why'd I have to cart this rotten flesh around on claggy old bones!"

"You're excessively tetchy today." The countessa walked by her side, dressed in finery and accompanied by a personal drone shade that hummed overhead.

"Why in Gothendore's name you couldn't have brought that blasted machine with you to the Red Orchid, I don't know! Making me sit in the sun all afternoon like drying leather."

"It is a gift from my daughter." Morantha gave a delicate shudder. "Always eager to show off whatever new wonder she has dreamed up at Capital Hall!" Her surgical smile faltered. "I'm still divided about the value of a debutante working in a technical laboratory, even if it is the country's finest!"

"Clever girl. Still young enough to use her intelligence and not grow fat on complacency." Grizmare sniffed as she laboured to take each step. "I grew fat. Oh, tosh – I don't mean physically! I never did eat enough to turn into one of those society dames with quadruple chins and bellies like giant turds. No, I'm talking about an organ like the brain, which should be wiry and well-used. My mind has gone flabby through lack of use. Sometimes I envy those young men and women put to work for the war effort. Oh, he's a clever one, my son! Cunning enough to

73

persuade even this country's elite to sacrifice their own children to his cause!"

Morantha shooed her off the path. "Sit down, Grizmare. You're getting delirious and shouldn't be walking in this heat."

"Not without one of those fancy shade drones, I shouldn't!"

Grizmare was in enough pain to follow Morantha's lead and they took a seat on a small stone bench in her favourite nook of the garden, beneath a giant moss vine that provided heavy shade. The drone hovered a foot or so clear of the vine.

Grizmare raised her eyes to the machine. "That thing's wise enough not to entangle itself in the branches."

"It is the gel frill. Senses the impact potential." Morantha shrugged. "I do read, you know! Being born to privilege doesn't preclude intellect."

"Maybe you could explain that to Harriot!" Thinking about their ridiculous friend, Grizmare snorted and rested one hand atop the other on the handle of her cane. "Meanwhile, you can lend me the thing. I'll send it out on a hunt for my son."

"Still no word from High Judge Titian?" Morantha did the nun's trick of staring out at the garden whenever she asked a difficult question.

"I think I represent his conscience," said Grizmare, enlightening herself with the thought. "He sent Kali away. For that, I love him as a son and loathe him as a man."

Morantha fell into silent contemplation. Wafts of her expensive perfume reached Grizmare's nostrils. Ticklishly sweet and underpinned with age.

"You smell like church, Morantha." Grizmare wrinkled her nose.

Morantha ignored the comment. Instead, she sat straight-backed, face beautifully carved. "Grizmare, you must be careful. You've always been loose-lipped. Coarse even, I know you won't care me saying it. But if word gets out that High Judge Titian no longer has you under his protective wing...? There are assassins, spies, Resistance fighters who will take advantage." She leaned in, scars silvery at her hairline. "Watch out for yourself, Grizmare."

"And change the habits of a lifetime? I won't be silenced."

"You say that now and yet you have been. Silenced, I mean." Morantha laid a hand lightly on Grizmare's knee. "I wasn't there, of course. I have never stepped foot in a courtroom my entire life and I intend to keep it that way. But as I understand it from the datestacks, you sat in the gallery for Kali's entire trial, and at no point did you attempt to defend your granddaughter, or pour down abuse, or otherwise run amuck!" The countessa batted her false eyelashes. "Grizmare, I love your posturing, I always have. Few things delight me more than hearing you chew out a pompous waiter or arrogant young officer. But when it comes to more serious matters – state versus family – you need to know when to be quiet. If only the Vary would behave with such dignity!"

"Dignity? Huh. And how much did my son appreciate my dignity? I chose him over Kali and he instantly forgot me."

"I believe you chose the nation rather than your son."

Tears burned the corners of Grizmare's eyes. She pictured Kali, seated at a distance through all those hours of evidence and hearsay. Throughout the entire trial the young woman had barely moved, as if she had already spilt every drop of her blood and turned to stone.

Shrugging off the memory, Grizmare fixated on the whirring drone. "Get your daughter to order me one of those bastards. The sun gets hotter every day. Soon there'll be no place left to shelter."

"Why do you wear the Perversionest brand?" The Lieutenant pointed to the neon symbol on Groff's left cheek.

Groff shifted around. The sand mattress was unforgiving and faintly damp. "My full name is Groff de Rubon," he said. "I am thirty-four years old. My father was third generation Bleekland Vary; he still had his family book, pages so old they'd crackle if you tried to turn them. The book told the story of my ancestors' passage from Raestan. The only other evidence was a small wooden doll reputably carved by a Raestanese carpenter. My mother kept the doll on the kitchen dresser, between her Fire Night candlestick and the urn containing Grandmother de Rubon's ashes. Legend has it my great great grandmother acquired the doll from a pauper who called by the house in need of alms. With the innocence of a child, she offered her mother's string of raven pearls. So moved was the pauper by the outlandish gesture that he refused the pearls and asked for black bread instead. He carved the doll from a stick of wetwood by way of reward for the young girl's kind gesture." Groff shrugged. The memory of the doll and his mother's kitchen was grainy, like photostats faded through long exposure to the sun.

He went on. "I was raised in Soagre, a mining town. You know it?"

The Lieutenant nodded. "North of Nilreb."

Groff suspected that the Lieutenant remembered a whole lot about Soagre from her time in the National Guard but didn't care to share. Just as well, he told himself. He didn't want to know which of his neighbours she'd had executed.

Instead, he opted to tell her about the man he had loved. "His name was Ju. A nightclub singer, born and raised in Nilreb. We met one evening twelve years ago. I was a student nurse living in halls on the east side, near the universium." Groff laughed softly. "I was a homely sort. *Bread*, my mother called me, meaning welcoming to the eye and always a comfort. My experience with sexuality was restricted to a neighbour's daughter glimpsed naked through a bathroom window." He remembered the girl. Angular where he had expected curves, the down where her thighs met at odds with her smooth skin. He had not felt as he knew he should. Instead, it was another six months before he visited a bathhouse and saw the beautiful young men walking naked through the corridors, their long lean limbs and taut buttocks unfolding his desire like an orchid blossoming.

"Ju and I met one Fire Night. The moon was rosy. Sort of

eve my mother would have said had blood in it, which was why I very nearly didn't go out. I'd developed a soft spot for a student named Glen and I wanted to stay in the dorm to see if I could talk to him. But my friends, Len and Ezra, would not hear of it. Fire Night is a time to fear Mama Sunstar and all those years ago when she opened up the throat of this world and rained down magma and ash. It is also the best excuse to drink, puke, and dance until your ears bled." Groff smiled sadly. "At least that used to be the way of things."

The lieutenant tucked her hands beneath her armpits. "It must be nice to celebrate something traditional. My father hijacked every celebration to toast his own greatness."

Groff couldn't help wondering what it had been like for Titian's daughter growing up. Hers must have been a cosseted if formal existence. Unlike his own. "Len was a city boy. He'd found this place behind a big old temple covered with graffiti, the sort inked by Bleek Youth Guard. The nightclub was called The Golden Note and it was just the kind of dive students flock to. My friend Ezra was an artist at heart who'd been pushed into nursing by his overbearing father. He lapped up the place with, as I remember it, all these candles in jars, rickety chairs, and tiny lanterns strung up like jars of lava. There was a bar, of course, selling mezcals, tequilas, algae wine and clay cups of jalapeno aquavit hot enough to burn a hole in you. There was a stage too, with a tin piano and a big old Jalwest Indian playing ragtime tunes."

The memories were sweet and sour. Tears pricked Groff's eyes and he breathed in hard. "Ju was first up. He was the new boy – hadn't paid his dues yet. So he got the cold slot when patrons were still trickling in and hadn't soaked themselves silly in liquor. But when he got up on that stage? To me, he was ten types of glorious." Groff nodded to himself. *Wasn't he just?* He didn't tell the Lieutenant about Ju's lips, sticky and full. Or how, later that night, he sank himself in up to hilt between Ju's buttocks and thrust and dragged at that tightly yielding embrace.

He kept those memories close, polishing them over in his mind.

"He sang well. Old favourites from the cradle to the grave. Len thought he had Ju all sewn up. But Ju was wily. 'No more city boys', he told me when we put the lights out that night."

"Where is he now?"

Groff swallowed. "The National Guard took him. He was caught leafleting for the Resistance." Pain spread through him like a needle weaving in and out. "My hope is he died a long time ago."

The Lieutenant was quiet a few moments, just a shape at the end of the bunk. Eventually, she sighed. "Sometimes I worry that with all the history which was lost during the Skyfall, we ended up going backwards."

A kiss to the forehead. Lips at the nape of his neck. A hand skimming down to the hard peak, a crush of thigh beyond... Mohab kept these thoughts at the fore of his mind as the sun beat down. Anything to distract from the endless exhaustion of the work. All around, the air resonated with the hack of picks on rock and the crack of sledgehammers. Every so often, the trammel rumbled into action, its great cylinder rotating and steaming. The loud clinking noise signified the drop of rocks being screened by size. The panting of the prisoners who drove the crank wheel was lost to the sounds of quarrying basalt.

Mohab used a forearm to wipe the sweat from his eyes. Everything was salt – the crud at the corner of his mouth, the grease across his skin. The rock smoked with dust where it had been freshly cut.

A pair of water boys made their way to him, battered tin cups strung on chords around their necks. One poured a shot of water from a leather bladder. Mohab snatched the drink. Peering into the tarnished cup, he drank the liquid down in one gulp. Too soon he was handing back the cup.

The water boys moved on. Mohab cursed the sore muscles in his arms and back. He was damaged goods now and no amount of Groff's ministering would put him back the way he used to be. Yet, he had the advantage of having recently enjoyed extra rations in the infirmary. In contrast, his fellow Vary were living skeletons, forced to break stone with blunt tools. It was hard to maintain his ambivalence in the face of such suffering. But what were the choices available to him? Take on his father's role and become the counter-voice to High Judge Titian? Lead the Vary to victory – or, at least, the outer wall of slice-wire before their nicks were activated and the desert flooded red.

"Get back to work!" A guard came towards him; just another clone in black shirt sleeves and boots.

Except, that wasn't true. Up close, Mohab recognised the guard who had smacked his skull repeatedly with a beater. His scars ached, inside and out.

"I know who you are now, Speaker's son. When I broke you before, you were just another dog wouldn't do as it was told." The guard came in closer; Mohab could smell the tang of schnapps on the man's breath. "I'll let you settle a while, shall I? Wouldn't want to deprive the Commandant Superintendent of his favourite toy too soon."

"I thought Joltu's favourite toy was Lieutenant Kali Titian." Mohab braced for the beater.

Instead, the man laughed thickly. Nodding, he put a smokestick between his lips and lit it. "The Super's welcome to it while she's still got meat on her bones." He eyed Mohab, smoke dribbling from his parted lips. "Why don't you finish her off for us, Speaker's son? Put the bitch in the furnace." When Mohab didn't answer, the guard shrugged. "Likely as not, we will see your father made into ashes before the Lieutenant." He turned around, reluctantly Mohab thought. His beater knocked against his thigh as he walked away.

Mohab swung the pickaxe, chipped off a piece of basalt and threw it into the trammel. Everyone expected something of him, whether it was the guard intimating he should kill the shamed Lieutenant, or his father staring up from a soiled cot and wanting to pass on the mantle. Why couldn't he just crack the rock and await death like any other?

For the remainder of the day at least, he was left alone. After eleven hours of agonising labour, he watched the sun dip at the horizon. It was sweet relief after the brutal heat of the day. He walked between the trammel and the rock face on legs he could barely feel. Each stone added its grime and scratches to his skin.

The guards still hadn't given the signal to exit the quarry and line up for roll call. Mohab gritted his teeth and drove the pick forward again. But at the instant the prong made contact with the rock, a tremendous force radiated out from the spot, powering across the quarry in a seismic pulse. Guards and prisoners put out their hands to steady themselves. Mohab kept a grip on the pick axe, every hair on his body reacting to the rush of energy.

When the wave receded, Mohab heard the guards instructing everyone to "Ignore Demonia's belches. It's just a tremble." He glanced back and, seeing the guards huddled together and animatedly engaged in discussion, leaned forward against the pick and strained to prise away the rock shard. It came free in two rectangular rock slivers, each the size of his hand. Mohab picked up the rocks. They were strangely weightless as he turned them over and found the underside had an obsidian sheen. The light was failing but he thought there were markings. Natural ridges in the rock?

There wasn't time for further inspection. The guards returned to racking up the number of returned tools on their gel sets. Falling in line, the first lot of prisoners started for the assembly yard outside the barracks.

Mohab knew he should drop the rocks and follow after. But in the time he spent processing the thought, he had already stowed the oddly weightless rocks inside his jacket. He dragged his pick axe over to the tool pile and trudged in line out of the quarry, all the while aware of the strange rocks tucked against his heart.

THIRTEEN

Magma flowed below Abbandon in a fire strip, born of the great Skyfall when the air swirled with red hot ash and the cities burned. For half a millennium, the heartbeat of the planet had oozed wherever the plates rubbed and separated. But finally the fault had appeared to stabilise and the earth had cooled, forming a crust of basalt which sealed the blood back in. There were exceptions like the Nedmac Traps, where molten rock still puddled the surface, and, more recently, concerns over the integrity of Geno's foundations. Mostly, though, the lava aged down into hardened layers, with occasional buried treasures waiting to be prised free.

Perched in his corner of a bunk, Mohab held up a lit smokestick taper to the rectangular pieces of rock and examined the engravings. If his bed fellows noticed the light, they just clutched to sleep the tighter.

The markings were deliberate; there was too much method to their arrangement to be otherwise. Similarly, he thought they represented letters. He couldn't begin to translate the script. Before the persecution of the Vary began, life for Mohab had consisted of steed racing across the desert flats and educating students about sulphur crystal anomalies and magma springs. His father, though, carried the knowledge of the ancestors.

Mohab knew his family's history, having had it drilled into him over the years. It was his father's role to travel through the Vary quarters of the great cities – Geno, the garden city, with its ancient cave network and complex underpinning of irrigation systems to support life out in the desert, and Nilreb, the capital, a sprawling nest of financial districts, weapons factories, municipal buildings, palaces and slums. In each, his father had stood on his soap box in Speaker black and shared his tales as if breaking bread.

Speaking the stories was a sacred skill – at least, his ancestors had encouraged such a rumour, dining out on the fact for hundreds of years, right from the very first Speaker – a poet called Ahill, who, legend had it, was a charismatic old dog who enjoyed his measures of sour gin as much as the under-bushes of young ladies with breasts yet to bud. Regardless, he captivated his audience and, in so doing, found a way to keep his coffers stocked and his prick greased. Ever since, the Speaker's children were required to speak out and speak up in a manner which saw them hunted and hounded across the centuries. Always, the task was to carry and keep the secrets of their people, locked up in family books and the crevices of memory, only taking them out when safe to do so and then to polish them up like gem stones to be admired. Mohab's father had accepted his calling as the Vary's hope and truth, and they had loved him for it. But now he was old. Now he was dying. And the knowledge would die with him.

Mohab snuffed out the taper, eager to save the light. He was reluctant to move; he so desperately needed sleep. But he was touched by the agonising sadness of his father laid out on the filthy stretcher. If his father was broken physically, he could at least stimulate his brain with the puzzle of the rock pieces.

Clambering down off the bunk, Mohab made his way over to the low cot. Moonlight filtered in at a ventilation gap below the corrugated roof, exaggerating the Speaker's sunken cheekbones and hollow eye sockets.

"I have something to show you."

The old man wheezed and cleared his throat. "Quiet now. Blocker bastards will punish the whole barrack if they hear you."

"I need to show you what I found at the quarry today. I think they might date from the Stonemakers." Mohab held the rock slivers over his father, angling them as best he could to catch the light.

"I do not know what those are. But if they are Stonemaker in origin, get them as far away from you as possible." Choking on his breath, the old man waved him away. "Sleep, Mohab. They will beat you again if you cannot work hard tomorrow."

"I will sleep soon, Papa. But first, tell me what these symbols mean. You see them? They remind me of letters."

"So now you want to talk?" His father laughed, but his voice was threaded with pain. "You've had barely three words for me since you got here."

"The rocks, Papa. Do you know these symbols? I think they are in the ancient language. Can you translate it?" Mohab shook the rocks in front of his father's face. "Come on. We all know how much you love your words now, Speaker."

"And yet my son has no use for them. Or for his own." The old man shuffled in his bed. His weak eyes settled on the stones. "It is language, yes. The Glagolitic alphabet of old East, I think. The triangle – it is bisected by two lines. Perhaps it has common origins with the later Cyrillic word, TEHb, meaning 'language.' In which case, yes, they are Stonemaker in origin. But I am at a stretch here. They are a fascinating find, yes. They are also a death sentence. Get rid." His breathing deepened and the creped eyelids closed.

Mohab slid the rocks back inside his jacket. He watched his father sleep.

"Where did you find them?" said a woman's voice.

Why was the Bleek bitch talking to him? Mohab remembered Kali Titian perched beside him in the haulage wagon, smelling so clean after the reek of the Vary slums.

"You spoke to me on our first day. It's what got you beaten by the guards." She squatted down beside him. "Have the rules changed?"

He scowled across at her in the half-light. "Just because my father abides you doesn't mean I will, Lieutenant. You want to know my secrets? Ask me again when we're both burning in the hell fires."

"The nurse, Groff, requested that I speak to you. I'm to ask you to take your father's place." She said it as easily as if she had been asking for help to fold a blanket.

Mohab shook his head in disgust. "My father is still breathing. What else would you like me to take? This cot, perhaps? His boots?"

"I don't care. Your father spoke up for me once, so I am returning the favour. As for the dalma plates you are smuggling there, I don't know how you acquired them, but you'll be lucky to see out another dawn if the guards get scent of them."

"Or you report the matter to the Commandant Superintendent. After all, you have his ear. And other parts."

When Kali didn't react, Mohab found his curiosity piqued. "What are dalma plates?"

"Data hives that act as neuro systems for warcraft. At least that is their modern application."

"But I dug them out of the rock at the quarry. Even given the geological shifts after the Skyfall, we are still looking at these being buried for 500 years. See for yourself." Taking the rocks out of his jacket, he passed them to her.

Kali turned the rocks over. "I haven't seen dalma plates with this level of schematic detail preserved before." She brushed dust from the engravings and held them up to the moonlight.

"Are they glass-sheet?"

"Not glass-sheet. Dalma plates must be conductive. It's a rare element, not native to Bleekland." She stifled the desire to smack the Vary male hard across the face and call out for her fellow guard. Instead, she reminded herself that time had shifted. Circumstances had evolved. "Once upon a time, I'd have had you executed for having these in your possession. Now…" Sickly hope washed through her. "There has to be a reason why my father outlawed Stonemaker artefacts. I used to presume it was to guard against any corrupting influence of the past on our present. But then I came to understand that my father needed to control the technology, to harbour and hide it. To mine it."

Crouched in the gloom, the unearthed dalma plates between them, Kali told the Speaker's son about the day she first recognised the debt.

"You are aware of the Nine Bridges of Nilreb. Each straddles the dry riverbed. I've always thought they were beautifully constructed in that way Vary have of taking a simple material and shaping it well. 'It is on account of their physicality,' my father used to tell me. 'Long arms, broad thighs, their need to pattern-make.'" In her mind, she also heard him say, 'If only we could have found a way to harness that side effect of their mental retardation. We put them to work in the labour camps, but they are a wilful species, too base to create to order.' Kali tried to block out the sounds of the damaged males sleeping around her, the faint whimpers of their haunted dreams.

"This particular morning, I made a visit to the seventh bridge on official business. I took a subunit of guards disguised in the ponchos and embroidered caps of your people, filter masks too as dust-handlers no longer worked the slums. It was a dark and sullied world. At least that was how I viewed it at the time." She could still remember the fug of the unfamiliar enveloping her like putrid steam rising off a fumarole. Her troops had moved incongruously through that crumbling neighbourhood with its dank odour of strange spices and meat slops. Vary young had played in the ash piles alongside wild maw cats.

"Wicke's Emporium was on the seventh bridge, squeezed between a stinking butcher's and a boarded-up tailor's shop. I remember the bell above the door jangling like a noisy canary. Maybe you can imagine it, how the antique dealer's smile of welcome visibly melted at the sight of me?"

"… Good morning, mada…"

Kali had pulled off the black poncho, revealing her guard uniform. "You are Oliph Wicke, owner of this establishment?" Her eyes wandered, taking in the strange ephemera crowding the shelves, so perfunctory to the cesspit of the slums.

The male nodded while kneading a leather duster between his hands. He was typical of his species, with teeth so large as to press against the lips, threatening to protrude. His skin was dirty-looking and sluggish. His nose was broad and unrefined. An effort appeared to have been made to deliberately disguise the length of his limbs beneath baggy clothes.

"Oliph Wicke. We have received intelligence that you are harbouring Stonemaker archelogy, as outlawed by the Historical Cleansing Act."

The male widened his weak eyes. "Artefacts from the pre-Skyfall period are extremely rare and highly illegal." He gave a shudder, agitating his flaccid neck folds. "In fact, it is not even permitted to allude to *Stonemakers*." The term was notably overenunciated, betraying fear. Oliph continued to pull on his leather duster.

"So, you deny the allegation?" Kali held up a hand and the guards spread out, blocking the doorway, window, and a short corridor leading to a second, inner door.

"Of course I do!" Throwing the duster down on the counter, Oliph folded his arms in new defiance.

"Stonemaker antiquities are stored on these premises. Whether you willingly reveal the location of the items or withhold that information will directly impact your punishment."

"I assure you, all items for sale are entirely legal. I vow so, on the heart and stomach of Mama Sunstar." The Vary male signed out the circular thumb to index finger gesture that symbolised his faith.

"Funnily enough, your vows mean nothing to me. And so, I repeat. Where are the antiquities?" At Kali's signal, a pair of guards moved either side of Oliph and held him firmly by each arm as she reached down and slid out a long thin service blade from the side sheath of her boot. She saw the Vary male flinch. "It doesn't help in any way to keep secrets," she said, and drove the blade hard up under the male's chin, straight through to the back of the throat.

Oliph made a hideous gurgling sound. Blood frothed from his lips, spattering down onto his shirt.

Kali cleaned her blade with the leather duster. "Point."

The Vary male tried to speak. He was choking on his blood.

Kali lent in. "Point."

A trembling hand reached up and a long finger pointed to the corridor and the inner door…

"What did you find?" Mohab interrupted Kali's narrative. She could see that he was fighting to control his revulsion for her.

Taking no pleasure in recounting her past violence, she stuck with the facts. "We found the dalma plates hidden inside an old datastack receiver. Parcelled up in sheets of stone-wool like forgotten birthday presents." She felt a frisson of wonder at the recollection. "I had never seen Stonemaker items in reality." Kali nodded towards the dalma plates. "I couldn't help it. I immediately began to question what I was seeing. How could dalma plates exist pre-Skyfall? They are fundamental to Titian warcraft. These stones, these alien carvings, were dangerous enough for my father to outlaw any talk of Stonemakers and their technologies. And after holding those ancient stones up to the light of day, I worked out why." She swallowed; it would never stop hurting her to go against her people, but she made herself press on. "There is a direct parallel between those crude antiquities and the water tech of the ancient Vary. Both use datascripts to process information. Stonemakers used water to infill the shallow channels cut into the rock. Bleek use gel – which is a self-oscillating polymer fluid, or 'soft robot' if you like. Both rely on secret codices, on language, to store and activate data."

Mohab ran his fingers over the dalma plates. "You think High Judge Titian outlawed all reference to the Stonemakers because he harnessed their technologies in the past and didn't want to admit so?"

"From what I unearthed prior to my arrest, the very latest gunner schematics have Stonemaker tech at their heart."

"And your father is ashamed he stole from this country's past?"

Kali let her head fall back. She stared up at the oppressive beams of the hut's ceiling, imagining the expanse of blue-black, star-speckled sky above. "My father has stolen from *your* past.

The ancient Stonemakers were Vary."

Mohab fell silent. Kali could understand. The idea that her father had not only ordered the imprisonment of the Vary but stolen their history and manipulated it as his own was as shocking as it was numbing.

"If these pieces of rock aided Titian's ascent to power, they might as well be stained with the blood of my people."

Kali sensed his new distaste for the stones. She took them from him and cradled them in her arms like the ancient treasures she believed them to be.

"I will hide them under my corner of the mattress. If I am caught with them in my possession I will not be bled out on the spot. You might not be so lucky." She went to walk away, but then she stopped and said over a shoulder, "My father has stolen your legacy, Mohab. I suggest you think of a way to steal it back."

FOURTEEN

Three Months Earlier

Something had been growing inside her granddaughter for a long time. To call it guilt would be to overegg it and miss the subtleties of the change. Looking back to the sparrow-killing child she once was, Grizmare could see that Kali had altered immensely over the years. Throughout her trial at the Nilreb Imperial Court, Kali had remained cold – ultimately feasible as a Lieutenant in High Judge Titian's National Guard. Less so in her role as a Vary sympathiser, intent on polluting her nation's rationale. Kali had crossed the line by abusing her elite access to the datastacks and publicly criticising the regime. Grizmare might have made this point to her granddaughter if she thought it would do any good. Instead, she instructed her driver to pull into the underground docks at the court dome and made up her mind to endure Kali's predicament. After all, the girl had tied herself up in knots!

"What can I do?" Grizmare muttered, shifting her weight between her aching feet as she waited on the elevator.

"What's that?" The latest in a series of personal companions paid for by her son stared at her with almost rude intensity. This one – apparently named Lizabeth – was a nun, and young as a prostitute from Geno's red-light district. Wearing the traditional black habit and wimple of her order, she looked like a child playing dress up.

"Mind your own stinking business!" Grizmare masticated her gums. The fire-lamps were too bright in the basement; they made her old eyes hurt.

The lift arrived noiselessly, the reflective inky panel sliding back to reveal a softly lit interior.

"So, should I ask which floor we need? Or is that none of my stinking business either?" The nun waited by the panel of gel patches as Grizmare hobbled inside the lift.

"Well, you're a spicy little minx." Grizmare nodded to the numbered patches, many of which required an identification scan to activate. "Floor forty-three. The main court room. Unless my granddaughter's act of treason has been bumped to a smaller court in favour of a worse felon."

"A worse felon does not exist." The nun thumbed the gel patch and the doors closed silently.

The motion was imperceptible. Grizmare outstared the nun, who had the most perfectly Bleek green eyes. "My son would like you," she said, jabbing the floor with her ornate cane.

The nun's mouth twitched; a micromovement. The doors slid open, letting in the noise from the corridor.

"My son's secretary promised me it would be a civilised proceeding." A few steps from the elevator and Grizmare was already recoiling against the flashes of gel film and an assault of questions from the datakeepers.

"Madam Titian. What do you say about this charge of treason?"

"Madam Titian. Have you spoken with your granddaughter?"

"Will High Judge Titian intervene?"

"Did you know Kali was going to post a personal manifesto on the datastacks?"

"Were you in on it?"

"Were you in on it?"

"Were you in on it?"

Grizmare didn't answer their questions. Instead, she barged on through, whacking shins with her cane and muttering, "Get out of my way, lice!"

The nun, too, proved her worth. Pulling Grizmare back by the shoulder, she pushed her way in front and held up the crossed swords pendant which hung around her neck. "Let us pray to Lord Gothendore to lend us intelligence and listening ears in the trial ahead, ladies and gentlemen. Let us pray."

The whole corridor fell into a begrudging silence. *No respect for the mother of their great leader*, thought Grizmare darkly. *But you fools prostrate yourselves before a piece of tin on a chain!*

"Oh, holy divine, the sacred, the iron rod. Keeper of benediction and salvation. Grant us weight to our ambition. Purity in our blessed design. And the humanity to shine longest and brightest. Lord Gothendore, hear our words." The nun brought the pendant to her lips, kissed it, and led Grizmare through the crowd as if parting water.

"See how straight she sits?" Grizmare nodded towards the distant figure. "I taught Kali that. Drummed it into her with a choice between pound cake and a backhander." She nodded smugly. "The National Guard will take credit for that posture, but I bred her that way since the beginning."

"Bred?" The nun stared at the solitary figure in the dock. "I understand you keep a zoo, Madam Titian. Do you enjoy the company of animals?"

Funny girl, this Lizabeth, thought Grizmare. *Was there intent behind her words?*

"I find comfort in the retardation and spontaneity of beasts. We —" she nodded to the rows of dignitaries and datakeepers in the main hall below. "...are cut from the same cloth. It's all entirely too dull."

"And yet you failed to breed the wild animal out of Kali when you made her sit up straight." Lizabeth fixed Grizmare with her sharp green eyes.

Oh yes, there is intent there! "Could it be, Lizabeth, you would have benefitted from a stronger hand in your own upbringing?"

Before she and the nun could pursue their verbal dance further, a clerk's voice boomed out below and brought the court to order. The judges materialised at their bench. Like flies on shit, Grizmare told Lizabeth out the corner of her mouth. She held up a hand and, from a distance, 'captured' each judge between a thumb and forefinger and pretended to squash them flat.

Last to arrive was High Judge Titian. Her son. Although, looking down on him from this angle, she would never have recognised him. He wore the black uniform of the National Guard with added stripes and medals, despite having seen no active service of course. Grizmare couldn't keep in a snort, attracting the attention of one or two of the vultures below. She produced a handkerchief and mimed choking into it.

"Imbeciles. My son, he walks well though." She nodded towards the man striding to take his central seat at the bench. "Pound cake or a backhander."

It was the first time she had laid eyes on her son in a month and a half. His hair was thinning, she decided as he placed his peaked cap on the long table and took his seat. And Kali? How did she look? It was impossible to tell from that far away. All Grizmare could do was interpret the outline of her granddaughter, dressed in the washed-out grey of a prison smock behind a translucent wall of glass-sheet. Kali sat so very straight. Unflinching.

"That's my good girl," Grizmare said softly. It took all her steel not to throw herself over the rail and fight tooth and nail to reach the child she loved the most.

FIFTEEN

High Judge Titian was to make an inspection of Abbandon. Kali
heard the news in the holding bay, her father's name resonating
between the prisoners like the strike of sledgehammers in the
quarry. She pictured Titian in his uniform, boots laced up his
shins like scars. His close-cropped beard had always reminded her
of the monks who wafted incense through Geno Benedictory;
she had visited often as a child, her grandmother having a
penchant for the sour gin produced by the monks using the
benedictory stills. For a moment, it would confuse her to imagine
the grey hue of her father's skin, and then she would remember
the lungrot which had struck him down like her mother, and how
she had received weekly reports on his progress while she took
over the country's pompadours. Seeing him again might evoke an
instinctual sense of comfort; after all, he was still her father. But
then she would remember where she was and on whose order,
and all false hope evaporated.

"Will he be moved to see you?" Groff worked to uncoil
cabling from a drum, feeding it up to her.

"I can assure you my father is not coming to see me." She
patted the gunner's underbelly. "This warcraft is the more likely
candidate. I haven't seen a gunner like this before. The fact its
fuselage is blown after re-entry suggests it's still experimental.
And there is a far greater degree of bio-engineering going on
beneath these bolt plates than I'm used to." She sent sparks flying
as the cabling synced and fed into the magnetised clips. "The only
way my father will see me is as the ghost of a girl he once knew."

"I don't know how a father could be like that with his
daughter."

Groff visibly jumped when she looked at him, as if expecting
a new outburst in defence of her origins. But Kali knew he was

just voicing the same sentiment as the Speaker had when she first arrived.

Sparks fountained around her like Skyfall. "I never set out to harm my father. We just disagreed on his politics." She shook her head. "Increasingly, I think I have been very stupid, Groff." Her voice cracked with the sentiment.

Groff squinted. He didn't look as monstrous as he should have. Kali remembered the tooth of the Vary male killed by the blocker at the spinning machines, how it had reminded her of the milk teeth she lost in childhood.

"I have lived in a cage made of lies," she said.

"Why did you speak up for the Vary, Kali?"

She expected to feel sickened by the presumptive use of her first name. Instead, she felt almost grateful for Groff's attempts at kinship. And so she told him the truth. All about the time a year and a half ago when, on her father's orders, she travelled north of the Nedmac Traps.

Commandant General Ricklan, an elite member of her father's cabinet, had met her off the passenger wagon and guided her through his Cull System with wind in his sails and wild gesticulations. As Rickland had explained it, the bedrock of pumice was carved out by the first cargo load of Vary to arrive at the site. Once seven large trenches had been cut, the first shipment were stripped, made to lie face down in one of the trenches they had dug, and bled out via their nicks. The first rows were soon submerged under subsequent layers of bodies.

Arriving alongside one of the trenches, Kali had peered down at the mess of hair and limbs and faces, and had thought how much the bodies below looked like melted wax dolls. Seeing movement at the sides of the trenches, she had watched as a pair of guards clubbed the survivors to death with their beaters. Up close, it was more difficult to put aside the fact that the Vary were in fact not wax, but flesh and bone. The mix of putrefying bodies and the expulsions of those who had opened their bowels in their last few desperate moments was staggering to the senses. Death clogged the nostrils; Kali tried to breathe through her mouth only to find its crud on her tongue. She had ordered executions, but a signature on a gel frame was a far cry from the moral inferno she saw before her. These Vary were the pregnant and the elderly. They were neighbours, gardeners, maids, teachers, lamp lighters, stone masons, glass-sheet workers, surgeons, actors, engineers, and lawyers. They were blonde haired and brown haired and pale skinned and dark skinned. They were tall and short and round shoulderd and straight backed.

Ricklan had turned to her, bloated with pride. "We eradicated fifteen thousand these last two days alone. A dusting of lime salt will melt the remains back into the lava flow. It will be as if they never were."

Standing on the precipice, Kali had finally understood the cancer at the heart of her nation. Hearing the tale, Groff had hardened his face to her and, for the first and only time, it had seemed to Kali that he could have killed her there and then with his bare hands had he been free to do so.

The tremor had knocked out the security coils around the house, gardens and zoo. Grizmare hadn't noticed immediately. Neither had the groundsmen who only worked a couple of days a week now. Harriot had heard about the break-in from her staff who had been gossiping with Grizmare's stable hands and she was quick to call, offering her condolences. Grizmare didn't say much. There was real sadness to her day. Boohoo and Shy-lo, the mating pair of desert otters, were missing. No doubt they had been stolen by opportunists and sold for a pretty penny. Grizmare kept thinking about the menu at the Red Orchid hotel, the listing for highly prized desert otter and a price to reflect their rarity. She didn't like to think of Boohoo and Shy-lo ending up on the chopping board of some impartial chef and served up bruised and braised in wine stock.

"I cannot talk right now," she told Harriot. "I have the coils to reset and charge, not to mention five otter kittens to hand-rear.

The little bastards probably won't take to the bottle. But we're not monsters, are we Harriot? We have to try these things."

Harriot made it clear that Grizmare should forget the animals and concentrate on barricading herself back in. "There are unpleasant rumours, Grizmare. Enemy combatants infiltrating our forces, warcraft shot down over Nilreb. Naturally, one doesn't believe a word…"

"More's the pity."

"Now you are just being antagonistic, Grizmare. Loose lips cost lives."

Grizmare had heard enough. She cut the wire phone connection. Her day was already bad enough without Harriot's inane contribution. The truth of it was that even Bleekland's grand dames were forced to fight over scraps of information about a war taking place above their heads. The datastacks still broadcast the same patriotic diatribes and overinflated numbers of defeated enemy. The skies still smoked and glittered with warcraft. And now her son had disowned her.

"Not literally, of course," she told Lizabeth later that afternoon after several sour gins. The otter kittens were playing in a makeshift sandpit below the water clock. After a couple of hours mourning the loss of their parents, all five had bucked up and taken to the bottle with the brutish insensibility of the animal kingdom, pleasing Grizmare greatly. "But he has put me to one side. And I…" Her eyes greased. "I should have done a better job of raising my granddaughter, but I thought she would shake free of her father's influence in time. To be quite honest with you, Lizabeth, I thought this entire nation would shake free of my son's ideals long before now."

Lizabeth wasn't scrimping on the measures of sour gin for once. Grizmare was wise to the young woman, though. She was actually surprised that it had taken Lizabeth this long to try her luck. Often the nun had appeared on the verge of saying something meaningful. She had talked of injustices in the world and corruption of the church. *You have an ulterior motive for taking care of an old fart,* Grizmare had concluded. *One day you will show your cards. One day I might show mine.*

"Grizmare," Lizabeth began, Grizmare's insistence on the nun's use of her first name having finally stuck. "I feel we might broach an unpopular subject today." She nodded towards the otter kittens, lulled to sleep by the chimes of the falling water against the bells. "After a tiring day, we have peace at last."

Grizmare nosed her glass. She had no intention of speaking first. Let Lizabeth struggle through her bit; it would be more amusing and put Grizmare at the advantage.

She was taken aback when, rather than confess her secrets in a mess of tears and weakness, Lizabeth returned to the drinks tray and, uncorking the decanter, poured herself a measure of sour gin. Grizmare was in her usual place of residence in front of the wall of glass-sheet which gave out onto the garden. Grizmare sat in her favourite recliner while Lizabeth opted, as usual, to sit on the chase lounge, perched on the edge as if Gothendore himself might disapprove of the privilege of comfort.

Grizmare made no comment on the gin. Just watched and waited. Everyone had stories. It was one of the things that irritated her the most about her aging acquaintances. Everyone was so enthusiastically, desperately eager to tell their tales of privileged lives – tales of daring, exoticism, flamboyance… to Grizmare's mind, so gut-wrenchingly dull.

But Lizabeth had a far more interesting story to tell and Grizmare wanted to hear it. The woman had admitted she deliberately gained a position on High Judge Titian's staff. More specifically, she had wormed her way into being Grizmare's personal companion. Now Grizmare wanted to know why.

After a long sup of gin, she said, "Go on then, girl. Spill your guts. And feel free to take that ridiculous wimple off and lose the eye contacts. None of it looks comfortable and I've seen through your ruse since the day we met." She pursed her lips. "Good effort, though."

With a sigh, Lizabeth pulled off the wimple, revealing short black hair cropped tight to the scalp. She didn't remove the green contacts. "My real name is Eva," she said firmly. "I was born in Zochgeng, five kilometres outside of Nilreb. My family were embroiderers, my mother, my father, and my twin younger sisters. Only my older brother escaped the family calling to become an entertainer in the city." Her hand started to shake and she drowned the remainder of the gin. The liquor appeared to calm her slightly and she rolled back her shoulders, as if shaking off the emotion. "I suppose it is fair to say I always envisioned a different path for myself as well. I wanted to be an actress. Like my older brother, I wanted my time in the sun. Once I was of age, I think my parents knew I wouldn't stick around to stitch vesils and mantles and family flags." With clear pride, she said, "A vesil is a ceremonial pair of gloves. The mantle is an embroidered silk scarf worn for worship. The flags are tradition. But a clever woman like you, Grizmare, already knows these things." Lifting a hand to her face, she touched a fingertip to one of her eyeballs. "Do you see? No contacts."

Grizmare didn't quite believe her. "But you are Vary. Vary have black eyes."

"Black, green, blue, grey, brown, hazel and every shade in-between. But you are right in that, over the past 50 years or so, Bleek have been at pains to maximise the green-eyed gene. These" – She pointed to her clear emerald eyes – "...are all mine and they have helped me to move in circles I should never have been allowed in."

Grizmare folded her arms and tutted. "I can see where this is going. Your family have been arrested and you come to beg for clemency. Befriend me first, of course. So as to seal the deal."

"That is not it at all!" The nun banged the arm of her chair with the flat of a hand. "Nothing so mundane. Oh, I know you better than that, Grizmare… Madam Titian. You wouldn't entertain anything so mediocre and I certainly wouldn't approach you for it. Besides, my family are all long dead. Mother and Father first. Executed for religious crimes, according to the official documentation. Because they manufactured outlawed items – which they did – and were murdered for those self-same gloves and scarves. My sisters were rounded up during one of the National Guard's sweeps and sent to the Killing Fields. I survived because I was auditioning in Nilreb. And since then, I have survived because I am a fucking good actress and I was born with the ability to pass."

Grizmare pulled at her chin hairs. She was disappointed in herself. Yes, she had picked up on the nun having some driving purpose beyond attending to the toilette and eccentricities of an octogenarian. She might even have known that, deep down, Lizabeth – *Eva?* – was Vary. But the eyes – so blindingly green, so pure – they had really thrown her.

"You are quite the spectacle, Eva. My son's scientists would call you a genetic anomaly and perform unpleasant procedures on your eyes in a bid to explain them."

"Fortunately, my official data trail testifies to my Bleek heritage."

"I warrant it does." Grizmare continued to pluck at her chin. She narrowed her eyes, the better to see Eva, the truth of her anyway. "Counterfeit data like that is worth killing for. Liable to get you killed, too."

"It is. But I wasn't about to give up on my brother, Ju. When our parents and sisters were killed, he chose to work for the Resistance, putting together pamphlets using a printing press hidden in the basement of the Universium library."

"Why are you telling me this? Why would you think I have the slightest interest in you and your role playing, or your dead parents, dead sisters, most likely a dead brother too?" Grizmare nosed the gin glass. She took a spicy mouthful. "I suppose the real question is, what do you want from me?"

The nun – was she even that? – fetched them both a fresh measre. She took her perch and returned her gaze to the garden. "Grizmare, I can confirm that, as of last week, Kali was still alive. But that's where the reassurance ends because our informant was recently executed inside the walls of Abbandon. As for what I want? Quite simply, I want you to help us rise up and act. I want history to testify to the fact that you, Grizmare Titian, matter. You are not just a grandmother, not just a mother. You are so much more. You can help halt the extermination of an entire ethnic group in this country. You, Grizmare, can be a burning star in the insidious night."

Grizmare rocked back in her seat and honked with laughter. "Oh, Eva! You've me pinned as quite the modern rebel. It's hilarious and fantastically sinister. You, girl, have been stalking me for some time then? You and your merry band of revolutionists. I hope I have forced you to watch me take several hundred shits and pick my nose! And you think I would betray my own flesh and blood? High Judge Titian is my son!" The light went from her eyes. "He is my son," she said more gently, her heart breaking just a little.

An uneasy calm settled over the room. The nun's words repeated over in Grizmare's mind. *Rise up... You can matter. You can matter!*

She felt a deep shifting inside, like bones breaking and resetting.

Eva reached out. She laid a hand over Grizmare's very gently, as if she was handling precious china. "High Judge Titian is your son, but Kali is your granddaughter. As history tells it, you stepped in when her mother died. High Judge Titian was absent for the most part. You raised Kali – and he took her away."

"That is a ridiculous thing to say." Grizmare's lips clamped shut. There was a small flicker of a nerve under one eye. Remarkably, though, she didn't take her hand away from Eva's. In that moment, she felt more alone than she ever had, even when her husband died and left her to bring up a squawking infant, even when Kali was arrested and she had hidden in the darkness of the house for three days straight rather than face the pain of sunlight.

Grizmare's shoulders slumped. "Some part of me will always

take responsibility for creating the beast which rules this country. I didn't set out to raise my son to be wicked. If you ask me, the fucker was determined to turn out that way. And for the longest while, I thought Kali was destined to follow the same path." She took back her hand and nursed her sour gin, taking sips to fortify herself. "Kali should have talked to me. Maybe we could have worked out a wiser approach to the whole rebellion thing. I found her notes, you know."

Eva became acutely alert. Grizmare was reminded of a desert otter, sitting up on its hind legs, nose twitching.

"Yes, I thought you and your rebel kind would be interested in that little fact."

"What notes did Kali leave for you?" A stillness settled over the young woman, as if she feared the slightest movement would make Grizmare clam up again.

And she was tempted; in so many ways, Grizmare wanted to go back to keeping everything inside – all the anger, all the rage, all the guilt for what she might or might not be responsible for. But she was tired of it all. Or was it more a final conceding that she, Grizmare, did not hold the same views as the holy nation of Bleekland? In fact, she vehemently opposed them?

"Kali never has known quite which side to come down on. Good, bad, she's always been a bit of both. But I am older, crabbier, and one thing I know for sure: if I can breed a monster, I can help find a way to stab that abomination in the heart. High Judge Titian took my Kali away," she said numbly, wishing she could peel time back from its blood and muscles. Instead, she drained her glass and held it out. "You'd better fill this up, Eva, and then I suggest you explain what it is you and the rest of the Resistance want from me."

SIXTEEN

The blockers were at the door to the barracks at first light, barking insults and hacking up tobacco grinds. Mohab unrolled from his corner of the bunk, hearing his joints crack. The need to piss was overwhelming. He hurried to the slop trough at the far end of the shed, desperate to relieve himself before others crowded him out or the blockers bustled them into the assembly yard. It was pitch-black near the trough. He didn't need to see to know his stream of urine was peppered with blood; one of his testicles had been crushed during a beating by a guard even before his transfer to Abbandon. A thin wire of pain backed up his urethra.

"Get up, hogs! Get up!" The blocker threw the insults like grenades, bouncing them off the weary men. Groans accompanied the lengthening out of stiff muscles. Others sobbed in their sleep and were prodded awake by a neighbour; one slacker could see the nicks activated for a whole bunk! In a matter of seconds, the Vary males were shuffling out into the dawn.

Finishing up at the trough, Mohab secured his trousers and hurried over to his father. "Roll call. It comes around too soon each day, I know…" His voice trailed off as he saw two figures crouched alongside the cot. Groff, the nurse, and Lieutenant Titian. Both glanced up as he approached. Groff had a hold of his father's hand.

"The Speaker is dead," said the Lieutenant. Matter-of-fact, as if passing comment on the weather. She visibly softened, shoulders slumping. "Your father is dead," she said, reminding him the body on the cot was not just his people's spiritual and political leader. He was the man who had told Mohab stories on the porch and who had taught him to ride red racers. 'Firm in the saddle, knees soft at the flanks.' His father's voice, now a ghost's.

"When?" The question was gritty on his tongue, like a mouthful of sand.

"In the night sometime." Groff stroked the dead man's hand. "It was peaceful."

"I will ask about a burial." The Lieutenant nodded vacantly at her own suggestion. "I'll speak with the Commandant Superintendent. It may be possible to arrange it." She turned her head towards the demanding voices from the doorway. "We need to make roll call."

Groff stood up. He patted Mohab's shoulder. "Come away now, Mohab."

Following the Lieutenant, Groff made Mohab put one foot in front of the other.

Outside, the yard was already crowded with men blinking and stumbling on emaciated limbs. Silently, they fell in line. Words singled a person out.

Despite the suppression of their voices, the Vary still managed to react to the arrival of the visiting officials. Breath came a little harder. Feet shuffled. The existing guards made no attempt to contain the reaction; let the Vary express their awe and fear in the face of their great leader!

High Judge Titian walked ahead of the rest, flanked by the Secretary of State, Magne Kirkland, to his left and the camp's Commandant General, Håkon Drescher, to his right. Behind walked Commandant Superintendent Joltu, and several of his higher-ranking officers. All wore the black uniform of the National Guard, collars stiffened with beet starch, wide razingstock leather belts at their waist.

Two rows from the front, Kali had a clear view of the inspection party. The coarse pyjamas she wore rubbed her skin, but there was lightness to the prison clothing that she had never felt in all her years dressing as a guard. Her organs weren't constrained by the belt. Her neck was free of its starched brace. The National Guard, meanwhile, sweated under their peaked brims.

The sight of her father almost broke her and she had to fight to bring her emotions back under control. In red boots and matching lapels, he looked as officiously neat as she had ever seen him. Here in the desert, where the sun baked down and the earth steamed, he was the picture of control. Before him stood row on row of starving Vary and he was so utterly put together.

Bile rose into Kali's mouth. She swallowed the sourness back down.

The sun was rising, but already the temperature was uncomfortable. All around, Vary swayed on unsteady feet, struggling with light-headedness and the fear of blacking out. On the far side of the yard, and separated from the males by two walls of slice-wire, the women and children stood and stared.

High Judge Titian talked amongst his staff. Occasionally, he gestured to a barrack building or pressed a handkerchief to his temples.

The usual roll call went ahead, with the weaker of the Vary picked off and led in the direction of the firing range. The invalids made no complaint. Kali suspected the poor devils had long forgotten why they were in Abbandon. She hoped their nicks would slice deep and deliver them from the pain.

It was not enough that her father come and survey the Vary's decay. It was soon apparent that he wanted to rescind their belief in false gods.

"Where is the Speaker?" he demanded in the screech tone which characterised his orations and was entirely alien to Kali's homelife.

The question activated a chain of command which went from Commandant General to Commandant Superintendent to the block chief to his bully boys. The bark went out to, "Bring your father here, Speaker's son!"

Kali turned her head as much as she dared and saw a figure pulled out of line four rows back. She had a sudden, overwhelming desire to step forward too. 'Do not expose yourself,' she repeated silently as Mohab was dragged towards her father.

✗✗

Mohab remembered the weeks each summer when the red racers would require breaking in and his father stayed home awhile.

"Let me tell you a story," his father would say of an evening, settling into the old rocker on the porch and giving the seat beside him a pat. Mohab would climb up alongside his father and look out at the coarse prairieland of his family's homestead and the low sun at the horizon. A first few stars would brighten, tiny diamonds ahead of the rush of night.

Those evenings, Mohab would listen sleepily to his father's stories of patchwork men, magic gourds, gilded lilies, tarnished knaves, white crows, and three young sisters enchanted into teaspoons – one brass, one silver and one gold – and a blind minister forced to taste his soup with each. All the triumphs and suffering of the Vary, lifted from the family books of all the hundreds and thousands of Vary descendants out there in the world. No matter how many times the Vary were driven from their homes, beaten, and degraded, the stories endured.

Kneeling in the dust on the day his father breathed his last, Mohab finally thought he understood their value. They had kept his father elsewhere for most of his life, but they were also the only thing that felt solid any more.

"My father is dead." Mohab forced back his shoulders, steeling himself against a second blow.

The blocker went to raise his makeshift beater, but a voice snapped, "Stop!"

Mohab had only heard High Judge Titian speak on the National Broadcast, transmitted three times daily. But he recognised Titian's voice from that one word and felt a reflexive jolt of fear.

The blocker nudged him between the rows of prisoners to the very front.

Mohab had seen enough photostats and parodies of the man to recognise High Judge Titian. He was stouter in the flesh, his cheeks slack and faintly grey, and he had the same delicate pale green eyes at Kali.

"Speaker's son." Titian focused intently on Mohab's face. "Where is the body?"

"In the sweat box."

"Sweat box?"

"The barracks." Mohab's throat flexed around a surge of grief.

"He died of natural causes?"

Mohab wanted to scream, 'No, you rancid fucker! There was nothing natural about my father's death. He was starved, beaten, and repeatedly humiliated.' The words stayed unspoken. What was the use speaking to Bleekland's High Judge in a language of truth he could never understand?

Instead, Mohab just nodded.

"Fetch the corpse."

Corpse? Mohab's pain crystallised. *What words! What terrible, festering words to say to a son!* His rage was self-replicating, swelling to take up every last space inside of him.

Titian repeated the order. Commandant Superintendent Joltu stepped forward.

"Get your father." Joltu nodded to a couple of guards. "He will need assistance."

"To carry the body of one old man? I think the male can manage," said the Commandant General.

Joltu stepped back, overruled and superficially unmoved.

Mohab walked away, watched by Bleek and Vary alike and feeling the weight of so many eyes.

Inside the gloom of the barracks, it took him a few moments to see again. Oppressive with body heat at night, the air inside was even more cloying in the sweltering day. The smell was animalistic – the shit-soaked slats of the bunks, the sulphur stench of opened orifices, and something new: the oaky putridness of a dead body.

Mohab considered sitting down on the floor beside his father and waiting for death in whatever form it might take. But something about the instant degradation of his father's body made him want to escape back into the light. He considered dragging his father's body out on the low cot; he didn't know if he wanted to touch him.

"Hurry up, boy."

A guard stood in the doorway. Mohab struggled to lift the body. The lifeless head lolled against his shoulder and he cradled it there, reached behind the knees and lifted the body up into his arms. He had no doubt that his father was feather-light, but in that heat, with High Judge Titian waiting on him, the body was a tremendous burden.

As the guard barked his demands, Mohab laboured to put one foot in front of the other. His father had opened his bowels on death, expressing the crud of his used-up existence. Mohab stumbled forward, immersed in its stench.

Two rows back, Kali watched the Speaker's son stagger from the barracks with the body in his arms, face straining under the weight. No one said a word as Mohab made his way slowly across the yard until he arrived at last in front of her father and stood, swaying under the strain put upon him.

"Check the pulse," Titian said to the air.

Joltu unbuckled a cylindrical nick key from his belt. He checked for a pulse at the Speaker's neck, undid one wrist nick, checked again and undid the second nick. "No pulse." He threw the set of nicks to one of his officers, fastened the key back onto his belt and stepped back.

Kali's heartbeat quickened. *What now?* Crucify the body in a public place? Or would the fennec foxes get the best of the meat out in the desert? It was all so pathologically brutal. The man deserved a proper burial.

"The Speaker has left his stain on this camp," her father announced in his screech voice. "He spoke of change that wasn't his to offer! Abbandon will not become a germ centre for fresh sedition. If other countries fear the gross indoctrinations of

107

conscience and morality, we Bleek alone will embrace the label of barbarians. We will root this nation in acts of eradication in order to break down the core disease. Variness shall be made stagnant and it shall be made to burn."

He addressed his staff, but the oration was meant for the prisoners. Kali wanted to rush out of line and put a hand across his mouth. She did not love the Vary the way she had her own people, but the words which had once uplifted left the taste of ashes in her mouth. When the National Guard knocked their hands against their breasts in sharp salute, she wanted to break every arm. How could her people embrace barbarianism when they had language, architecture, schools of learning, music, poetry, dance, performance, and philosophy?

There were no notions of beauty in her father's next utterance. "Take the body to the factory and throw it in the furnace." This, to the Speaker's son, still cradling his dead father. There would be no burial; Kali understood that in the harshness of day. But to demand that a son cremate his father like a bag of slop at a slaughter house went against everything Kali understood about belonging to a cognitive species.

"You cannot ask that!" she called out. "The man is dead. Why further the suffering?" With no way back, she stood up straight, imagining herself in uniform once more.

Her father stared at her. He looked tired momentarily, as if he hadn't slept for days. Mohab collapsed to his knees, his father's body limp in his arms, head lolling.

"We are not a cruel race," she said, the same logic she had employed in court and knowing, as she had then, that her words were diaphanous next to his father's hefty jingoism. She persevered, despite the dread in the pit of her stomach. "If we treat the Vary as animals, what is to say we won't turn on our own? How long until we persecute the old, or weed out the elite amongst our children and execute the rest?"

"You do not get to talk in terms of 'we'! You have no Bleek affiliation," said her father with the maniacal conviction he used for his sermons. His features corrupted. "Bleek blood was flushed from your veins the day you betrayed your nation and joined the Vary swine." He snapped his head aside and, addressing the Commandant Superintendent, said, "Do with her as you wish." Turning his back, he walked off in the direction of the political offices, accompanied by foreign minister Kirkland and their personal guard, leaving Kali with the roaring swell of anger in her ears.

You would abandon me again. The reality struck her hard in the stomach, making her bend over and retch. What now? Would she be led to the Killing Fields? Or would her nicks be activated where she stood?

She straightened up and wiped the back of a hand across her mouth. The Commandant General eyed her while fanning flies from his face.

"Commandant Superintendent."

Joltu stepped forward.

"I leave this matter in your hands." Drescher turned to the waiting officers. "Finish roll call and get the swine to the quarry and the factory. Too much of the morning has been wasted already." He left in pursuit of Titian.

Joltu glared at Kali, whose emotions oscillated between blind fear and perverse excitement that death would bring relief. "You will help the Speaker's son carry his father's body," Joltu said quietly. "You will throw the body inside the factory furnace and then return to your work duties." He blinked. "For the time being."

Kali glared at the Commandant Superintendent. She hated his passive wretchedness. None of the Bleek guards would risk Titian changing his mind about her – which meant she could rage against the regime of hate all she wanted. No one would take notice. She was not Bleek, but neither was she Vary. She was a silenced voice.

With no alternative, she helped Mohab move his father's body because she was told to. At the factory, she took the

Speaker's feet while Mohab supported the head and upper body. Together, they staggered down a metal staircase to the boiler room. There, in that putrid atmosphere, she worked with Mohab to lower the body onto the wheeled tray. Lifting the grate to the giant furnace, she shielded her eyes against the heat and the sight of a son forced to feed his father to the flames.

Later that afternoon, Commandant Joltu poured himself an excessively large glass of wine and sat down heavily in the chair behind his desk. He drank deeply then pressed a thumb and forefinger to the bridge of his nose, squeezing away the tension.

Helping the Commandant General to host High Judge Titian and his staff had been exhausting, both on a professional and personal level. Ever since the High Judge had signed off on his own daughter being sent to one of Bleekland's labour camps, no one took their position for granted any more. Admittedly, it took a certain degree of conscious rebellion to find oneself in Kali's reduced circumstances. All the same, it paid to be careful.

Joltu let his head rest against the back of his chair and closed his eyes. Everything ached – his jaw, his teeth, his shoulders. Another uncomfortable emotion niggled at him. It felt suspiciously like pity. However, the idea that he might feel sorry for the Vary was too simplistic. What he felt was closer to frustration at the way this slow decay of living creatures was being drawn out by their life inside the camp. It could all have been brought to a decisive full stop just by activating wrist nicks. After all, if you are going to kill the bastards, why not get it over with? Commandant General Ricklan had the right idea with his Cull System, disposing of hundreds of thousands of Vary swiftly and effectively. No prolonged suffering. No need for guards to watch the physical breaking down of a species.

But it wasn't High Judge Titian's desire to fully exterminate the Vary any more. Not only were their numbers providing a free and increasingly essential workforce during the war effort, but Titian and his doctor generals had new plans for the Vary.

Joltu learnt as much after roll call earlier that day. He had taken a seat at the long table in the guards' quarters, and was joined by the Commandant General, the High Judge and his attendant cabinet.

"The purpose of my visit here today is twofold," High Judge Titian had explained from his seat at the head of the table. His voice was quieter than Joltu was used to. More refined. "Firstly, I wish to thank those guards and officers in charge here. The Vary are well-mastered and the quarry and the factory are at peak production. Secondly, I wish to inform you all of a potentially revolutionary application of science to the Vary problem."

That voice, so soothing... Those eyes, pregnant with happy possibility... Joltu pictured Kali's childhood with this man. Titian had been an occasional visitor to the family estate, not unlike Joltu himself. Both attended politically sensitive dinner parties at the residence. He had even heard High Judge Titian enquire as to which staircase led to his daughter's nursery since he could not be expected to remember. "A lot has happened since my last visit," he had told the servant. "We have gone to war!" As if the conflict at large explained why he couldn't remember the route to his own daughter's nursery!

Presumably he and Kali had encountered one another now and then inside the house, or out in the grounds, or in Grizmare Titian's infamous and obscure zoo. What then? Had the High Judge scooped the girl up into his arms? Had he showered his only child with presents and compliments, in lieu of affection?

Joltu thought about that morning and Kali speaking up for the Speaker's son despite the very real threat of the wrist nicks above her pulse points. The Commandant Superintendent had studied the High Judge, standing a few short steps away. From a distance, Kali would have thought her father unmoved. That wasn't true, though. Up close, Joltu had seen a trace of sadness in the man's face. Titian's breathing had quickened too, the rise and fall of his chest counting out the seconds of tension between father and daughter. Watching the High Judge rise above his parental emotions, Joltu imagined Kali naked in his office. She was his reward and his punishment.

Sitting at the long table that afternoon, he was distracted by the High Judge introducing a newcomer, a Doctor General Tristan Harris. Harris was faintly ghoulish in appearance. Thin grey skin stretched taut over his prominent skull and his clothing looked a size too big, as if his body had shrunk in the coffin. When the doctor spoke, he showed off his pale pink gums like an enraged primate.

"Thank you, High Judge Titian. Thank you," Harris chattered, spreading his hands out on the table as if to assert a calming influence over it. "And thank you Commandant General Drescher. It is very exciting to be setting up this new laboratory in Abbandon. We shall start small, of course. But I am confident that an intense timetable of procedures will lead to excellent results."

"Procedures?" Joltu liked to understand the everyday running of the camp. "We have an infirmary. Are you talking about another ward? Something more specialist?"

"Indeed, indeed. Commandant Superintendent Joltu, isn't it?" Harris showed his gums again. "But don't let me dazzle you with words. I will reveal my plans for the Vary through practical demonstrations."

"Now, to other business." High Judge Titian turned the discussion to other matters – new reductions in rations for the Vary ("Ravenous as rats," Harris had interrupted and High Judge Titian had smiled); an increase in stone wool quotas; the proposal to extend the quarry, and the lowering of the age of children working its surface from seven to six years old.

After Titian had brought an end to the meeting, he called Joltu back.

"Commandant Superintendent. Stay a moment."

With a small thrill of fear, Joltu turned back from the door. He saluted. "High Judge Titian."

Titian held his chin characteristically high, as if tilted to meet his own personal sun. He'd aged over recent months, thought Joltu. Acquired a new depth to the wrinkles at his mouth and eyes, lending him a permanently sour expression.

"My daughter is still alive." He said it matter-of-factly, if with the slightest hint of surprise. "Her breeding aids her resilience."

"Naturally, High Judge Titian."

"She is a disruptive force?"

"She can be. But she is a useful conduit between the Vary and the Bleek." He didn't say how she drove his mouth to the salt lick between her legs. How she bit and thrust like a she-wolf. How the dust engraved her navel like unpolished wood and he feasted on her knots. Instead, he stayed silent.

Titian pursed his lips. "A document will be sent to your personal datascreen. I want you to put your name to it."

With that, the High Judge strode from the room and Joltu had followed after. Now though, tucked behind the door of his office, legs spread, wine in hand, Titian's words came back to haunt him. 'She is a disruptive force…?' 'Put your name to it…'

Opening his eyes, Joltu sat forward, drained the glass and reached for the remainder of the bottle. 'Do with her as you wish,' the High Judge had told him out in the yard that morning, in front of Kali and so many listening ears. In truth, though, back behind closed doors, Titian held both his daughter's and Joltu's fates in his tight grip.

Joltu shook his head. When it came to Abbandon, it didn't matter which side of the fence you lived. Freedom was a fallacy!

PART TWO

SEVENTEEN

The journey had been an irritant. While the first-class passenger car provided a smooth ride over the slipstreams, Grizmare had found her patience wearing thin as the minutes passed achingly slowly. A simpering waiter with greased-back hair and a limp moustache had offered her desert otter for luncheon. "A rare and uniquely palatable dish," he had announced superciliously, indicating the listing on the gel frame. Grizmare had thought about breaking the menu over his head or hobbling him with her cane. She would have rather liked to watch that officious face crumple in agony.

But she had resisted, demanding instead that the meat be discontinued from the menu in future. She had ordered the curd and fennel pie, enduring – and enjoying – the surreptitious glares of her fellow diners now deprived of their desert otter.

With her journey finally complete, Grizmare found Nilreb as unmanageable and overbearing as she had remembered it. While Geno rose from the basalt bedrock in great stalks of glass-sheet which were almost organic in nature – at once striking and as one with the fractured landscape – Nilreb was a sprawling mess of brutal architecture.

Seated in the back of a limousine sent by the hotel, she got the impression that the driver was going out of his way to keep to the most impressive boulevards. To either side, huge glass-sheet palaces shouldered the heart and lungs of the government's municipal buildings. Among them was the Grand Library with its spiral columns and domineering bust of High Judge Titian erected relatively recently above the entrance. Soon she was passing Capital Hall, which was the country's political hub and the pinnacle of Titian architectural design. As he had been at pains to point out to her in the past, the smoked walls were underpinned by a curving spine of gel and grey-stone amalgam to allow for quake movement. Even the hotel, a huge grey-stone rotunda called The Perpetual, was a testament to her son's skills in taming elemental things and producing rigidity and order.

Grizmare, though, thwarted the driver's attempt to pull up in front of The Perpetual. Jabbing her cane into the back of his seat, she told him, "I am not finished with my sightseeing yet! I want to see the city at sunset. I want to see the Seven Bridges!"

The driver aborted his turn and gave a small cough of annoyance.

"Go on then, man!" Grizmare rooted around in the onboard wet bar and found a half bottle of sour gin. She didn't bother with a glass, but took a big gulp, enjoying the fire and tears it brought to her throat and eyes.

"Speak up!" she spat when the driver muttered something from the front seat.

The man cleared his throat. "Nilreb may be much changed since you last visited, Madam Titian." His speech was accented with the forward sounding vowels of the capital. "You can't just move around the city any more, can't go wherever you please. We've got to keep the city clean, so Vary are quarantined to the East Quarter until every household has been processed." He waved a hand to the colossal structures either side – great citadels of power with their moulded emblems. "Look how beautiful these streets are. High Judge Titian has given us clean air, a city to be proud of."

"Yes, yes. It is all very big and impressive. My son is the patron saint of dust handlers!" She gulped from the bottle. "All the same, it's insipid. I want to see the Seven Bridges. I've always liked their argy-bargy, all that colour, all that life!"

The driver gave his silly cough again. He was the kind of man who was worn by his uniform and not vice versa. Grizmare was newly irritated.

"Speak up again man! All I can hear is buzz, buzz, like I'm being driven around by a blasted botfly! Have the spine to spit your words out!"

"The Vary slums are not a tourist destination. They are not suitable for a person of your standing, Madam Titian."

"Fuck off!" Grizmare thudded her cane against the back of the man's seat again. "I'm the VIP. You are the chauffeur. So show me the Seven Bridges, or I'll feed you to my son or my tiger dog. And, trust me, neither option will be pretty!"

The driver didn't need any more convincing.

Half an hour later, Grizmare learnt that a border control unit had been established at the very edge of the East Quarter – or, as it was now named by thick lettering sprayed over the outer facing wall of the guards' office, 'Pig Town.' On the approach, both sides of the street were dominated by billboards playing Bleek propaganda. The underlying message was 'Stay Where We Can See You', Grizmare concluded, and she took in the sight of shiny faced Youth Guard manning the border. As the limo pulled up, four uniformed teenagers approached the driver's door. One girl marched forward of the rest. Grizmare noted that she had the horse-like bone structure so common amongst Bleekland's upper class. Her nose was long and straight. Even the two small moles beneath either eye were eerily symmetrical. In every way, the girl appeared to represent Titian's ideal of balanced perfection. It was soon clear that she was bred with the self-assurance to match.

The driver opened the windshield at the front of the vehicle.

"Papers," said the girl. Demanding it of a grown man as if he were beneath her.

She would make the perfect daughter-in-law, thought Grizmare – and chomped at her gums as if she had tasted something sour.

"No papers. I have with me a VIP on a visit to Nilreb and they have instructed me to show them the slums. You would be advised not to delay us." The driver shook off his lengthened vowels and spoke with clipped efficiency. "As per section 259 of the Nilreb Transport Code, any official on state business may move unhindered through Bleekland and its border dominions."

"But not every official has filed and had authorised the

necessary data stamp." The girl's long nose twitched officiously. At her back, her fellow youth got a slight twist to their mouths, as if trying to suppress their delight at the threat of disorder.

Grizmare lost patience. She tapped on the roof with her cane to indicate the driver should open the shield fully. As sunlight dawned across her face, she took pleasure in the reveal.

"I am Madam Titian, mother to the High Judge, Lord Elect. I have business at the Seven Bridges and you will allow this vehicle to pass unhindered or I will have you excommunicated, you idiotic child!"

The confidence drained from the teen's face, like so much hot air squeezed from a lungrot sufferer's lungs. The girl nodded curtly and stepped back, leaving the driver free to pull onto the road beyond the billboards and to slide the shield back up into place.

This much Grizmare saw on her unofficial tour of the Seven Bridges and the Vary slums. Poverty – swathes of it, infecting the streets – alongside boarded-up shop after boarded-up shop. Where the tremors had cracked the sidewalks and gone untreated, fat clumps of feather gorse had broken through. Grizmare knew from experience that the plant was rough to the touch while the stem had a coating of sticky sap which caused a rash and had been known to kill the very young. Where the wind had brought in ash at broken doors and windows, thick grey crusts had collected. The quarter and its bridges, once potent with families, artistry and commercial wealth, was now squalid and diseased-looking. Girders hung loose beneath the bridges. The dry riverbed was pocked with newly ruptured steam vents and bloody lava pools. Grizmare couldn't quite piece together what she was seeing; it was as if the streets and the riverbed had been turned inside out, their rawness exposed and rotting.

"What has happened here?" she said aloud, mainly to herself but the driver took it that he was required to answer.

"It shows you how uncivilised the Vary are when left to their own devices. A shock, I know!" He shook his head vigorously.

"Bleekland owes High Judge Titian a tremendous debt for keeping the Vary in order for as long as he did while they moved amongst us. But we've got the segregation in place at last and an end to their persistent leeching of the city's resources."

Even from the backseat, Grizmare could hear the righteousness pouring off the man. He was one of the zealots – fans so committed to her son and his teachings that they would happily sacrifice their own children to prove their idolatry. His kind terrified Grizmare more than the sunken eyed Vary trudging the streets.

"You even talk like him. My son. 'Leeching the city's resources'. 'Keeping the Vary in order'." Grizmare lifted the sour gin bottle to her lips, drinking deeply. She wiped her lips with the back of a hand. "Tell me, did you swallow every one of my son's tracts, page by page?"

The man was too quick in his response to have understood the criticism. "But of course, Madam Titian. My family is grateful for High Judge Titian's efforts to cleanse this nation of..."

"Shut up! Shut up! Shut up!" Grizmare took a fresh mouthful of liquor and swilled it around her gum to get rid of the crud the man was spouting. "Oh, I can't abide sycophants. Worse still, ignoramuses! Tell me, what is your name?"

"Rogber, madam."

"Tell me, Rogber. How close have you really come to the squalor you and your kind helped elicit?"

"I'm not sure that I understand, madam..."

"Lower the shield, front and back."

"But, Madam Titian, the Vary will see you!"

"Will they? Will they really, Rogber? And what will they do when they see me? Will they infect me with their fetidness? Will they make my teeth grow, my limbs lengthen? Will I lose my faculties? Have my mind dulled?"

"You could inhale lungrot."

"I risk that by sitting in my own garden, you ridiculous man! Lungrot doesn't care who is rich and who is poor. It's the eternal leveller! Now" – she wielded the bottle like a cosh – "Let the real world in!"

The driver didn't argue further. He lowered the shield and the darkness of the cab gave way to searing sunlight.

Six weeks after the death of the Speaker, Mohab sat on his father's low cot and whispered to the men in the barracks.

"There was a man once – tall as a saguaro cactus and just as spikey on the inside. The man's name was Master Huck and he was a swineherd. His house was fourteen storeys high. Master Huck had built it from the ground up, taking pride in the placement of every brick and each smear of mortar. The windows were hand-glazed, the washhouse paved with imported slate. A generator was installed in the basement of the house and powered by excrement – both his own and that of his pigs.

"Yes, Master Huck was a self-made man, and the tighter the rein he kept on his swine, the more neighbouring farmers and other swineherd wanted to learn from him. 'Share your secrets of success,' they would beg, offering up family heirlooms, I.O.U.s, pension funds, and loyal daughters.

"Soon, Master Huck – once a lowly swineherd shin-deep in pig shit – was an esteemed business man. 'It's all a matter of hard work, self-belief, and quality control,' he would tell the farmers and neighbouring swineherds, and, soon enough, the farmers and swineherds in the next state, and then the next state after that. 'My Swine System,' he called his patented approach, explaining how he separated males and females, and rehoused the piglets with an old sow that acted as wet nurse. The adult pigs were fattened with a mix of vegetable peel, brewing sops and a chemical bio agent, Zyklan B. When the time came to slaughter the livestock, he processed them in batches, saving only the strongest for future breeding.

"It was a fine and worthy approach to animal husbandry and, before long, Master Huck was far more than a businessman. He was a government minister and, soon, the sole advisor on the processing of swine. His marketing message infiltrated the country's economy and everyone prospered because Master Huck understood pigs.

"As his System spread far and wide, Master Huck assembled a fleet of hot air balloons, each grander than the last. Beneath gas-filled polyps, he would ride in a great wicker basket accompanied by his trusted advisors and the bold young cadets who had embraced his Swine Solution with zeal.

"The largest of the fleet was the High Hunt, named so because, on occasion, Master Huck and his favoured staff liked to lean out of the basket and take pot shots at the fields of swine below. The guns would recoil back against their shoulders and the air would crack while the ground turned red.

"But there was one factor Master Huck had not accounted for. Through his efforts in selective breeding, he had accidentally homed in on a gene which emphasised intelligence. In other words, pigs being the clever motherfuckers they already are, were being bred exponentially wise. And with this increased intelligence came the ability to rebel.

"So came a day when Master Huck and his crew flew overhead and, while taking their pot shots, noticed how the herd banded together.

"'What are those swine doing down there?' asked one ballooner, a whiskery man with a penchant for pigskin boots.

"'They are running from us,' said Master Huck, peering down at the strange behaviour.

"The swine broke out of their pens, kicking up buckets of pignuts as they went. It appeared that they were intent on swarming directly beneath the High Hunt.

"'What are they doing now?' said a second aviator, a woman with a fat mole on her chin and dripping emeralds from a lifetime farming swine.

"'They are just stretching their necks,' said Master Huck, and he pointed his gun at the misbehaving pigs.

"But even though he picked off a good number, he could not

halt the incessant swarming below. Pigs clambered over pigs which, in turn, clambered over pigs until soon there was a discernible hill of swine rising ever closer to the craft.

"'What do we do?' asked a third occupant of the basket – a young man with excellent blue eyes and hair that had the sun in it. He used his gun on the pigs below, grinning with every shot.

"Master Huck was busy demanding the balloon's pilot take them higher. But unknown to Master Huck, the pilot was a friend of the pigs and, instead, he helped the balloon descend. With the mountain of swine drawing closer, Master Huck was forced to act. Out went the man in the pigskin boots, hoisted over the basket and dropped into the squirming mass below.

"But they were still going down – which meant more ballast had to be jettisoned. Out went the woman with the mole and the hefty emeralds. Out went the young hunter with the blue eyes and hair full of sun. Even the pilot was shoved overboard. (The pigs cushioned his fall and one particularly reasonable hog insisted on transporting him far away from the warzone to a very fine coffee house.)

"Free of his compatriots, Master Huck felt the balloon start to rise. Except, again Master Huck had not accounted for one factor – an added weight that began to drag that basket down in spite of its buoyant balloon.

"The mountain of pigs knew what the weight was. Broken on the ground and taking their last breaths, the man in the pigskin boots and the woman with the mole and the emeralds and the young man with the blue eyes and sunlit hair knew what the weight was. So did the pilot, watching the decent of the High Hunt from a safe distance while sipping an espresso.

"Despite his prowess as a swineherd, business man and politician, Master Huck had not accounted for the weight of his sins against the swine. As the mountain of pigs peaked, he drew level with the topmost creature.

"'You shall yield to me, pig!' cried Master Huck, and he threw off the last bags of sand ballast in the hope the basket might rise. But it kept on sinking and rested at last aloft the pig mountain.

"'And now you are among us!' said the topmost pig, and he gave a great snort and all the pigs assembled below answered in kind until the ground shook.

"And so ends the tale of the greedy swineherd and the intelligent pigs. As to what happened to Master Huck, well, they ate him, of course, shared out in the tinniest slivers so that even the youngest got a taste. As to the fate of that grandiose balloon, the High Hunter, the old sow who had acted as wet-nurse climbed into the basket and set sail for bluer skies."

Mohab got up from the low bunk, knees cracking where the joints had prematurely worn. Had the story been subtle enough? He glanced over at the two blockers who listened in at the doorway. They appeared intent on chewing their tobacco wad. There was no raising of the alarm, no taking matters into their own hands and beating him senseless. Hopefully only the men in the barracks, those listeners treated daily like swine, would understand the story as a call to rise up when the time was right. Maybe even commit the ultimate act of sacrifice to liberate their fellow prisoners.

All around, men sat in quiet contemplation. For a moment, Mohab worried about the quality of the story. He wasn't his father. He hadn't studied the family books of the Vary, or told his versions of these tales over decades. But he had grown up as the Speaker's son, even if he had done all in his power to forget the fact. He had listened to bedtime stories, fairy tales, songs from the old country, and poems in honour of Mama Sunstar. To conjure up the parable of Master Huck and his rebellious swine had felt like breathing. And, after all, what was the point of rejecting his family legacy any more? He was swiftly approaching his end days, his body all but used up. He might as well do a service to his people before he went. Maybe even find some comfort after the final loss of his father.

The doubts fell from his shoulders as, slowly, men placed

one hand over their hearts, thumb to forefinger – sign of Mama Sunstar – and, in so doing, signalled their agreement with the plan disguised as a story.

EIGHTEEN

Kali had often wondered what happened to Mister Thatchett. Did the old man finish packing up all those empty boxes himself and make a successful journey to Augland, a sanctuary where, even now, he and his friend sat in chairs opposite one another, sucking their gums and berating the weather? It was a picture which appealed to Kali's new sensibilities. Except then she would remind herself of all the years which had passed since that day when she ran from an old man needing help. And she would force herself to confront the reality of another, deep-seated memory – of all that took place the day after.

Gathering in her grandmother's driveway, the guards had arranged themselves in pairs standing shoulder-to-shoulder. Watching from her hidey-hole in a large bush of feather gorse near the open gates, Kali had noticed how serious the guards looked – ten of them, dressed in long boots which came just short of the knees. She felt a mix of feelings in the pit of her stomach. Awe, because the guards looked so innately uniform, jacket buttons dazzling like tiny bites of light, and caps worn low over the eyes at an identical angle. Intimidation too, because there were so many of them, and because they moved as one.

To the fore of the group stood the sergeant; Kali had not known the woman's rank at the time, but there had been a clear indication of leadership in the way she stood apart from the others and spoke with efficiency. Kali couldn't hear more than a murmur, but the woman commanded the rapt attention of her unit.

Soon enough, Kali had begun to feel uncomfortable in her hiding place. The plumes of feather gorse had appeared soft enough, but now she remembered her grandmother's warning about the sap which oozed from the plant's exposed roots. 'Give you ants in your pants!' Grizmare Titian had warned, puckering her lips like a maw cat's anus.

Her grandmother was right. Kali's bare legs were beginning to itch.

She emerged from the bush, blotchy legged and ratty haired, just as the guards were marching out of the gates. Shading her eyes with the flat of a hand, Kali thought about calling out, just to see if any of the soldiers broke rank. What would happen if one of their number disobeyed an order, or allowed themselves to be distracted? Would the sergeant beat them for insolence? Would she produce a rock shot pistol and shoot the dissenter on the spot? Would she turn her gun on Kali?

In the end, as much as Kali was desperately, almost perversely, keen to find out, she was distracted when the National Guard marched dead ahead onto Mister Thatchett's driveway and the sergeant approached the old man's front door. 'Too trusting', her grandmother had always called the gateless property. Watching the guards smash down Mister Thatchett's front door, Kali wondered if any number of gates would have stopped their assault.

"What are you gawking at there, child?" Her grandmother was coming down the driveway, floor length kaftan billowing, her thin grey hair disguised under a turban.

"National Guard," said Kali, matter-of-fact. Opposite, the guards charged inside the white sugar cube house.

Grizmare Titian huffed. She knitted her hands together, the generous sleeves of her kaftan covering them as if a deliberate effort to contain her natural emotions. "I told Tomlin to have you help him pack his things away. I hope you did."

"Uh-huh." Kali rubbed at her scarlet thighs. She hoped her guilt wasn't too obvious.

"Let's hope Tomlin set out on his journey before... Motherfuckers!"

The guards were emerging back into the sunlight with the old man between them. He's walking funny, thought Kali. All heavy on one side, as if he was the halves of two different living men stitched together. His right trouser leg was bright scarlet at the knee, and the whole of the right side of his face was blood-stained from a gash at his temple.

"What's the meaning of this?" Her grandmother stomped between the gates. Kali hurried to catch up, heart skittering with the excitement of the blood and her grandmother' anger.

The sergeant moved to the front of the unit. The woman's height was exaggerated next to Grizmare, who looked like a hairy old goat wearing a bedsheet she had run through.

"Madam Titian. I am Sergeant Yorsef of the Bleekland National Guard. This man —" She nodded towards Mister Thatchett, who stood blinking against the sun's glare and clutching a pair of embroidered bloodstained slippers. He didn't appear to notice Kali, even when she stared at him hard, mentally begging him to look her way. 'I see you in a mess', she wanted her eyes to say.

"This man has been placed under arrest for conspiracy to trade in Stonemaker contraband."

"He is rich, you imbecile! He collects historical artefacts." Grizmare was spitting now; Kali half-expected her grandmother to start frothing at the mouth like the tiger dog. "Mister Thatchett has been my neighbour for ten long years. I can vouch for his innocence."

"It is shocking the kinds of illegal activities one's neighbour can get up to behind closed doors." The sergeant towered over Grizmare. Not that Kali had the impression her grandmother gave a jot for the woman's attempts at intimidation.

"This is thuggery, pure and simple," Grizmare said with a snarl. "The man is bleeding!"

Kali was caught off guard as her grandmother grabbed her by the arm and thrust her forward.

"This child helped him pack those boxes. She was witness to their contents. Tell them, Kali! Tell them what you saw."

Kali felt as if she stood on sand that was funnelling away

from beneath her, threatening to suck her under. All eyes turned her way. Her voice became scratchy and small.

"Gloves. Lots of gloves. And a scarf thing, and a knotted belt. Everything smelt old, a bit like the zoo smells. And there was a big old book, where Mister Thatchett said the stories live."

Kali didn't get to find out if her revelations mattered. At that instant, there was a jolting cry of "Halt!" from behind – both sharp and impassioned.

Begrudgingly, Kali peered back over a shoulder. Her father stood between the open gates, hands behind his back, chest barrelled.

"Ah, good. You can call off your moronic guard here! My neighbour has already been assaulted to within an inch of his life." Grizmare carried on snorting and grumbling. Between the guards, old Mister Thatchett swayed, the blood soaking his shirt bib.

Kali walked over to her father and put her hand in his. Her father's grip was firm, reassuringly so, and with a heat that radiated.

"The male has been placed under arrest, High Judge Titian, as per our earlier consultation," said the sergeant.

The hand let go and Kali felt a sense of loss.

"This is my house!" her grandmother was squawking, a new haggardness to her expression that reminded Kali of a wicked witch. "You might have purchased it once upon a time, but it is my name on the deeds."

High Judge Titian paid his mother no mind, just gave a stiff salute to suggest the guards should go about their business. The sergeant returned the salute and Mister Thatchett was bundled into a waiting truck. The rest of the guards climbed aboard at the back of the vehicle, hanging off foot and handholds.

The truck pulled away in a cloud of dust, leaving behind broad skid-marks from its tyres and a patch of drying blood on Mister Thatchett's gateless drive.

The temperature was unbearable. In the factory, the furnaces belted out thick welts of smoke without pause. Bones splintered in the grates. The living raked out the crud of the dead. Occasionally, overhead, the filmy trail of a gunner left its ghost upon the sky. On battle days, the tiny black stars of smaller craft – twin tanks, F-22s, and coil-wings – were ever so faintly visible in their thousands. Whispers suggested High Judge Titian was on the verge of pushing through the airspace over Augland. But rumours festered inside Abbandon and it was hard to trust anything that came from the lips of broken men.

In the weeks since his father's death, Mohab had gained the ears and eyes of a Gothendore Sister and, with them, another side to the story. "Titian is up against it, as are his allies. Jonet and Greater Sangolia are plagued with infighting. Greater Sangolia's troops are losing ground to the ice." Sister Eva kept her voice low, her crystalline green eyes lost to the shade of her wimple. "We've been circulating photostats from the border. Fuck! You should see the soldiers' chilblains where the skin is exposed. Great fiery birthmarks, as if the breath of Mama Sunstar herself had touched their skin." Pretending to be loyal to Lord Gothendore, Sister Eva worked her prayer beads through her hands as a couple of blockers passed by. "Cross the arms!" she said loudly, pointing at the body on the ground. Mohab did as he was told. The blockers spat aside mouthfuls of tobacco and moved off.

"And do we have movement on the United Dominions Alliance?" Mohab straightened out the legs of the corpse.

"Nothing solid. Raestan still won't move against Titian without the Augland Neutrality Patrol entering into active alliance. There is a summit coming up in York Central. We wait on the outcome." Sister Eva counted off her beads as the bone cart arrived. A blocker climbed down and hoisted the body on top of the rest. Sister Eva drew a finger across her chest in honour of Gothendore, All Immortal. Secretly, she let the movement flow into a tiny circle and faint flex of the fingers.

Barely perceptible, the sign of Mama Sunstar.

"Show me the next one."

Mohab led the way past the guards, who muttered into their coffee jars about the sister's poor choice of assistant. Their hatred for Mohab ran deep, but Sister Eva had the final say over who worked as her whipping boy. No one questioned the erratic ways of the Sisterhood, at least as far as their interactions with the infidels was concerned.

A dead boy, no more than eight years old, had been left to rot in the sun. Mohab stared down at the body. Sister Eva drew her finger across her chest prematurely.

"We have found a pilot," she said in a whisper.

Mohab waved away the flies as he squatted and tried to rearrange the child's arms. The bones had already set. He yanked on the bare wrists, heard something snap like dry tinder and worked to control his gag reflex. Faces haunted him, those of his sisters in the final days before the lungrot took them. Skin, the colour of clay. Cheeks caving.

"This pilot. They any good? Needs to be once the bastard guards start shooting up the sky."

Sister Eva muttered over her beads. She nodded to the far end of the quarry, where the gate lay with its twin guard towers. "Those will have to be taken out at the first opportunity. In truth, I've no idea if Titian's daughter is any good as a pilot. She was a decorated member of the Bleek military and she's all we're got."

"Lieutenant Kali Titian is the pilot?" Mohab's disbelief read hard in his eyes. "Has she really embedded herself so thoroughly? The woman tore apart families, ordered executions, decimated Resistance cells."

"Precisely. The Lieutenant has been in combat and she has survived!"

The nun fell silent as the bone cart rattled up. Cradling the boy's body, Mohab tossed it up on top of the other bodies.

As the cart moved off again, Sister Eva beckoned a water boy over. She gulped down a cup of water and insisted the cup be refilled for Mohab. He drained the cup and the nun waved on the boy, who was no older that the body they had so recently stacked amongst the others.

Mohab tried to process the idea of Kali Titian assisting with the plan. Kidnapping a gunner at the precise moment it was restored but not yet rerouted to the war effort already struck him as a desperately dangerous prospect. Confiding that plan to a former Lieutenant Colonel of the National Guard – not to mention, an immediate family member of High Judge Titian himself – was suicide, nothing less.

"I might as well bite chunks out of my own wrists."

Feeding her hands inside her bell sleeves, Sister Eva grimaced. "The Resistance has already found a chink in High Judge Titian's armour. It is very risky, a shot in the dark really. I do not want to say more. We both know that secrets tend to buff up and shine brighter the more people who handle them. But if the sabotage does succeed, it will greatly aid our plan." She titled her chin. Sunlight filled her exceptional eyes. "You've already entrusted the stonemaker relics to Titian's daughter. She has not betrayed you. More than that, she stood beside you against her father."

Mohab thought about the ancient stones he had unearthed at the quarry. Dalma plates, the Lieutenant had called them. He had wanted nothing to do with his discovery at the time – just as he had wanted nothing to do with his ascension to the role of his people's Speaker. The stories were his father's burden. So many twisting helixes of words, like a genetic restructuring, until every last molecule of the father Mohab had yearned for was gone.

Except, then his father had died, and he – and, yes, Kali as well – had eased his father's remains onto a slab that had housed so many thousands before. In those final moments before he fed the body to the flames, Mohab had finally seen his father freed of the weight of words and he had looked light as dust.

"The Lieutenant cannot atone for the sins of her past. But she has been abandoned by her own kind. And while she will never be like us, she is like me." Mohab snorted. "In that no matter how much we might despise the fact, we are both destined to lead armies." He took a deep inhale and nodded. "The Lieutenant has kept my secrets these last few weeks, as you say. If she *is* our only real option for a pilot, we must trust she can keep more."

NINETEEN

"Where's Groff?" Kali glared at the blocker, who slung his hands into his pockets and leaned back, groin presented to her like a handshake.

"Suckgap? Fuck knows." He used his makeshift beater to push Mohab forward. "This one's bust up from working the quarry but there's muscle enough to last another fortnight. One of the sisters sent him and I'm not going argue with one of those soul suckers."

Kali hissed through her teeth. "I've spoken to the Commandant Superintendent about keeping the same men on the job. It's wasteful to dispose of quality workers." What she wanted to say was 'I've grown used to Groff and now my kind may have killed him and I want to kill you in return.'

Apparently, she didn't hide her intent too well. Mohab put his hands on his hips, intercepting her path to the blocker. "Groff's been assigned to the medical suite permanently."

Reassured to know that Groff was still alive, Kali winced as the blocker brought his beater down on Mohab's shoulder. The Speaker's son cried out and stumbled sideways.

"Bastard chatterbox! It's none of the bitch's business where Suckgap has fucked off to." The blocker leaned in by Kali's ear. He grabbed her hand and rubbed it against his crotch. "At least unless the Commandant Superintendent tells me otherwise."

His breath was stale. Aware of Mohab's gaze on her, Kali didn't flinch but let the guard rub and buck against her until the nausea became too much. Snatching her hand away, she glared at Mohab and tossed him the wrench she had booked out. "We're using the second riser rig. You'll need a tool roll."

"Stupid cunt." The blocker moved off in the opposite direction.

Kali pressed a hand to her throat to keep the bile in.

Mohab massaged his shoulder, bruised to the bone. For a moment, he looked as if he was about to say more. But then he turned his back and walked off to join the tool roll queue.

Even as a child, Groff had been a peacemaker. If there was a fight between some boys in the neighbourhood, he would wait for all parties to exhaust themselves then suggest a game of Odd Ball, with him as the target. Weaving in and out of their legs, he would unite the squabblers in their mutual pursuit of him. This ability to placate had led him into nursing, where, to Groff's mind, a body's physical state of illness was a form of conflict in itself. His job was to alleviate suffering. Sometimes he nursed patients better. Other times, he held their hand as they slipped away.

But now that he was set to work in the medical suite, Groff had neither the tools nor mental capacity to ease the suffering of those tortured within. The senior medical officer was a Doctor General Tristan Harris, newly arrived at Abbandon and yet to wear the expression of regimental boredom which characterised those Sisters and guards about the place

As far as Groff could make out, Doctor Harris selected patients according to his erratic criteria and the ever-changing pool of Vary available to him. He chose the strongest males for sub-volcanic immersion and children for chemical stunt agents. Those individuals with lighter skin, birthmarks or above average intelligence were given over to the gas chamber and dissection. The children he singled out were subjected to the cruellest experiments.

Unlike the rustic shed of the infirmary, the medical suite was a series of pristine and sanitary wards located in the grounds of the factory. Unlike the infirmary with its promise of respite, the medical suite was a direct road to deformity and death. To Groff's mind, it was an evil place.

"You will arrange for the child to be bathed then place her in the chair." Harris nodded towards a girl perched on one side of a riser trolley, legs dangling.

Groff reached out to the child. "Come on, bumblebee. Legs up. Time to get clean. Warm water too. And soap. It smells a bit funny. But it kills those itchy lice." Leaving the doctor to finish his round, Groff guided the trolley to a shower block where a sister waited for them. Lifting the girl down, he steadied her on her feet. "Go on in." He nodded encouragingly towards the shower block. The child pattered over the bare tiles and the sister followed after, rolling up her black sleeves.

Groff exhaled heavily and leaned back against the trolley. The ward was quiet now the doctors had moved on. A couple of beds were occupied by children wearing eye patches. At the opposite end of the ward was a boy with bandaging around his chest where his underarm lymph nodes had been removed. He cried at night according to the sisters; they would be glad when his 'treatment' was complete.

Otherwise, the ward was empty. Groff was glad. He hated his work in the medical suite. It was worse than being spat on by blockers in the factory or witnessing the sisters' cruelty in the infirmary. He suspected that, overall, Harris preferred to protect members of that so-called holy order from the detritus of his experiments. Groff, though, was not only medically trained but Vary, which meant he was useful if disposable.

The eye-op children whimpered in their sleep. Shuffling onto his side, the lymph node boy kept his eyes tight shut; no doubt it was preferable to pretend the outside world didn't exist. Left alone with those suffering little children, Groff realised that he was the only adult in the room. Tears pricked his eyes. *This must be how it feels to be a free man!* Just standing here in this room, breathing air. Forced to witness these emaciated children with their tears and imposed monstrousness, his mind remained in chains.

"She is ready." The sister ushered the child out from the shower block.

Groff felt his shoulders tighten. The girl was naked. Her starved body was anatomical where the bones showed through. He found a spare shift and dropped it around the girl, who shivered despite the heat.

"There may be lice on her yet. Tell Doctor Harris. Her head needs shaving." The sister floated away. As she passed his bed, the lymph node boy cried out in pain. She kept walking. In her stiff black habit, she reminded Groff of a spook from one of the Speaker's son's tales — the sort that sucked the life from the lips of sleeping children.

The pen vibrated as Mohab kept pressure on the handheld operator switch, guiding the riser rig up and around the gunner's outer walls. From that height, it was possible to finally get to grips with the scale of the thing. The surface tiles shimmered in the sunlight, the blue-black diamantine reminding Kali of her grandmother's house. She marvelled at the geometric skim and bruise blocks left proud of the surface and designed to act as shock absorbers if the craft encountered turbulence. She didn't entirely understand this new model's schematics; it had been years since she passed out from the Military Academy in Nilreb. She was a reasonable engineer, a better soldier. All the same, she longed to roll back the door which sat flush with the epidermis and lose herself inside the gunner.

"You've Seconded an engineer before?" She nodded at the riser's operator switch in Mohab's hand.

"I've used a riser rig at the Nedmac Traps when I was collecting lava samples." Mohab squinted at her. "I taught geology at Geno Universium."

Kali pointed to a hole in the gunner where the tiles had buckled at impact. "Take me in." Mohab guided the riser alongside the hole. Up close, the edges of the impact looked melted rather than punctured.

"Log out the scrappers. Both of them."

Securing the riser rig, Mohab knelt and undid the tool roll

which opened out into a flat bed of tools with its own data screen. He logged out the scrappers and handed them over. Kali trimmed the nearest fold, using the scrappers to pare back the constituent.

"Why hasn't the hull repaired itself? I thought the point of the tiles was to create a self-healing environment." Mohab snorted. "I thought it was meant to be Titian's not-so-secret bargaining chip with Jonet and Greater Sangolia in exchange for their support?"

"The metal-matrix is artificial bone, meaning it's fantastically lightweight and, yes, living cellular material with the capacity to mend itself. But only if the underlying weft is intact. Now, hand me the swarthe light." She passed back the scrappers, waited for Mohab to log the tools back in and took the swarthe light when he handed it up. The handle was telescopic; she whipped it out in front of her, protracting the beam into the dark wound in the hull. "The arterial layer has been compromised," she said, taking in the damage to the tube twists and avionics. There was a bad smell coming off the hole, like something rotten and left to the flies.

"You ever worry we're so busy messing with nature that we'll give up our flesh and turn back into stardust?" Mohab stood close behind her. Kali felt his proximity as a physical pressure.

"I don't worry. I hope," she said, and snapped off the light. "I can't do anything from the outside. You'll have to take us further in." Sheltering her eyes against the glare off the sunlit gunner, she turned to the guard platform opposite.

"We've got to fix her from inside! Once it's done, we'll use the crawl space behind the epidermis and exit via the slush shoot." She prayed the craft's youth and recent damage meant it had been brought in before the slush shoot could impact with waste.

A guard held up his arm with its glinting wrist cuff. Kali understood his meaning; the nicks had rubbed her skin into fat callouses over time but the blades could still punch in any time they were activated.

Mohab leaned out over the railing. "We need another swarthe light! It won't let me log a second out."

The guard knocked elbows with his neighbour, who shook his head and drew on a smokestick.

"We will manage with one." Kali nodded at the tool roll. "Bring that. They'll have to let me log out the weft agent and hook anyway. If we're lucky, there may even be a drag tool to clean down the walls of the slush shoot before we use it."

"There won't," said Mohab.

Kali flicked out the swarthe light. "No, there won't."

Groff made it a rule never to ask a child their name. The heart had a finite capacity for pain; swamp it and the veins got saturated. He led the girl out of the ward and did his best not to look at her. Her hand was flimsy in his. He could feel her birdlike bones.

As they walked down the corridor, he became aware of a tug on his sleeve.

"Will they cut me?"

The question was matter-of-fact. Groff didn't mean to, but he was so taken aback that he looked down. "It is a small operation. They will give you anaesthetic." He hoped Doctor Harris didn't make a liar of him.

"Will they wake me again after?" She stared up at him, eyes unusually blue. Her teeth looked big in her mouth where the fat had dissolved from her face and lips.

Groff wished he had something soothing to say, but all he thought was, 'Is it her eyes they want? Will Harris store them in a jar like lumps of polished glass?'

The girl gripped his hand tighter. Her palm felt damp. "My name is Shola. Shola Ricks."

The name was out before he could shush her. Groff's stomach knotted. 'Don't remember the name,' he told himself. The niggling, sadistic part of him repeated 'Shola Ricks' over and over until the name was engraved into his mind.

"I am nine," said Shola. "Mama and I lived in Geno. I had a chuckle bird. His name was Laurel Lee. I used to fetch him bugs from the balcony of our apartment. Big whistlers, fat as your finger. Spiders too. I caught them in my shoes." She stopped walking in front of a pair of opaque glass-sheet doors. Shaking off Groff's hand, she patted one of her shoulders and stroked the air there. "Laurel Lee doesn't like it here."

"Come on." Groff didn't want to use her name, but when the girl made no attempt to move, he relented. "Come on, Shola. It'll all be over soon and you'll be back in your bed."

Shola turned her strange eyes to him and shrugged. "That's what I'm afraid of."

"The Commandant Superintendent. Why do you go to him?"

"More light."

Mohab brought the swarthe light closer. Kali worked a set of clamps between the tube twists.

"Do the two of you have an arrangement? It can't be in exchange for rations or kind treatment. You're as broken as the rest of us." He knelt, directing the beam up into the mess of the gunner's innards and catching Kali in the eye so that she was forced to squint. "Is it possible you like it? Like *him*? Is that it, Lieutenant? Do you like the Commandant Superintendent? Was he your plaything even before you came to this camp?"

Kali logged out a small blade and focused on paring the severed ends from two of the tubes, ready for soldering. The Speaker's son had a mouth on him. It had been easier to work with Groff.

"He was not... *is* not my plaything," she said evenly.

"You certainly aren't his. It's not as black and white as that with you." Mohab dragged a hand back through his hair and sighed. "Look, I don't give a fuck who you like, Lieutenant. It has no bearing on me or any other Vary. But one thing I do know." He dipped his head under the mess of tubes. Closing in, he put out a hand and laid it flat against her breast, above the heart. "No matter how hard you work to sweat it out, you'll never get clean of sin. It bleeds black from the pores. Your only option is to live with it."

In that moment, Kali despised the Speaker's son. He was right, of course. She would never work her way free of the stain. But he'd misinterpreted the sex.

"I fuck the Commandant to get clean, not because I live among swarms of Vary, but because he is fat with life. There are threads of citrus flesh caught in his teeth from breakfast; I root them out with my tongue. I stick my nose into his armpits; he stinks already where the heat gets to him. But I can still make out the slicks of frangipani grease. The bones of his arse don't bite at me like the Varys in my bunk." She brought her face millimetres from Mohab's and felt his breath on her lips. "His cock is very pale and has a small mole near the shaft. When I suck it, he tastes of brine soap." Her hand went to his groin. "You would not taste so sweet."

He clutched her wrist, above the nick. She felt the pressure at her pulse point. "So you remain a selfish bitch, fuelling your need to feel alive with each new fuck?"

"Precisely."

"I could fuck you now. Work up a bit of that glow for myself."

"I'd break your ribs first. Your freedom doesn't lie between my thighs."

"Where does it lie, hmm, Lieutenant?" His glistening eyes bored into her. "Can you tell me that much? Is there nothing you can offer to wear down this daily sense of pointlessness?"

She shook her head and stayed silent. She couldn't begin to conceive of a way to soothe him.

"What do you want from me?" she said at last.

"Solidarity."

Kali caught her breath. The word carried weight. "Solidarity in death?" It was hardly a new idea. She had expected to offer as much within minutes of walking into Abbandon. It was only

Mohab's father who kept her alive.

"In life." Mohab stood very still, the sounds from outside the gunner coming to them as through a blanket of stone-wool.

"Tell me a story," Groff would say to his grandmother night after night, as was the way of the Vary. It was the stories which connected them through the centuries, whenever walls fell and children were grabbed from their beds. When all else was taken, it was the stories which drifted above the heads of their enemies, always out of reach. And they were potent, these stories, infused with the agonies of his people. Even after the last of the Vary had been slaughtered, some whisper of them would survive.

Laid out on the stretcher, her head wrapped in black lint, Shola Ricks was not going back to the children's ward. Groff cursed the temperamental pneumatics of the stretcher. He gave the riser a thump and the mechanism woke up. The stretcher undocked from the bolt plate and Groff eased it out of the operating room.

"Luna La lee," sang the girl through her bandages. "Luna la lee!"

Groff chuckled. "Funny little song you've got going on, Shola Ricks." He steered the stretcher out into the corridor. Fire lamps crackled either side.

"You keep singing, Shola Ricks," he told the girl, glad of her lungful of dream gas.

At the far end of the corridor, past closed doors and pharmaceutical cabinets, was the lock up. There was no need for guards in the medical suite where the aim was to dissect rather than restore. Nonetheless, Harris and his team liked to keep their more dramatic surgeries safely stowed away. Groff guided the stretcher inside.

Entering the lock up, Groff thought about the dark fairy stories his grandmother had told him and decided they were true. Harris' experiments were housed inside several glass-sheet cubicles. Five had been boys. Three had been girls; Shola Ricks

143

made four. The cubicles were fed with an invisible cell accelerant; Groff had seen bones restructure, skin adapt, teeth migrate, and all manner of biological change take place behind those glass walls. Shola would be no different.

Lifting the girl off the stretcher, Groff carried her inside an open cubicle. He lay her down on the low coat and stroked her bandaged head.

"Sleep, Shola Ricks. Who knows? Maybe the doctors will have given you a gift. Second sight, perhaps. Or the ability to fly." He shook his head, walked back out of the cubicle and locked the glass-sheet door.

"Actually, we have spliced her germ-line with that of a fennec fox," said a voice behind him.

Groff turned to find Doctor Harris standing in the doorway – and felt his stomach clench. He didn't like it when the doctor spoke to him. It didn't pay to attract the man's attention.

"The skull has been bioengineered to suit the gene grid, the ears in particular. I am interested in the dissipation of heat and auditory improvement. We may be blessed with evolutions of bone structure and other shifts at a molecular level." Doctor Harris approached Shola's cell and examined a handheld data frame by the door. The feed from the cell's environment pleased him; he peered in at the sleeping girl and hummed softly.

"I have high hopes for this specimen," he said, maybe to Groff, maybe to himself.

Such joy in the face of so much suffering! Groff wanted to break the doctor's skull and tear out the dark matter that pioneered such cruelty. Instead, he stood very still, hardly daring to breathe.

Harris slid the handheld back onto the wall-mount. The scrubs he had worn to the operating room were soiled down the bib.

"Do you have a name?" He stared at Groff, his eyes illuminated with the excitement of his latest operation.

"Groff de Rubon."

"You trained as a doctor?"

"Nurse."

"General or specialist?"

"Paediatric and Minor Maxillofacial."

"Ah. The assigning officer has made good use of you then." Fixating on Groff's arms, Harris swung his own absentmindedly. "The afflictions of your race are manifold. Such cumbersome physiology. Arms that dangle as if stretched by some mechanical means. Teeth made for chewing the cud." He indicated that Groff should follow and moved on to the next cell along.

"Here. The subject has been aligned with razingstock genes." He tapped on the glass-sheet and a boy of sorts stirred inside. Groff was familiar with the child; the first time he had seen the creature, bent over on all fours, vast shoulder blades protruding like wings, he had fled the room and vomited in the corridor.

"The splayed hooves allow for a better distribution of the bulk, allowing the mule to carry heavier loads over greater distances. I am heartened to see the breeding programme is enjoying success. This is science in the making and you and I are the first to witness it."

It was a singular moment in Groff's time within Abbandon, this suggestion that he had eyes with which to witness a thing and a mind with which to process what he witnessed.

"You would make cattle of us," he said quietly.

Harris clucked his tongue. "I am trying to save your species. In a virgin state, the Vary is mentally malnourished and physically substandard in every way. These paranimal procedures will pave the way for a worldwide breeding programme."

Groff watched the creature lumber up to the bars of the cubicle as it had been taught. Harris picked up the cell's handheld and ran a finger across the screen. Inside the cubicle, a feed slot opened; the hybrid lowered its muzzle and came up again, churning its jaw as bits of wingnut pellets scattered the floor. Naked, the one-time boy arched his tailbone and sprayed the back wall of his cubicle with diarrhoea.

"As for making cattle of you…" The doctor cocked his head towards the cell. "I would make your lives of value," he went on, examining the boy with cold intensity and recording his latest stats on the handheld. "Rather than execution through mass genocide, the Vary will be re-engineered as livestock. I am also very optimistic that these current experiments will result in viable bio weaponry. The evolution of your species may even help Bleekland win the war!"

Groff's emotions seesawed between fear and rage, and he considered the desolation of death. Better to go while he was still whole than some genetic pariah! And yet, even faced with these horrors of the future, he still couldn't break free of his desire to keep on living. Things still mattered to him – the wild blue of the sky, the togetherness of his people, all the great and terrible stories, and the voices which kept them alive.

This is just another story, he told himself as Harris moved on to the next cubicle and an eight-year-old girl carved into a spine lizard. The monster behind the glass was just a morality tale, designed to stop children straying from their beds and to keep men in bondage.

"You see the fringe scales down both sides of the throat? It is the first signs of self-sustaining body armour. And the eyes. Have you noticed them? The pupils are smaller; they dilate less to aid in the perception of UV light." Harris added his observations to the relevant handheld then replaced the set. Leaning in, he rapped the glass with his knuckles.

The girl spun around on her heels. Mouth gaping, she produced a deep hiss and expanded her throat to show a bright green collar of flesh.

"Glorious. Just glorious." Harris looked to Groff, like a child awaiting applause.

"Every gunner has a keycode – the master command to activate the engines. The keycode is reconfigured every twenty-four hours via a wire feed from the datastacks. The only way to gain access is via the gel frame which is located in the Commandant Superintendent's office."

Kali understood what was being asked of her – to steal the keycode during one of her and the Commandant Superintendent's trysts and thereby aid an escape plan. Mohab didn't say 'Do this and make amends', or 'Finally, you can wash your sins away.' But the suggestion hung in the air between them.

"This gunner is a new type of ship," she said. "Where are you getting your information?"

"A reliable source."

"A resistance spy." Kali grimaced. "Who is it? That bastard guard stationed at the furnaces? He likes to have a grope before he burns a body."

The words had barely left her lips when Mohab struck out, the sting of his open hand resonating against her cheek. On instinct, Kali drove the small blade towards him, pulling up short of his left eye. "You are an academic. I am a trained soldier with ten years' field experience. Odds are you will lose if you take me on."

Mohab wasn't listening. "So, any fucker stupid enough to help the Vary has to be a pervert or a gun for hire. Why do you always degrade us? It takes nerve to infiltrate a camp like this, more for a person to risk their life seeking out the cracks." His voice caught. Leaning in to her blade, he said between gritted teeth, "Why do you insist on making animals of us?"

She saw herself reflected in the cold circles of his eyes. "I have been raised wicked," she said numbly. Mohab flinched as she stroked his face with rough fingertips. "I was taught to see differences, where maybe there were none."

"We are the same and your kind has slaughtered us."

"Yes." She dropped the blade from her hand. She couldn't stop stroking his face. "And you want the chuck key to be my token of 'sorry'."

"You cannot be sorry for the war you have helped wage. Sorry has no more substance than if I were to rub the air between my fingers." He mimed the fact.

"But I can help. That is tangible. I can fly the craft too, I think." She let her hand fall back to her side. Despite her intentions as a recruit, she'd never had the chance to pilot a craft the size of a gunner. But she did have experience in mesospheric flight. "How hard can it be?" she said quietly.

"It will be the closest you come to forgiveness." Mohab retrieved the small blade from the floor and handed it back.

TWENTY

Love is complicated. Like an egg held in the palm of the hand, it can feel smooth and pleasing. But hold it too tightly and the shell will break, and love becomes a mess of mucous leaking through your fingers.

Kali was twelve years old when she and her fellow Youth Guard made the decision to break open the zoo. Grizmare had long suspected Kali would one day be lost to her entirely. Already the girl had demonstrated her father's propensity for cruelty – so many sparrows had lost their fragile little lives to Kali's gun. When High Judge Titian, in a rage over a soiled rug, took the family dog outside and shot it between the eyes, Kali had insisted on running to the garden to watch. She got there too late, apparently, the execution having already been carried out. But when she returned inside the house, Grizmare had endured lurid descriptions of the blood and brain matter. Her granddaughter's eyes had gleamed with enthusiastic innocence, as if the girl balanced so precariously on the edge between good and wickedness.

She is so young, Grizmare would remind herself while reading fairy tales or combing the knots from her granddaughter's hair. *She doesn't know any better. All children are nasty little fuckers. All children worship death.*

Except, then Kali was twelve years old. Taller than most girls her age. Muscular too from all the years of climbing whatever she could and taking gymnastics classes and sprinting the full length of the grounds. Teeth bared. Panting with a wild, breathless glee. "I like to run until it hurts," she had explained once.

The girl was studious, too. Not in the same way Grizmare might describe herself or Kali's father. Classical art, the ballet, the theatre – these were wasted on Kali. Instead, by twelve years old, the engineer in her was starting to stir. She took apart the house's security system – and got ten lashes of her father's belt across her hand for the trouble. She rewired the fire lamps inside the house to interact with the intelligent glass-sheet walls. And as a final triumphant farewell to childhood, she threaded a kill-switch down through the roof into the main data gate and unlocked the zoo – all thirty-three cages.

Grizmare could still recall Kali and her friends, dressed in their immaculate Youth Guard uniforms, hooting and howling with laughter as the beasts came nosing out into the garden. Standing below, wielding a glass of sour gin and a scowl, Grizmare had watched in horror as her precious herd devoured one another in order of size or savagery. Mew cats hunted desert otters. Razingstock thudded through the cacti beds, tiger dogs snapping at their heels or felling a beast with a leap. Tiny timid sand bears came blinking blindly into the light – and had their throats torn out by a mating pair of screech hawks. Even the lumbering Frillbream emerged to investigate the garden. Leaving great orange dung pats steaming in the sun as it walked, the frillbream gave a shake of its huge neck collar, sending a wave of fluting sound through the environment.

"Away! Away with you!" Grizmare had done her best, running into the fray without a plan or a weapon. All she knew was these desert otters, these maw cats, these sand bears – this frillbream! – were her life's passion. Waving her hands manically, she danced around while the carnage played out before her.

It was the unmistakable putt-putting growl of a tiger dog which made her turn around. Hunkered low a few feet away, the bony spines proud along its spine, the tiger dog had her in its sights.

Grizmare would never forget how she felt in that moment. The sickly wrench of dread. How did she intend to fight off the tiger dog? It was a mass of muscle and long, needle-fine teeth. Grizmare's bowels gave way and a tiny mew of fear escaped her lips.

The rock shot slammed into the tiger dog's flank, spraying blood like a sneeze. A second shot punched through the skull and stayed embedded.

Grizmare gasped and doubled over, choking and wheezing. At her feet, the tiger dog lay dead, its dark eyes cooling.

Laughter reached her ears. While the shit was still warm as it ran down her leg, she looked up to see Kali standing in the middle of her gang on the roof of the zoo, the butt of a rifle resting against her shoulder.

Love. A strange, breakable emotion. One moment it is whole and smooth, the next, it is a mess of shell and gore slipping through the fingers. Grizmare never forgot the cruel streak which marbled Kali's personality. But love. Breakable, messy love. That kept Grizmare adoring Kali across the years and despite the horrors her granddaughter had inflicted. It was love which motivated her now to follow in Kali's footsteps and open the gates to a different zoo.

"There were once twenty-five razingstock tied up inside a rickety old barn. The razingstock were owned by Mother Goose who kept them tethered and fed them measly portions of pignuts. She housed the beasts so because she was jealous of their usefulness and scared of their strength. Night and day, the razingstock would appeal to her, saying, 'There is no sense in this, Mother Goose. We are good and willing members of the farm. The plough does not till the soil unless we pull it. The produce cannot be got to market unless we are hitched to the goods' wagon. Your family will die over winter without our milk and the cheese you make from it.'

"But Mother Goose was a sour woman. She did not want the razingstock to feel they had more use than she. And so it was that she persuaded the chuckle hens to act distressed, thereby attracting the razingstock to enter the barn – whereupon she locked the creatures in. And after, how she had danced, arms raised to the skies as if she had made herself a god!"

Perched on his father's old cot, Mohab eased back his shoulders. He went to lie down, but the men around him reacted with discontent.

"What?" He sat back up. "What else is there to tell you?" Bringing his face into a shaft of moonlight, he stared out at the sea of men. "Do you want to hear about those razingstock? Twenty-five of the finest specimens in the herd. Are you praying they escape, having broken free of their bonds and having killed Mother Goose while she was still dancing? Do you think that ending is likely?"

"Isn't that the point of the story, Speaker's son?" hissed one of the crowd. And another, "Tell the story the right way. How's a man to have hope otherwise?"

"How indeed?" Mohab spread out his hands. "Where is our hope if not in the twenty-five strong razingstock and the chance they might overwhelm Mother Goose? These twenty-five who are the redeemers, the thinkers, and the brave. Good strong beasts who have resisted Mother Goose's best efforts to break them. In accordance with the rules of the story, do we not all will these beasts of burden to revolt against their master, these same beasts who have been beaten, chained, and made to work themselves to death? What hope do the rest of the herd have if those twenty-five do not rise up and take the reins from Mother Goose?" He could hear his voice cracking. What use were words unless he could knit them into something worthwhile?

It was Groff who said, "And why did Mother Goose choose to imprison twenty-five? Why that exact number?"

Clever Groff, wise Groff with his questions about the details of the story, which was, after all, a ruse to disguise their new-born escape plan. "Five a-piece. Five to distract, five to overwhelm, five to steal Mother Goose's wagon, five to guide it, and five to open the gate and lead the other razingstock to freedom. All healthy, all right-minded, and most importantly, all ready to sacrifice themselves for the survival of the herd."

The men had fallen quiet. Mohab imagined he heard a

woman's breath, and, not for the first time, he wondered if Lieutenant Kali Titian would really keep their secrets and her promise to man the gunner? The whole plan rested on her shoulders, which was why he hadn't shared that particular detail with the other Vary. After all, why sabotage the only escape plan they'd ever had? And hadn't Kali proven herself already? She had stood up to her father – stood up to the entire Bleek nation, in fact. She had carried Mohab's father, taking half the weight. And now she was to acquire the gunner's keycode from the Commandant Superintendent, at great personal risk and with no support system. Kali Titian had worked and suffered and cried like any other. Her face bore the same scars. Her body had the same exaggerated hollows.

But Kali was still Bleek, and she had still hurt his people more than most. All he could do was join the rest in having hope.

"Twenty-five then," said someone, and a murmur of 'Twenty-five' went through the ranks. Mohab wanted to tell the men to quiet down even before a blocker appeared in the doorway and demanded they fall silent. In the almost darkness, the men crawled back onto the bunks, interweaving their limbs to all fit in.

Mohab lay down on the rickety cot and closed his eyes. Hunger and exhaustion clutched at him. He tried to picture a different environment – the cool sheets of his bed back on the farmstead all those years ago. In the saddle and riding across the parched ground on his favourite red racer. Lying between the thighs of Lilith Gutsing in the grain store, basking in body heat...

When Mohab finally slept, he was dead to the world.

TWENTY-ONE

Shola Ricks crouched at the far end of her cell. She looked smaller than ever, a shrinking girl wearing dress-up ears. Only, Groff knew all too acutely that there was nothing make believe about her physical alterations. The ears stuck up from her head, twitching occasionally. A halo of brown fuzz covered the girl's face and naked body. The grafted tail was painted with bright blue iodine to prevent infection.

"So there you are, Shola Ricks. I know you heard me coming." Groff opened the trap at the base of the glass-sheet door and slid a bowl through. "They've adjusted your diet. Ask me, they may have improved it. Handful of greens and a couple of hoppers. Not exactly what you're used to, but plenty of folk would be glad of the protein."

He didn't say any more, just watched as she drove her face into the bowl. She lifted her head, cracking the insect casings between her molars. Hopper juice bled down her chin.

Groff cocked his head, trying to understand the abomination of a creature which had so recently been a little girl. "What can I tell you, Shola Ricks? Life. It shouldn't be anything like this. You and me, we've got to believe that. Mama Sunstar is wild-hearted, but I do not believe the likes of your alternations are within her philosophy."

The fox girl scratched at one of the newly stitched ears and chuntered in discomfort. Groff checked over a shoulder. They were alone momentarily. He had only salve and words with which to soothe her.

Leaning towards the cage, he smiled his gappy smile. "I am different too, Shola Ricks." He tapped the neon brand at his cheek — and tried not to think about the pain of receiving it. "Once upon a time, or so history tells us, people believed they

154

were free to love as they wished. I loved a man. I know that is shocking to you. How could any sane individual behave so? By which I mean, choose to put themselves in danger. Except, it isn't a choice, you've got to believe me on that, Shola Ricks. In recent years, Titian's rule has meant folk like me being tossed out into the shadows." He nodded. "Yes, you and I, we are outcast. Good job we have each other."

On the other side of the glass sheet, Shola Ricks stared back with painted eyeballs, her sore, stitched ears rotating slightly like orbiting satellites.

Doctor Harris was an intelligent man, Groff gave him that much. Harris behaved and spoke like a monster, but some small part of him understood that there was a reason to hide what he did from the world at large. What else explained his reluctance to have more than a couple of Gothendore Sisters assist in the medical suite, or his decision to leave the bulk of the nursing to Groff? Somewhere inside that black heart of his, Harris knew his actions would be condemned. Surely that was true?

Except, as Groff stood feeding sheets stained with every bodily fluid to the medical suite's incinerator, he found he was not the only one entrusted with Harris's secrets. A nun entered, her face lost to the unforgiving folds of her wimple, and closed the door.

Groff didn't like the idea of being shut in with one of Abbandon's resident witches. He padded the floor and looked abashed.

"Can I help you, sister? Are you lost?" He tried to force a smile then remembered his missing teeth. The smile faltered. "This is the medical suite. Could be you are after the infirmary?"

The sister didn't reply. Just stood, back to the door, the faint outline of her features becoming more visible as he stared into her dark hood.

"Sister?" Groff felt a fresh wave of fear. What had he done wrong? Was this his moment of deliverance? Except, he and the sister worshipped very different gods. Lord Gothendore was an armoured warrior, blinding his followers with incandescent light. Mama Sunstar, on the other hand, was all earth and fire. Would that affect his passage to the afterlife?

The face moved forward very slightly. There was something gut-achingly familiar about the nun's features…

"Groff!" The nun gave a little yelp, like a smothered sob, and suddenly threw her arms around him.

In that moment, nothing made sense to Groff except the nun's embrace – because of course, he recognised her now as Ju's younger sister, Lizabeth. Suddenly he was breathing in everything familiar, and it hurt so fucking much! "Lil… Lizabeth." There were more questions, but in that moment, he couldn't form them.

Instead, Lizabeth pulled away and held him by his shoulders. "I do not have long. I volunteered to deliver a new child at Doctor Harris's request, may Mama Sunstar bless and keep that poor creature! But I needed to see you. I *needed* to see you." She stroked his face – the spot above his brand – very gently, and Groff couldn't help it. The tears fell and his bottom lip quivered with the effort to keep all he had endured contained.

"They took Ju," he said, the pain of the fact breaking over him anew. "The guards pulled him out into the street. His beautiful face… it was…" He broke off; Lil didn't need the details. "They dragged him away. He wouldn't have lasted a month in one of these camps!"

Lizabeth caught her breath. She forced the emotion back under. "I knew he was gone. I felt it in my bones. There is no record of him at any camp. I found you, though. At last I found you."

"But this work you are doing…" Groff looked at the door instinctually. "Any moment you might be discovered. There will be no mercy, Lil. They will drag you out into the sun and they will kill you, and they will throw you into the furnace along with all the others. I do not want that for you, Lil. Ju would not want that for you."

"I have come too far on this journey to stop now." Lilzabeth inhaled raggedy and sighed. "Listen, Groff. I must go. But know this much. I am here. I am working for the Resistance in Ju's name. The end is coming, Groff. One way or another, the end is coming for you and me, Groff. Stay strong. Know that I love you. And Ju loved you. He loved you so very much." This time, the sob broke through, and it was Groff who pushed a hand to Lizabeth's mouth and eyed the door in panic.

But Lizabeth recovered herself.

"If you see me here, my name is Sister Eva. Remember, Groff."

With one last tender brush of fingers down his cheek, she turned, passed through the door once more and left him behind.

The hole in the hull had closed up, the diamantine skin having melded together without leaving a scar. Kali couldn't help but experience a pinch of regret. She had enjoyed creeping beneath the skin of the gunner and pretending she was free.

But now the hull had healed and work had turned to the interior levels. Coming into the holding bay that morning, Kali's regret was soon replaced with anticipation, reminding her of the very first time she ever set foot inside a gunner. All the plans in the world were meaningless without prior knowledge of this new vessel's layout.

"But you've been aboard hundreds of other ships," Mohab had reasoned earlier when she expressed her concerns.

"Yes, and the blueprint is probably very similar to what I'm used to. But this is an imperial gunner, barely out of the dock before it got shot up." Mohab's tone had irritated her. At first it had been enough that she should pilot the craft. Now she was meant to be an expert on its interior as well!

Fortunately, Kali's superior engineering skills meant that she was selected to carry out the majority of the more complicated repairs and upgrades to the gunner.

"New scanners are to be installed in medical," said a guard, pointing to several large polythymer boxes and a riser trolley.

Kali didn't want to say any more, but if she didn't, how authentic would her behaviour be? She swallowed and spoke up. "My field of expertise is bio-engineering not hardware. Am I the right person to fit these scanners?"

The guard struck her hard across the face with his beater. She stumbled back as the world squeezed down to a pinpoint of light. Calling on her military training, she shook off the blow and stood up straight again.

"The right person? You are a bone bag, a rancid bitch who takes turns at getting fucked by the Commandant Superintendent and the fifty Vary you share a sty with. Traitors don't get to describe themselves as a person. They're diseased like Vary." He jabbed the end of the beater against her cheek and forced her to look at the polythymer boxes. "Fit the fucking scanners."

The guard stepped back, twisting his beater in his hands and watching Mohab closely as if deciding whether to strike them both down.

"Let's go," said Mohab softly. He didn't stop to see if Kali was all right, just kept on walking.

TWENTY-TWO

The smell from the furnaces was stronger than usual. Nothing had ever prepared Mohab for the reality of starving to death alongside the constant stench of roasting flesh. His stomach was a dried-up ball.

He was glad to leave the stench behind. Entering the gunner at the airlock, he followed three guards through the corridors. Kali walked at his shoulder. Behind came the scanners on a riser trolley, the reactive bio-chord of each pallet tied in to their nicks. Mohab was thankful for small mercies. He wasn't sure he had strength enough to lift let alone carry the scanners. Working in the quarry had used him up. Likewise, no doubt Kali's face ached where she had been struck. Mohab understood why she had spoken up. If she felt she had been assigned the wrong role, it would never sit well with her. Bleek were raised that way. To the best of his understanding, they settled into a career in early puberty and tended to stick by that decision. Very rarely, one went against the prescribed path and switched direction. In the case of Lieutenant Kali, they even swapped sides.

The corridors made an echo chamber around them. Mohab imagined the gunner in flight, the warm pulse of its revolving rings and the banter of its crew. He envied those who manned the gunner. Inside that ship, they could rise above the horrors of the world.

"This is the first circle level," said Kali quietly. "Mess hall, sleeping berths, leisure hall, store. Next level up is medical, officers' quarters, and the Captain's suite. Third level is the bridge, navigation deck, and weapons systems. Fourth level is the viewing platform. We won't get that far." She cocked her head towards a set of smoked glass-sheet doors. "The mess hall." Further on, she nodded to an open galley fitted with burners, water coolers and manual preparation equipment. "The base kitchen. For the use of crew. Beyond it is the main preparation galley, manned by domestic staff."

Mohab dragged a hand under his nose and sniffed. "I'm surprised you know this level so well." He directed his eyes up. "Officers and captains being housed elsewhere, I mean."

"I've always taken an interest in all ranks."

"But the next level has the officers, you say? They were more your kind, surely." Mohab heard the bite behind his words.

The lieutenant gave him a sideways glance. "I've dipped in and out of both camps, but it's less complicated to screw the crew. Less hassle, less gossip. You understand?"

"I understand that you never fitted in with your own kind." He stared dead ahead. "Or does it turn you on to rough it?"

"I think she answered that question the day she hooked up with Vary swine like you," shot one of the guards. The man double-backed and Mohab felt a wave of nausea. Had the guard overheard everything that he and Kali had discussed? Not everything, he realised as the guard flashed Kali a filthy smile but then turned back around.

His pulse settled as the man joined the others leading the way again through the corridors. Behind him and Kali, the riser trolley gave off its percussive buzz.

"I will show you what I can," said Kali under her breath. "Stay close. Listen hard."

Mohab gave the slightest dip of the head.

In Groff's mind, he had murdered Doctor Harris a thousand times. He liked to imagine Harris' blood as a red slick across the tiled floor. He found the idea beautiful. Today though, he pushed the fantasy aside to reach into the cabinet and pick up the concentrate bottle. He froze just short of slipping the concentrate into the hole in his waistband. Had he heard something? At his back, the cells were in darkness. Carefully he hid the bottle and closed the wire-mesh across the medical cabinet.

"Got any poison for me?"

A phantom solidified at the front of the cell opposite. Shola Ricks pressed her newly aquiline face to the glass sheet and stared out at him. One of her grotesquely stretched ears twitched; she squatted down and used a back foot to scratch at it. In doing so, she revealed her inner workings, those soft whorls of flesh between her legs.

"I didn't know you spoke still, Shola Ricks. It's nice to hear your voice. Nice to have company. Your friends here have given up using words." Groff held his hands out to the other cells.

"Poison. Can I have some?" Oranged eyes shone out of the darkness.

"You mean the medicine I just collected?" Groff patted the waistband of his pyjama pants, checking on his contraband. "I'm not sure a dose of this would do you much good. Plus, I have been tasked with keeping you alive. Keeping you alive keeps me alive." He swallowed. "The Vary need me, at least for now."

"Kill me with your hands then. Please, nurse. Do what they won't yet."

Her pleading tore at him. Shola Ricks had been made monstrous by Harris and his butchers. The stitches were exceptionally neat, but where the ears had been stretched and further modifications grafted, the skin was inflamed. Shola blinked repeatedly. The needle marks were visible where the ink had been pumped into her eyeballs.

"Shola Ricks," he said quietly to himself. The girl who had forced her name upon him. Reduced to this living patchwork. This un-thing.

"Do it now, Mister Groff. Before they come back."

He heard the desperation in her voice.

"I can't do it, Shola Ricks," he said, staring above her head into the darkness. "Too many lives depend on me." Approaching the glass sheet, he peered in at the wretched girl. No one should have to endure Harris's foul practices, let alone Shola Ricks.

"You will save everyone else, but you will not save me?" A

sob broke from Shola's lips and she squatted on her heels, open to the world. Tears gave way to pitiful mews. Cries of a cub separated from its mother.

"Now, now, Shola Ricks. Hush now. You'll bring them running."

He said it too late. The sound of heavy footfall rang out from the corridor.

"Do not betray me now," he told the fox girl. "I am needed and, time allowing, will soon be fixed to save you."

"There's nothing left of me to save." Shola faded back into the shadows as a pair of doctors strode into the room. Harris followed them in, scratching notes into a handheld.

He glanced up to see Groff step away from Shola's cell and he smiled.

"Well now, subject three. You are quite the chatterbox. Isn't she, Groff?" Harris peeped in at Shola's cell. When Groff didn't respond, the surgeon turned to him in expectation.

"I don't like the look of those stitches," said Groff. The hidden vial of concentrate felt too light. Had it started to leak? Paranoia made him sweat.

"It is a delicate procedure, Groff. How are we meant to advance these paranimal trials if we do not take risks, hmm? But I am sorry to hear you are concerned."

Groff kept his back to Shola's cell. Harris's tone was faintly mocking. The doctors with him stayed aloof.

"There is inflammation, at the sites of the ear grafts in particular." Groff tongued the gap between his teeth.

"You have applied iodine soak and salt salve?"

Groff nodded. He was remembering Shola's muffled whimpers as her wounds were bathed. The salt salve had burnt up her nerves, an agonising process he was sure of it. The iodine soak had made the seams in her skin look mouldy.

"Bring her out."

Groff frowned and Harris gestured to his colleagues. "So that we might examine the specimen under natural light." The doctor pointed to the dark cell. "I'm afraid subject three may mind the light since her eyes are still healing, but the sensitivity cannot be helped. In fact, it is a crucial tell sign in the subject's development."

Any other time, Groff wouldn't have thought twice about obeying the order. With the concentrate tucked into his waistband, he swung between feelings of rebellion and secrecy. "She is in a very delicate state, Doctor Harris. The light will cause her considerable distress." Groff licked his lips. The three Bleek doctors stared at him with dispassion.

Harris cleared his throat. "Fetch subject three from her cell, Groff. After all, you were the one who raised the subject of festering stitches. As much as I am sure you will nurse the subject to the best of your ability, there is the possibility that further surgery may be required."

Groff felt the motivation to keep fighting ebb.

Harris squeezed up his eyes. "Are you unwell, Groff?"

"I am fine, Doctor Harris." It was only a half-lie; organ failure and worn joints were everyday ailments in camp.

"You look like a man harbouring the will to do harm. Is that right, Groff?"

Groff thought about the calcium fluoride compound he had stolen. He imagined the compound activating, its colourless gas rising to the heavens and eradicating all life on the way up.

"I have a toothache."

"That, at least, is treatable. Be grateful your pain isn't more acute. And now, subject three if you please."

Such a polite request! Harris was also skilled at keeping his own brand of poison hidden.

The doctor entered the key pass into the handheld alongside Shola's cell. The door slid aside.

It pained Groff to step inside that cell. There were folk tales about girls who endured the sleep of the dead in glass coffins and princes who touched enchanted objects to the dead girls' brows and awoke them. He was no prince, though, and the girl was far too young and visceral to seduce him. A swirl of flesh on the bed, she reeked of pheromones and animal musk.

"Come on now, Shola Ricks. The white coats would see you." He slid a hand around the back of her neck and was repulsed by the feel of bristles.

"Do they kill me now?" she asked with a trace of longing.

"Soon, Shola Ricks. Soon."

Together, they emerged into the light. The gravity of Shola's surgeries had left her limp and weak. Groff had to half-carry her into the consultation room, where he laid her down on a riser stretcher and activated the hoover kick.

He stepped aside as Harris and his doctors entered the room. Trays of instruments were recovered from white cabinets sunk into the walls. As Groff had feared, there was no dream gas to soothe the girl to sleep this time, only the brute application of sharps and blunts to already raw flesh. Groff edged towards the door, but Harris instructed him to stay. He couldn't be certain, but he thought he saw a spark of amusement in the doctor's expression.

The scanners reminded Kali of her father's personal gel frame, from which he accessed the load-codes and access passes for the entire data farm housed at Capital Hall. She thought about the day she had threaded her own manifesto between the warp and weft of the government's newsfeed. Dust motes had twinkled in the soft haze through the window and the heat of the sun had been welcome. Not like the savage blaze out in the desert. There had been a water clock ticking, she remembered that much, and in the space between, a sense of time stretching. It took less than a minute to upload the document, but in those moments of waiting she experienced a heightened appreciation of life and its dangers. 'I am the fox', she had told herself. 'I am the fox creeping in amongst the plump chuck birds.'

Months later and Kali felt like that fox once more stealing into the hen pen. Despite her objections, she had more than enough training to install the scanners. But she needed an excuse to give her and Mohab eyes on the bridge.

"I do not like the way these hinge." She banged the top of the scanners and pursed her lips.

"You get it right, bitch," said the guard who had eavesdropped on her and Mohab earlier.

"If you want it done right, we will need to anchor the scanners at the apex of the service trunk. It can be assessed from the bridge." She put her hands on her hips and stared down her nose at the guard. One of the men visibly flinched and she braced herself against the baton.

For once though, the guards appeared to be in agreement with her suggestion.

"You seen a gunner's bridge before?" said one to the comrade nearest.

"Only photostat."

"Do we have clearance for the upper deck?" The mouthiest guard eyed Kali. He was right to suspect her of an ulterior motive for visiting the bridge. Luckily, he wasn't able to fully process what that motivation could be.

"Hurry it up, then. We'll take the internal riser rig to the bridge. And Klein, Gilbert..." He fixed on his fellow guard. "You don't take your eyes off these two, not even for an instant. After all, it doesn't take much for that rebel bitch to whip up a shit storm!"

The three guards elbowed one another and laughed at her expense while, standing by her shoulder, Mohab stared dead ahead.

"Lead the way then, Lieutenant Kali," said the mouthy guard, waving her on. "After all, this gunner belongs to Titian's army. It's only right daddy's girl should head up this parade."

With her fluffy eyelids pinned open and her newly scarred irises being prodded, Shola Ricks was proving how she had learnt to howl. Back in the cells, the razingstock boy scuffed the floor with his bone hooves and produced his version of their low drawl. The lizard girl was equally excited. Groff recognised the dry rasp of her working neck folds and the tight keen which was her attempt to communicate. No animal liked the sound of another suffering. Except Harris and his fellow white coats.

Groff endured the child's distress. But Shola Ricks had sunk her hooks into him, and he folded his arms and dug his hands into his armpits. It was the closest he could come to a barrier between himself and what was going on in the room. Pipettes hovered over Shola's eyes; she screeched at the stinging drops, working up froth at the corners of her mouth.

"I'll wait in the corridor," said Groff, and he started for the door.

"Stay." Harris was drawing blood from the girl's arm with a suck syringe. Groff half-expected the doctor to the drink from the plunger.

He did as he was told, even as the cries of the hybrid children mingled with those of Shola Ricks. 'His name was Ju. A nightclub singer, born and raised in Nilreb...' In his mind, Groff recounted memories from another lifetime, telling himself the story as he had Lieutenant Kali. Memories from that first night soothed him – the lights in the trees, the crisp white tablecloths, the bite of schnapps...

"Lo-lany-lo, lo-lany, lo-lany. Mama, sing with me. Oh, Mama, wait a while. That's hurting..." Shola's nonsense talk turned to sobbing.

Groff grabbed at his hair and twisted the handful. He longed to retrieve the bottle of concentrate he had stolen and burst it under the noses of the brutes in that sterile room! It would be sweet relief to watch the Bleek bastards have their lungs and eyes blister, to watch them burn from the inside. Except, there was Shola Ricks lying prone on the examination table between them, and while he longed to end her suffering, he couldn't face the idea of watching her die like that. And so he stayed still, still as stone, and tried to convince himself that he wasn't really in that room. He was back at the nightclub with Ju, listening to his pretty songs.

It took him by surprise to realise that Shola Ricks had quietened down and was being carried back to her cell in the arms of one of the doctors. Harris patted the stretcher.

"Hop on then, Groff. Let's see about that tooth."

Tooth? It took Groff a moment to shake off the remnants of his daydream and remember his claim to have toothache. Whether that was true or not was difficult to tell when he lived with perpetual hunger and the pains of a body breaking down.

Either way, there was no getting away from the lie. And in part, he felt he needed punishment. Hadn't he stolen the concentrate in full view of Shola Ricks? Hadn't he been reduced to this phantasmal villain, this stealer of potions and tellers of lies?

He sat on the edge of the riser stretcher, feeling it give a little under his weight then settle.

Doctor Harris selected a set of pliers. "Yes, you may like to watch the extraction," he told the others, and all three doctors peered down as he lay back on the bed.

"Open wide, Groff, and show me which tooth is causing you bother. Prod it with your tongue. Yes, yes I see."

Harris leaned over and used the closed pliers to ease out one of Groff's cheeks and then the other. He glanced up at his fellow surgeons. "The decay is prevalent throughout the teeth. It is a Vary weakness. The elongation of the incisors and breadth of the molars means there is a differential between a healthy Bleek mouth and the oversized version you see here. It is a subtle demarcation, I grant you, but acutely marked by those who study Vary physiognomy."

One of the doctors cleared his throat. "If the malformation is inherent, why bother removing one tooth?"

Groff saw the man staring down into his mouth with abject fascination.

"Because this is Groff, and Groff has a way with children,

don't you, Groff?" Harris poked at the nurse's forehead, right over the branded P. "Now brace yourself, Groff. A few firm tugs and we'll have you relieved of another of those troublesome teeth you're so prone to losing."

The pliers widened before Groff's eyes and descended. He felt them clamp down and the sweat of anticipated agony broke over him. The false accusations wore away at him like acid. With Shola Ricks' suffering still ringing in his ears, he thought about the smuggled concentrate in his pyjama waistband and the dream of flying free in a gunner.

TWENTY-THREE

Mohab thought it must be strange for Lieutenant Kali Titian to stand on the bridge of an imperial gunner ship wearing a pair of nicks and prison pyjamas. It was just as strange for him to be at the heart of one of High Judge Titian's colossal war machines; it drove home quite how futile it was for the Vary to dream of freedom. Even if he and a handful of others made it inside the gunner and made good on their promise to destroy the camp, there would be other camps like Abbandon waiting for them all over Bleekland. If Titian had his way and struck out against his neighbouring states, there was the risk that camps like Abbandon would soon litter the Earth. And then what, when the last vestiges of freedom had been drained and Vary were on the brink of extinction?

He shrugged off the thought and concentrated on absorbing his surroundings. The bridge was a cube of black glass-sheet. Banks of datastacks and gel screens locked in and over one another. Riser stools sat flush with the floor, ripe for activation. The great living shaft of the engine's stem dominated the bridge.

Mohab imagined the gunner in flight, the docile hum of its kinetic engine. Did the stem oscillate or simply vibrate? He felt like an innocent inside a Tree of Knowledge.

Kali pointed to the racks of scanners and a row of spare hook-ups. "Over there." She spoke up for the benefit of the guards. "The hook-ups look secure." Dropping her voice, she whispered, "Dalma plates are part of the data system; they control the display systems, weapons, navigation, etc. You see those charger bays?"

Mohab followed Kali's eyes as they flicked sideways. The charger bays looked the same size and shape as the weird stone tablets he had dug up in the quarry.

169

He didn't dare make his interest any more apparent. Instead, he concentrated on logging out items from the tool roll as Kali worked to link up the scanners to one of the spare hook-ups. Behind them, the guards were curious in their own right. They poked about in the nooks and crannies of the bridge, no doubt imagining themselves sent to war in the romanticised setting of the gunner and not stationed amongst the slime and pestilence of a prison camp.

Mohab couldn't help it. Curiosity got the better of him. "The keycode brings the engine into play. The dalma plates...?"

"Hold a full interstellar schematic for trade routes, satellite rings, meteorological differentials and debris imagining. We have no way of knowing if there is any juice in the stones you excavated, but nothing in my study of the gunners or what I thought was Titian tech led me to believe they could expire." Kali looked past Mohab and her face went blank. She held out a hand. "Pass me a couple of jack pins and a bore gauge."

They were being watched. Mohab logged out the tools and passed them over. Assisting as required, he watched Kali work to fix the scanners in place, all the while aware of the guards at their back and the vast swell of the gunner all around them. He just hoped Kali Titian knew what she was talking about. The lives of every Vary in camp depended on her.

"There was once a raggedy old man who travelled far and wide on a broken riser stretcher pulled by a lame red racer. The man had gone in search of the Purpled Cathedral – a sacred place and his spiritual home. Ever since he was a child, the man had heard tell of the Purpled Cathedral, and he had longed to rest there. But the man, he had wolves at his back and at his door, and so he was forced to take to his broken rig and lash the lame red racer to it, and go on his quest through a land full of wolves. There had been terrible encounters – burly four-legged beasts which snapped at his heels and tore his clothes. The lame red racer was whittled down by their attempts until the creature was even more pitiful and the raggedy old man longed to put it out of its misery.

"All around him, the man saw his people beaten and tormented and slaughtered by wolves. There were days when he could barely find the will to breathe, and there were nights when his heart hurt like it was being carved out from his body. But he kept the vision of the Purpled Cathedral in his mind and journeyed on.

"For many years and over many miles, the raggedy old man travelled through the land until finally, just as the wolves had almost caught up with him and were baying for his blood, he saw the ancient towers at the horizon. The Purpled Cathedral glittered under sunlight, deflecting the cries of his attackers. Banked on either side by the snarling wolves, the old man drove the lame red racer through the crystalline gates. At his back, wolves impaled themselves on the spikes at the cathedral entrance, or curtailed their pursuit and wove around in figures of eight, whining for their lost prey and fearful of that grand Cathedral of righteousness..."

It had been clumsy in its way, this story of flight and pursuit. There wasn't enough detail about the why and the wherefore, and he pitied the red racer being forced to soldier on. But it had been the best Mohab could muster with so much riding on the events of the next day.

The nurse, Groff, sensed as much.

"Sometimes it must be difficult to find the words," he said later, taking a seat on the low cot alongside Mohab and handing over a small glass cylinder. "There's one more vial to go. I can get it tomorrow. I'll just need to find an excuse to bring it to the holding bay."

What Groff really meant was 'I need this last vial as leverage so you don't take off without me.' Mohab understood. And he owed the nurse in a way. Groff had done his best to put him back together again.

"We will need you to attend to any who get wounded," he said by way of reassurance and hid the vial in a secret pocket of his pyjama jacket alongside the other three which Groff had already acquired.

"We will have a very small window of time in which to board the gunner. The keycode changes every hour."

"And do you trust Titian's daughter to do her part?" Groff stared at Mohab in earnest. "Can she be relied on to deliver the code?"

Mohab blew out his lips. He'd asked himself the same question over and over since putting the request to the lieutenant. After all, betraying the Vary seemed the surest way to secure herself a pardon and acceptance back into Titian's fold.

Somehow, though, he didn't think she would go against him and the others depending on her. Was it because of a sense of morality? A need to atone for her manifold sins? Or a desire to outwit the Bleek bastards who'd brought her down? It might have been none or all those reasons. All he knew was when he looked Lieutenant Kali Titian in the eye, he saw the same cold resolve as he saw in the twenty-five Vary recruited for the escape plan.

"We must trust the child of our enemy. It's a ridiculous circumstance but nothing about our current existence is reasonable." Peering out into the half-light of the barracks, he said quietly, "Kali has chosen her side. She won't let us down."

"Hey – you two! Go the fuck to sleep or the next shit I take, you lick my arse clean!" It was the block chief, arrived at the doorway and flanked by his men.

While Mohab lay down flat on his father's old cot, Groff sloped off in the direction of the bunks at the back of the cabin. Holding his breath, Mohab waited to see if the blockers would shut him up in their own way. But then the block chief stepped away from the door and his men followed, leaving Mohab to breathe again and pray for the oblivion of sleep.

TWENTY-FOUR

People make assumptions about me, Grizmare noted to herself. *How comfortable I must be with a life spent among grandiosity and palaces and political power!* Except, hadn't it only been yesterday that she swept dust from her cave home and watched a young boy build towers using alphabet bricks? And – *Oh, the memory made her smile!* – hadn't she liked to kick those bricks down, revelling in the pouting rage on her son's usually stoic face?

Now, though, standing in the foyer of High Judge Titian's grand Capital Hall, she couldn't help feeling small next to the robust statues and soaring walls. The exterior of Capital Hall was tremendously imposing – part fortress, part palace. The tallest building in Nilreb, it was wholly characteristic of her son's love of utilitarian grandeur, consisting of twelve graduating tiers and being capped with five shards of dark grey bedrock surrounding one vast central dome. Internally, the ostentation continued. Grizmare stared up at the blank-faced statues towering over the foyer and she supposed she was meant to be admiring facets of her own son. Arranged in facing pairs, there was the gladiatorial aspect of her son, lunging forward while triumphantly holding up the globe of the Earth. The next pair showed his propensity for architecture, being seated, gel frame in one hand, a 'miniature' version of Capital Hall resting on the palm of the other. The third pair represented her son's steely ambition; much like the tiger dog, he had always struck Grizmare as gritting his razor teeth and powering forward. Each statue braced against an imagined wind while cradling a model imperial gunner craft against their chest. Lastly, and carved either side of a glamorous reception desk, were the most honest pair of figures. These emotionless giants each held up a piglet while taking a blade to its throat. Captured in the stone was the creature's ecstatic anguish – the only emotion in the entire series.

"Always have to go over the top, don't you?" Grizmare murmured.

The driver stayed silent at her side. In truth, she'd been grateful for his assistance – the doors to the building, even the smaller side ones as opposed to the giant set at the main entrance, took muscle to haul open. Also, the floor was tiled in cold blue shiny tiles, each with a sharp orange star at its centre; every time she took a step, her cane threatened to slide out and send her sprawling. The driver's presence was reassuring in that, if she were to slip, the man would catch her, and that, at least, would help her retain a modicum of dignity.

A group of school children milled around the foyer, no doubt waiting on a tour guide. The children paid her no attention as she hobbled between them. Even the tip-tap of her infamous cane had no effect.

"This country's future generations are entirely ignorant to the great mother in their midst!" she said aloud, munching her gums and rather pleased by the fact.

"Their parents should educate them better." By her elbow, the driver opened his mouth, preparing to speak up.

Grizmare poked him hard in the stomach with her cane, visibly winding him. "Shut up, you stupid man! I am not my son. I do not require an audience."

She did not stay incognito for long. The five receptionists behind the desk were beautifully trained, but could not hide their slight stiffening at finding the mother of High Judge Titian standing before them. One, presumably the head of staff, took charge and offered her a small bow of reverence. At the same time, a group of Youth Guard entered the foyer, that bit too loud and full of self-importance. They were better at spotting a dignitary in their midst and insisted on crying, "Madam Titian!" at the top of their prepubescent voices and standing to attention.

Grizmare thought the best way to deal with the irritation was to ignore the Youth Guard completely. Instead, she pointed a gnarly finger over the desk at the head receptionist.

"I am here on official business. I presume I simply make my way up." She flicked her gaze towards the distant ceiling.

The head receptionist held up a hand as if attempting to calm a wild beast and used her other to tap away at a gel screen. "Please forgive me, Madam Titian, but all visitors are required to have official clearance. In this time of uncertainty…" After a few moments, the man called one of his colleagues over and both took turns to scroll through information while frowning.

"Uncertainty? I haven't the faintest idea what you are referring to! I do hope you are not intonating that High Judge Titian is in any way uncertain in his rule. Or that the people of Bleekland are in any way uncertain of the divine path he has laid for them. Or that we are uncertain of victory over the United Dominions and their rabid attempts to corrupt our great nation and liberate the Vary to breed like roo rats and infest this country once more. Demonia's hell fires! What is the matter with you? I cannot abide incompetence!" Grizmare scrunched up her eyes and gave the floor a couple of fresh raps with her cane.

"My apologies, Madam Titian, but I am struggling to find you on our clearance system. You are extremely welcome to sit and wait until we sort this ou…"

"Don't be a dumb-fuck! Why would my name be on any of your lists? Wouldn't that put me in danger of assassination? I warrant there are a good few special security personnel who pass through this building and are not on that list."

"I am sorry to say it, Madam Titian, but even if their name is absent, they do have the necessary clearance codes." The head receptionist gave the knot of his tie a little adjustment. "I don't suppose you have a code?"

Grizmare leaned over the desk further than was commonly polite. "Tell me. Do you see another name on that list, that of my son, High Judge Titian?"

The receptionists looked newly flustered. For an instant, all five took it in turns to exchange glances.

"There is no need for us to check High Judge Titian's

details." The head receptionist raised his eyebrows. "High Judge Titian *is* Capital Hall."

"And I am his conscience. I am also Mother Elect of the Bleekland Nation and the single most important person in my son's life. If you think there are secrets within these hallowed walls to which I am not privy, then you are in danger of suggesting my word is not law in my son's absence!" Channelling her son – or, equally, her tiger dog – Grizmare pulled back her lips, exposing gums instead of teeth. Her words visualised through spit. Even the school children fell silent. "Now, stop screwing around and give me access, or I will have every one of you insipid jobs-worth's dragged out by those Youth Guard and immediately transported to Bleekland's labour camps to end your days breaking rocks with the Vary!"

A minute later, her hand was data stamped – a painless procedure with a reserved suck syringe and despite Grizmare having complained bitterly against being "branded like razingstock."

"This stamp will give you access to all areas, including the military offices above." The head receptionist blinked. Grizmare wondered if a damp stain grew down his trousers' front.

She thinned her lips and turned to her driver. "Wait in the vehicle. I haven't the slightest idea how long I will be and I don't want you hovering at my shoulder like a bad smell."

Making her way carefully across the shining floor tiles to a gilded elevator, she waited as one of the Youth Guard rushed to thumb the gel patch on her behalf and call the lift. At her back, the school children resumed their insistent babble. Grizmare shuddered; the noise was not dissimilar to the clashing thoughts inside her head.

"What do you want me to do?" she had asked Eva one month earlier, and the girl had talked about trust and lies and how Grizmare could make all the difference, if she had the nerve to. Within a matter of days, she had begrudgingly agreed to wear a blindfold as Eva drove to what Grizmare took to be the outskirts of Nilreb, judging by the length of time they were travelling. When they came to a stop, the nun guided the handle of the cane into Grizmare's hand and hooked her arms through the old woman's, leading her over warm ground and then a harder, cooler surface. A sixth sense told Grizmare that high vaults of stone loomed above.

"You might as well remove this blindfold, Eva. And the rest of you pussies! Scared of a little old lady? Paah! I'd bet my gizzard we're in one of the old cave homes out west." She kicked a leg low across the ground and felt her foot connect with something hard and rigged. "This floor's even got the ripple welts caused by the fault's movements."

Grizmare's blindfold was torn off and she stood blinking like a new-born as her eyes adjusted.

She was right, of course. Around the stone walls, fire lamps spattered out greasy light. Cave homes had always made good use of their nooks and crannies and those stubborn outcrops of rock the tunnellers decided to leave intact. In the case of this particular dwelling, a large stone shelf served as a table. It was piled high with gel batteries, data screens arranged in a stack, what looked like a physical map or maybe even blueprints, and a brace of rock shot rifles. There were chairs too, hard-backed and empty. Instead, the men and women who worked to bring down Grizmare's son stood around her in a circle, Bleek and Vary, shoulder to shoulder and silhouetted against the flickering light.

By her side, Eva still wore her nun's habit. Directly in front, and holding the blindfold, was a woman. Hair loosely tied over one shoulder like a fur collar, she looked about twenty years old and had on a National Guard uniform, momentarily taking Grizmare back to a time when Kali would call in on her as a recruit. Kali had been all grins, unlike the woman opposite who kept her face neutral, almost masklike.

"Madam Titian." The woman's accent had the soft lilt of the far north.

Grizmare elbowed Eva. "Who's your friend?"

"I am 94. Your friend the nun here is 116. The rest of these volunteers are also known by numbers."

"The old number system, huh? So the Secret Guard can cut off a limb but they can't kill the trunk. My name is Grizmare Titian and there is very little point us pretending otherwise. My face is emblazoned on the national coin for fuck's sake!"

94 held up a hand. "You are right. It is stupid to pretend we do not recognise you. What we do not know is whether you are truly committed to uprooting the status quo or are in fact data gathering for your son's spies?" 94's lips softened. "You may, of course, just be a little old lady playing games with your maid as a way to amuse yourself."

"You are right. I am all those things – well, not a spy for the Secret Guard, but that's only because I hate those bloodsuckers just as much as you lot! But a spy in my own right...? Well now." Grizmare plucked at her chin hairs. "Maybe, maybe. What should I report back? That Eva and I played blindfold in a crumbling cave out in the desert?" She did her trick of leaning in too close to the person she was talking to. 94 folded her arms to put a barrier between them.

"Do you think anyone's going to give a rat's ass what this old fart dreams up between popping pills to keep her ticking over and spending her days talking to the animals? There's not a soul cares, believe me." Grizmare raised her scrawny eyebrows. "But I would be missed if you chose to put a shot in me here and now."

"I do not doubt it," said 94 – even as Grizmare felt a throb of sorrow. In truth, she doubted she would be missed at all. Maybe the countess would regret the passing of one of her luncheon ladies? Grizmare wasn't convinced.

All the same, her name carried weight, Choosing to ignore her state of loneliness, she jabbed her cane towards the stone table. "These are your plans, I take it." She went over to the table and gave the physical papers a prob with her cane. "You intend to overturn High Judge Titian. My son."

"116 said you were an ally…"

"Oh, she is," said Eva at her back. "But Grizmare needs to have her fun first."

"That I do…" Grizmare peered closer at the paperwork and immediately recognised the design of the building on one set of blueprints. She lent her cane against the table and struggled to manhandle the sheet on top of the rest. "This –" she stabbed a finger at the paper – "I recognise. This is one place you may as well leave alone. The clearance levels are tighter than Gothendore's asshole. I know it. My son told me."

94 came over to the table. "And did he tell you anything else of interest? In the last week in particular?"

Grizmare snorted. "So, you think I may serve you best as a spy on my own son?"

"Isn't that why you are here? To stand against a regime you finally want no part of?"

"She is here because she wants to be." Eva moved to stand besides Grizmare, who noticed that even now, here amongst these Bleek rebels, Eva's nun's habit stirred feelings of fear and reverence in those around her.

"I want to ask something of you and your clan of reprobates. A favour. And I'm going to need a flash lamp and a measure string." Grizmare rapped the tip of her cane against the rock floor. The sound echoed off the stone walls. "I need two volunteers. One Bleek, one Vary. Don't tell me who is which."

Two men volunteered and endured Grizmare's poking and prodding as she lifted one arm then the other, inspected gums and teeth like she did her razingstock and maw cats, and made both stick out their tongues and even lower their trousers. Through it all, the volunteers remained courteous, if bemused.

Eventually, Grizmare threw aside the measure string and shone the flash lamp up under her own chin. "They both have brown eyes," she said, grimacing like a gargoyle. "Their skin tones are similar. One is missing a back molar. The other has longer limbs. This one has a wider girth, this one the longer cock. Both have a ripe set of balls." She tossed the lamp back to one of the men and pattered about on the spot, agitated. "I can't decide between them. Each is different to the other."

"And does that affect your conclusion?" 94's chin was down. She stared up at Grizmare from below hooded lids.

"Let's not labour the point. Clearly, I can't tell which is Bleek and which is Vary. Then again, I've had a feeling that might be the case for a long time now." She blinked rapidly – it wouldn't do to shed tears and show weakness, especially not with these rebels. She rather suspected, if anything, they would despise her more, calling out her display as too little too late. Instead, she remembered Mister Thatchett – Tomlin – her friend for fifteen years. She pictured him being dragged bloody-faced from his home. And she remembered Kali watching with solemn fascination – a child raised wrong. Or just inherently cruel?

"Show me the blueprints for Capital Hall," Grizmare said to 94, and turning to Eva, "I am old, young lady. Help me make this count."

Seldom had there been an occasion when Grizmare Titian wished to blend into the background. It wasn't that she liked to be admired. Quite the contrary. Grizmare couldn't care a jot what people thought of her. Only, that they did think of her, and did not treat her as less. In the early days of her son's political success, she had been treated with courteous compassion. Today, stalking the corridors of Capital Hall's Military Wing and forcing the guard employed in office work to back away, Grizmare was grateful to be recognised for the acid-tongued matriarch she really was. She strode forward, head high, face stern, accompanied by the battle march of her cane across the floor tiles.

In all her encounters, only one person questioned her presence. She was passing the window of one of the larger offices when a door opened and Chief of Staff, Secretary De Agnes, stepped out into the corridor. De Agnes had very small, colourless eyes, cheeks that sagged, and a jowly neck that reminded her of a shriek hawk's. He carried a low-slung paunch, like a forward-facing hump, and patted and stroked his stomach now as he blocked her way.

"Madam Titian. How wonderful to see you. High Judge Titian is away, overseeing manoeuvres. But you know that, of course."

Grizmare felt her hackles go up. The stupid man stood directly in her path, blinking his tiny eyes.

"Secretary De Agnes. I know perfectly well where my son is."

"Of course, of course. It really is exceptional news, is it not? About the advances on the western front, I mean." De Agnes stroked his paunch. Tiny as they were, his eyes had a way of boring into her.

"You mean the south-east strip." Matching De Agnes with her own glare of suspicion, Grizmare called on the intel she had gleaned from the Resistance. "The western front has lost hundreds of thousands of troops on land, and fifteen gunners and three fleets of smaller munitions craft in the skies. It is a travesty of poorly devised troop formation and feeble-minded leadership, *Chief of Staff.*" She used his title as a weapon.

De Agnes's mouth wormed. Clearly, he found her hostility an affront to his inflated sense of self-importance. "You are right, of course. And now, where are you headed? You mustn't go beyond the billing offices without the necessary permissions." He swept a hand back in the direction she had just come. "You would like to return to the main lobby, yes? I am passing that way as it happens. Let us go together and I will arrange for a cab to come and collect you."

"I am afraid, Secretary De Agnes, as joyous an encounter as this has been, it is not the true purpose of my visit here. I have further business on this floor."

"That business being?" The small, weak eyes burrowed hard.

"A petition on behalf of my granddaughter, Kali Titian." Grizmare patted the side pocket of her duster coat, as if indicate some hidden document. She kept her gaze steely.

De Agnes bent down to her level, hands on knees, slightly leaning in. "It is admirable that you can love your granddaughter despite her transgressions. Personally, I could never forgive. In fact, I think High Judge Titian was too lenient. I know Kali is his daughter but I think she should have been publicly executed for her crimes. Something to send a message to those bastard swine in the Resistance. I would have liked to see Kali Titian stripped and flogged bloody, and then hanged – not a sudden neck-snapping drop through a trapdoor. No, I'm referring to a slow death where the perpetrator is forced to lean, toes just kissing the ground as the rope progressively tightens, crushing the windpipe. As I understand it, that method of hanging is by far the most painful."

The Chief of Staff maintained his weak-eyed stare. Grizmare thought about smashing her cane through his teeth before yanking out his tongue like pulling up hog weed in her garden. Instead she reached out and gave his nose a sudden, hard flick.

"Fly," she said sharply, and caught the birth of a snarl at the man's lips as she turned away and stomped down the corridor.

TWENTY- FIVE

"What do you want from me?" Joltu slid his fingers inside the waistband of her pyjamas, but Kali broke free of him. She couldn't afford to let him touch her when the dalma plates were strapped to her bare stomach beneath her shirt. Instead, she pressed a hand against his chest and forced his back against the wall of the office. Keeping pressure over his heart, she undid the zip tie of his trousers and felt for the warm swell beneath her hand. He went to grab at her, but she tightened her grip.

"I want you to be still."

He liked that – she read it in his glistening eyes – the idea of being reduced to a thing of flesh and given instructions rather than dishing them out was liberating and seductive. She read the subtle signs in him – the curl of tongue at the corner of his mouth, the flush of heat and subtle flex of muscle under her grip.

She milked him, alternating between watching his face with dispassion and fixating on the rigid shaft. Joltu kept his eyes open, not entirely trusting yet given over to her. His lower lip trembled; she wanted to bite it. Not through passion, but some desire to sink her teeth in and make him bleed.

It fascinated and aroused her to have such a true grip on the man who bedded down with her in spite of the lice. His sex twitched under her grip, the muscles across his groin spasming. To Kali, the cock in her hand had its own life force. She stroked that blind and naked vertebrate, feeling its ridges and tender tip.

"Be still for me," she insisted as Joltu's breathing became laboured.

He cleared his throat, forcing the rising of breath and ecstasy to quieten. She stayed emotionless, even as she felt the pulse of heat and slickness pump between her fingers. It would have been easy to ride him, bucking and carousing as the sweat broke between them. It was a finer, tighter wire of discomfort to hold back and drag and tease until his face contorted.

"Argh!" He bucked, greasing her clutching fingers.

She continued to watch, noting the careful ease of motion and loosening her grip. If he had been her experiment, she felt her knowledge had advanced. 'I told you to be still,' she wanted to tell him, pinching his sticky red bud by way of punishment. Instead, she did not take her eyes away from him, just let her hands fall back by her sides and was still herself.

Joltu didn't have the chance to explore what lay beneath Kali's rough layers. A curt rap on the door was met with Joltu's sharp command to "Enter!"

A guard came into the room. The man was panting, his face red as rind fruit. "Commandant Superintendent! Apologies, sir, but we have a small group of insurgents directly outside this building. Shall we activate their wrist nicks now or wait until the prisoners are rounded up and take them to the firing range?"

"You interrupt me for this?" Joltu snatched his jacket off the back of his office chair and stormed from the room, leaving the door open.

Left behind, Kali waited a few seconds, breath rising high in her chest. She was very nervous, which surprised her. She had engaged in plenty of active service during her time in the guard. This was just another mission, albeit one where it was the Vary she called allies and her kin, the Bleek, who threatened her with discovery.

Forcing herself to act, she ran round to the other side of the desk and took a seat in front of Joltu's gel frame. Stealing glances at the open doorway and ignoring the itch of her nicks – made worse by the threat of discovery – she entered the string algorithm she had memorised from watching the Commandant Superintendent log in. Metadata spooled before her eyes. Seeing the streaming lines again made Kali nostalgic for the regime of her past and nauseously reminded of another time she betrayed another's trust.

To Kali, it felt like only yesterday that she typed her Discharge Manifesto into the country's metadata, calling for a kinder resolution to the Vary Problem. She had pressed SEND so easily. Was it strange that she stood by the contents of that document? Even after everything she had endured, her father's politics of ethnic cleansing struck her as clumsy. If she allowed herself to truly feel, they might even be perverse.

The key code was hidden beneath a firewall of bruise code and mundanity. She memorised the sequence of Bleek glyphs. Strapped against her chest by two lengths of braided stone wool, the dalma plates were her secret to guard – as was now the passkey.

She was about to step away from the gel frame when another folder caught her eye:

TITIAN K PRECEDURE NKR.

Kali checked the doorway. Still empty. The uproar from outside had subsided – which meant her window for accessing Joltu's gel frame was closing. All the same, she had to know what was in that folder!

The files were open access. Apparently she was the subject of a series of transmissions between a Doctor Harris and the Secretary of State, Weilen Von Kirkland. She gleaned what she could, eyes flitting across the screen as if the words she read there threatened to burn her retinas. She latched onto a smattering of phrases – 'Kali Titian', 'Subject 952187', and 'Under the Sanction of High Judge Titian.' A physical operation was described – talk of her suitability for the experiment and the bio-fusion of her chemical makeup and something called the NKR nucoid. She pressed a hand to her throat and held back the fear. She didn't understand the science, but the idea of being subject to cross-genetic experimentation was gut-wrenching.

The last communication had a feedback link from Joltu. He had signed off on the procedure. The date was irrelevant; with no concept of how much time had passed since her arrival in

Abbandon, Kali couldn't begin to know if Joltu had put his mark to the experiment before she had even arrived or in the moments before she jerked him off.

"Kali."

She looked up to see Joltu standing in the doorway. His face was hard. "What are you doing, Lieutenant?" He eyed the gel frame.

Kali stepped away from the desk. It hurt her to be discovered in the act. Her tasks had been so simple. Find the keycode. Deliver the dalma plates to the docking bay. In return, a pair of Vary martyrs would cause a scene outside the officers' quarters, giving her the opportunity to search Joltu's personal datastacks. Her part in the plan was paramount and now she had outstayed her welcome and been discovered. All for the sake of a glance through files she might never have had to worry about if the plan had come to fruition.

She went with the truth, a part of it at least. "I wanted to know if my father had enquired after me." She swallowed. "I wanted to know if he had tried for a pardon on my behalf."

"No. No, he hasn't," said Joltu, keeping his eyes on Kali as he came into the room. At the desk, he shut down the gel frame and sat down heavily in his office chair.

"Two Vary males decided to start a fight outside the building. They were bled out by their nicks on the spot." He gestured to the door. His eyes narrowed. "Mind the blood on your way out."

Kali had her arms folded like a barrier against Joltu's reprisal; she forced herself to lower them, aware of the stone tablets strapped to her skin. There were no apologies to be made, no admonishments or making up. She had overstepped the boundaries. There would be no more meetings in private.

She left the office, closing the door at her back.

This much Grizmare had learnt from the Resistance. High Judge Titian's gunners were winning him the war. While the United Dominions had inflicted considerable damage on Bleekland's smaller craft, the aerospace was littered with enemy debris. By all accounts, there was a chance that Bleekland would push through and secure a globe-wide surrender by the end of the year. Victory would give the nation free rein to commit genocide against the Vary and to spread out beyond Bleekland's sweltering, ruptured landscape.

"The war is being lost because no other country is willing to sacrifice its hardware so readily," 94 had told her at the rebel's cave. "The Bleek have Vary labour. No other country can boast those resources. It would take a miracle to sway the war's outcome."

Days later, it was time to test that theory as she walked a corridor lined with the offices of government, the occasional stretch of window giving out on a city that looked like a land of giants. Officials passed her now and again. All nodded in recognition. Not a soul thought to stop her. Grizmare carried on lurching forward. Hips crackling. Knees threatening to give way.

She had memorised the route from the Resistance blueprint. Finally arriving at the airlock, she used the inbuilt suck syringe to extract a fine spray of her blood and thumbed the gel patch. The door revolved on greased tracks. Beyond, a corridor stretched away to a distant square of black.

Titian blood. Grizmare smirked as she sucked her thumb and hobbled inside. The door revolved back into place and all noise cut out. For a few seconds, she was suspended in total darkness. The sensation was eerie; womblike. Then tiny recessed fire lamps burst into life on the floor, lighting a pathway. Pushing herself on, she made it to the far end of the airlock, where, with a small pish of releasing air, a second inner door revolved and gave her access to the inner sanctum.

TWENTY- SIX

The twenty-five were stationed around the circumference of the gunner. To the National Guard, they were Vary swine going about their daily labour. Males took to the riser rigs, logged out tools, poked and prodded at the shell of the warship, and tried their best to survive another day.

Officer Hockle never understood why the Vary strove so hard to survive. Wasn't the easier option to make a nuisance of themselves early on and get the painful part over and done with? By his reckoning, nicks were clean and controlled mechanisms which guaranteed death. But the bastards would insist on eking out their miserable lives, even as the fat melted off their bones and the lice and rot set in.

Hockle thought about his family. His youngest, Giselle, would have pitied the Vary perhaps. She was, after all, a solemn child with a tendency to cry at the death of a mouse or finding a bone in her jack rabbit supper. His son, Dolg, would have a different view. Hockle sucked on his smokestick and rested his elbows on the railings, staring down at the prisoners in the holding bay. He saw the Vary with the same dispassion he had bred in his son.

"It is a waste of Bleekland resources to endure them to live." Hockle could imagine his son's reaction to the creatures below — and yes, his son might have started to spout High Judge Titian's official indoctrinations with the same ease as childhood rhymes, but he had a clear way of thinking that Hockle envied.

Only once had he wondered at the purity of Titian's vision. Face-to-face with Lieutenant Kali Titian, he had asked himself what kind of monster could dispatch his own daughter to Abbandon. It made him sick to the stomach to imagine Giselle subjected to the humiliation and degradation of life in the prison camp. It hurt him to the marrow to know a child could betray her father as profoundly as Kali Titian had, but he still couldn't reconcile the violence of her punishment. As he explained to his wife at the time of her sentencing, "It wasn't like she committed murder. She just had a breakdown of sorts. Somehow those Vary swine must have polluted her mind, don't ask me how! But at the end of the day, was any harm really done? After all, it wasn't like her so-called manifesto made the slightest bit of difference. Sure, folk read it, and yes, it proved there was a flaw in High Judge Titian's datastack security, but nothing changed, did it? No one thought any differently because of her words."

His wife, Clara, had nodded in agreement. Her eyes, though, had gone to the far end of the room, settling on Giselle. Their solemn child – too long in the womb, the midwives had explained. Hockle's little girl, who didn't quite act like her Bleek compatriots. His precious Giselle. A child born different.

Staring down at the prisoners, Hockle dragged on his smokestick and dreamt of Giselle's sweet-smelling hair and ticklish feet. He allowed himself a smile. There were Vary enough to keep High Judge Titian appeased. As long as he kept Giselle in the shadows, she would be safe.

"There has been an outbreak of lungrot in the quarry," Sister Eva told the pair of guards stationed at the door. "I need to make an assessment of your workers. The disease spreads like wildfire."

The guards nodded. They knew all too well that lungrot could take out a colony in a fortnight and no one, Bleek or Vary, would be spared.

"This one's with me," she said, nodding at Groff. She might have been Ju's younger sister once upon a time. But today she was Sister Eva – tight-mouthed and efficient.

Who were the men to question one of Gothendore's Sisters? They stepped aside, envying the pitiful prisoner with the bleeding rag at his mouth. Lungrot was airborne and even that filthy rag was better than no filter.

More of the National Guard peered down from the balcony. They saw the two on sentry duty wave the sister in along with her Vary companion. They watched the sister direct the male to gather saliva samples from the Vary workers on the ground.

Groff made his way over to Mohab.

"You have it?"

Groff nodded. He slid the final vial into Mohab's hand.

Mohab frowned as he pocketed the contraband. "What happened to your mouth?"

Groff took away the rag. He opened his mouth and prodded a finger at a second gap in his teeth. The gum was soft red jelly.

"Harris took a tooth. It is nothing next to his usual butchery." It was difficult for Groff to talk. His speech came out mangled.

"Any idea where Kali is? She's late." Mohab was sweating.

Groff shook his head.

Sister Eva arrived and offered Mohab a spit pot.

Mohab put the pot to his lips and handed it back over. "Have you seen Kali?"

Sister Eva forced cups on a couple more workers and shook her head.

Mohab searched the hanger for Kali's face, remembering the day he left the infirmary and saw the lieutenant exiting the officers' quarters. Was it so surprising that she had chosen to fuck one of her own kind? Joltu was not just Bleek, he was Commandant Superintendent and one of the Bleekland elite, a club to which Kali had herself belonged. Was it so very unusual to want a taste of the familiar in Abbandon's alien landscape?

Except, at that moment, he needed Kali to put aside the reminder of her old life and prove her loyalty to the same people she had once tried to destroy. Staring at the men waiting on his order, Mohab felt the anger resonating off them. How much longer had they got until the National Guard sensed rebellion in the air?

"Where is your Primary?"

It was one of the guards. Mohab recognised the man; he was the same one who attacked him all those months ago, when he first stepped off the haulage wagon. The man's face was etched into his brain along with each thud of a boot against his ribs and each crush of a fist.

He steadied his voice. "She has not arrived yet."

The guard exhaled heavily, hand twitching near the handle of his beater. "Then how are you to do your work?" He leaned in. His breath was sweet with beer sops. "How are you to have a purpose?"

Mohab thought about driving his thumbs into the man's eye sockets. He wanted to scream into that dreadful face, scream and not let up until the bastard's ears ran with blood.

"The Commandant Superintendent wanted to see me." Kali arrived alongside them. She had been running. Her shoulders heaved as she struggled to catch her breath.

"Apparently the Commandant Superintendent likes to swim in the gutter." The guard looked Kali up and down. It surprised Mohab to see a suggestion of sadness in the man's eyes. Did he actually feel sorry for High Judge Titian's daughter?

"Get your tool roll and catch up." The guard turned away and headed for the nearest riser rig.

Kali choked against the back of a hand. "He saw me. Joltu saw me looking at his datastack screen."

"And he let you go?" Sister Eva tucked the clutch of saliva samples into her satchel. She retrieved a small grip pistol at the same time. It was an unreliable weapon in Abbandon's desert atmosphere. Little wonder the National Guard relied on nicks and beaters, thought Mohab. All the same, he wanted to break the woman's arm for a chance at the weapon.

He stifled the impulse. "The men are in position. Groff, we look to you to start this fight." His eyes went to Kali. "And we look to you to end it."

"Yes, yes." Groff padded the ground. Even given the circumstances, he struck Mohab as extraordinarily twitchy.

"There is a girl in the medical suite. I must break her out and bring her with us. I shall activate the chemical and then I must fetch her."

"There's no time, Groff. Don't be ridiculous!" Thrusting a spit cup into Groff's hand, Sister Eva directed him to use it with a sharp nod of her head.

Groff ignored her. "I delivered the girl into the hands of monsters. I cannot justify any escape attempt without trying to rescue her too."

"We will have enough to contend with," Mohab said, "without additional complications." He couldn't understand the stupidity of what Groff was suggesting. There wasn't time to delay. Everything must be done now, swiftly and effectively.

It was Kali who spoke up for the nurse. Taking in the perimeter of the hanger with its watchful National Guard and resting gunner, she said quietly, "Groff has his morality and he must shoulder it. As I shoulder mine. I will steer the gunner by way of the medical suite. If you aren't waiting outside with or without the girl when we pass, I will be forced to forget you."

Hers was a promise so absolute that it left the small group silent. In that moment, Mohab felt the mantle of his existence as the Speaker's son lift. There was no further need for stories, for the shape and sound of language. All that was left was the plan.

Mohab retrieved the four vials from his waistband, adding them to the spit cups in Sister Eva's tray of empties. She nodded and turned around. Stalking away from the gunner, she crouched down in a corner of the hanger and busied herself with the contents of the tray.

"Hi, sister! Are you all right there?" A guard leaned out from the balcony. When Sister Eva didn't answer, he signalled to a nearby pair of blockers. "Go help the sister. She appears to have fallen."

Mohab was vaguely aware of another guard calling down, demanding that Mohab and Kali get on with their work, threatening to activate their nicks and cursing their mothers' wombs. Kali fetched her tool roll from the rack, hoisted it onto her back and pushed Mohab in the direction of the gunner.

"Do not associate yourself with the sister, remember?" She gave him another hard prod in the back, forcing him forwards. "Each person plays their part."

Mohab could hear the blockers laying down tools and muttering into their chests.

"All is well," Sister Eva was insisting. Moments later, there was the sound of breaking glass followed by the sister's effulgent apologies. Mohab couldn't help risking a glance; Sister Eva backed away from the broken vials, pistol hidden in the lengths of her sleeves.

"You!" Officer Hockle pointed at one of the blockers in the pit. "Clean up that mess."

The man did as instructed, shaking out a hand when he nicked it on broken glass.

"Sure you are okay, ma'am?" Hockle leaned on the rail of the balcony and squinted down at the sister. Why the Commandant General abided those witches in his camp, Hockle would never understand. After all, the Lord Gothendore was an old wives' tale, left over from the dark ages before the Skystorm. Why hadn't the new age swept away all these ridiculous superstitions?

When the sister didn't answer, he unhooked his beater and knocked it against the rail.

"Sister!"

The crone lifted her head. "I have spoiled the samples. These hips of mine crack and moan in this desert heat. I feel the bones splintering inside of me."

Hockle understood the sentiment, except it wasn't his bones which suffered but his mind. The horrors of Abbandon never came close to healing.

"Go, sister. Fetch your fresh supplies. There's enough time left to collect your samples aga..." He broke off. His eyes were stinging. No, burning! His throat flexed and threatened to close. "I'm feeling... unwell," he said between breaths. "I need the nurse."

Collapsing against the rail, Hockle pointed a trembling hand at the prisoner, Groff. Something had a hold on him, something sudden, violent and profoundly terrifying. Warmth trickled down the corner of his mouth. Hockle put a finger to his mouth and brought it away. The streak of blood felt inevitable. His lungs began to scream.

Hockle's arms swung over the side of the rails. Below he could see the prisoners staring up at the guards' balcony, tools in hand. He made out the shapes of the other guards nearby. Some had collapsed onto the metal walkway. Others clung to the rails as he did, necks distended against the wracking agonies in their throats and lungs.

Why were the Vary so still? Panic scrambled his understanding of their environment. Why didn't the men below help? His eyes – his burning eyes! The pain was pure white heat. Molten tears streaked his face. Below, the filmy gas was just visible, coming from the broken vials and rising.

This was death, then? The fact clutched at Hockle's heart like a fist. It hurt him utterly, this sudden dissolution when Giselle was still a squeeze of softness on his knee. His wife too, so much life to her yet, the crow's feet only just beginning at the corners of her eyes.

His throat was completely closed now, his eyes tucked behind swollen lids. 'I wanted to outlive this madness,' his mind whispered. Faces came to him – High Judge Titian beneath a raging midday sun; Commandant Superintendent Joltu, stolid and unbending; Lieutenant Kali Titian, shining with a core of golden light; and Giselle. Solemn Giselle, who rarely smiled and who nested into the nook between his neck and shoulders.

The air turned stale in his lungs. Hockle kept his mind's eye on his daughter's face and slipped below.

The guards slumped over the balcony railings or collapsed on the walkway. Safe from the rising gas, the prisoners below stayed quiet, watching the dying. Only the blockers reacted. They ran at one another, demanding answers. It didn't take long for them to start pointing at the broken vials and then the sister. The mix of the hydrogen fluoride concentrate and air had seen sulphuric acid rise into the upper reaches of the holding bay. The idea had been Groff's, his nursing qualification belying the true extent of his knowledge of chemicals. Kali had witnessed the man's intelligence when he assisted as her Second in the holding bay and in their moments of hushed conversation in the barracks. 'The Vary will be safe below,' he had assured Mohab, a prediction proving true.

Kali pressed a hand to Groff's shoulder. "Your chemical weapon worked. We don't have long. Avoid the blockers. Avoid the guards. You should go rescue your charge."

Groff had tears in his eyes. Now the moment was here, it was overwhelming. "I have murdered men," he said quietly.

"Yes." Kali leaned in, examining his face intently. "Do not think about it or the wound will fester. Now go, Groff!" She gave his shoulder a squeeze. "Be outside. I cannot wait for you."

He nodded and broke free of her. Making for the door, he was approached by a blocker brandishing a makeshift beater.

"Get back!" shrieked the male.

A shot rang out and the male froze, arm raised. His look of astonishment turned to agony.

The blocker fell forward, revealing Sister Eva standing a few feet away, holding out her smoking pistol.

As Groff slipped out of the door, Kali felt the atmosphere crack and was struck by a sudden tide of noise. The Vary had been spurred into action by the sound of the firing pistol. Brandishing hammers, wrenches and torque bolts, they ran at the blockers, who lost all pretence of restraint. They went for the prisoners with their teeth bared. Kali had seen the same frantic anger in the wild cats her battalion used to capture for food. She would feel a jolt of pity to see the creatures hissing and snapping in the traps. But she would slip her blade into their throats just the same. It was no different with the blockers. She joined with the Vary and charged, a bolt gun in one hand and a mallet in the other.

She ran at the nearest blocker, offloading slugs from the bolt gun. The male crumpled inward, hands clutching his head. She drew back her arm and drove the mantle up under the male's chin. The head ricocheted back. Knocked unconscious, the blocker fell back and sprawled on the ground. Kali didn't hesitate; she brought the mallet down on his skull, crushing bone into soft matter.

Extra rations and preferential treatment meant the blockers stood their ground. Vary broke under their makeshift beaters. Kali didn't let up. The timeline was tight and, despite the blockers being stronger, the Vary outnumbered their betrayers five to one. Wild-eyed, the Vary punched and lashed out with hunks of metal. Kali aimed two slugs at a blocker beating on Mohab. Staying true to her military training, she went aimed for the pressure points – the groin, the eyes, the throat. The blocker pushed Mohab aside, raising his arms against the blows.

Kali stayed true to her military training. She went for the pressure points – the groin, the eyes, the throat. The blocker pushed Mohab aside, raising his arms against the blows. Once Kali would have balked at his long Vary limbs. Now she just saw a tall man with a generous reach.

A quick flick of the wrist and she switched to driving her mallet up into the man's belly. He stumbled back a couple of steps, recovered, and charged at her full pelt.

Kali had seen that expression of rage before, on the faces of soldiers during her training. The recruits were always the most unhinged. The gangly Vary was no different. A couple of shots from the bolt gun took out a portion of his skull. He grappled with her a few seconds more, clinging to life. Kali put up with his attack, feeling handfuls of hair ripped away and the pressure of the male's thumbs at her collarbone. The grip went slack. The blocker fell to the floor and bled out.

"Kali!" Mohab was on the nearest riser rig, hand

outstretched. "Leave the blockers to the men. Keep to the plan."

Easier said than done for Titian's daughter. Trained to conquer. Trained to kill. All around, Vary prisoners and blockers locked weapons, bellowed and bled. The sight made Kali bare her teeth. Not so long ago she had brought the Vary to heel. Now she was to be the one to save them. She should have felt relieved, but was disappointed to leave the battle behind.

"You'd think the blockers would try to muscle in on an escape attempt," she said, breathing heavily as she joined Mohab on the riser rig.

"Blockers have been turned against their own for so long they've forgotten what it means to be Vary." Mohab spat to one side as the rig took them up. A few moments later, it shuddered to a halt alongside the gunner. Kali entered the keycode into the gel pad. The airlock decompressed, and the door slid in and sideways.

Lights rippled down the length of the internal corridor.

Once, a very long time ago, when Grizmare was five or six years old, she had been taken to the museum by her own grandmother. The day had been hot, she remembered. Similar to the scorching white heat she had experienced up on the roof of the Red Orchid Hotel more recently. All those years ago, her grandmother, who had also been a formidable woman, shoed her into the temperature controlled cool of Geno museum. While so much of Bleekland's second city was still built into the rock, the museum was one of a number of new buildings, built above ground and cooled by turbines powered by the same flowing magma which made the city bake from beneath. This Grizmare had learnt from her grandmother, in-between their examining all the museum had to offer locked behind glass-sheet.

One display she remembered more clearly than the others. "Pre-Firestorm," the data recorder had informed her, in a clear female voice which sounded like it should be telling her to swallow medicine. "These water stones represent the blueprints for the communication stacks and energy rooters of early Vary settlements. While most examples of Pre-Firestorm technology were destroyed, these stones were unearthed at a quarry on the outskirts of Nilreb."

Even as a child, Grizmare had been in awe of the complicated patterns set into the strange metal bricks. Only as an adult, standing at the entranceway to her son's data farm, did she finally get to see the technology in action.

The warehouse was the height of two floors, she guessed. In place of fire lamps on the walls, small circles of low light were set into the smoked and textured glass-sheet underfoot. The farm itself was comprised of banks of tall stone monoliths. Each stone was etched with geometric designs – the same complicated patterns she had seen all those years ago in the museum. Only, now they were synched to one another using gel – that new-world constituent – instead of water. Every channel flowed with green-gold gel like blood through veins, which she supposed it was.

Staring at the data farm which was Bleekland's communication bank, Grizmare knew she was looking at her son's true heart. Here was the thing she had given birth to all those years before. Power to control. Power to suppress. Power to wage war.

She felt as if the room swelled and contracted around her. At the same time, the atmosphere was tight as a drumskin. If a single droplet of sweat had fallen onto the black glass-sheet floor, she could have sworn she would have heard its splash. No one rushed to throw her out. Instead the chamber resonated around her as Grizmare forced herself to walk forwards, the click of her cane echoing with every step.

Her mind filled with numbers – deliberately so since she didn't want to lose momentum, or courage, and run away screaming. As if making moves across a games' grid, she passed between the silent stones… Or were they? Now she was amongst them, she thought she detected a very deep, very soft vibration, like a universal hum which she might have heard as much through her bones as through her ears.

'Any moment they will find me.' The thought infringed on her steps. She brushed it away forcefully, pushing on against the doubt.

The keystone wasn't easy to find. She had been looking for something impressive, a match to the size of the towering stones, perhaps, or painted gold to indicate its significance to the entire nation. As it turned out, the keystone was a small, ornately carved oblong... No, a pair of oblongs, slotted so close together that their inner workings meshed. Water plates. Original Vary technology from the Pre-Firestorm period. Dug out of the earth and used for the blueprint on which her son had built his dalma plate datastream and, with it, an empire and space force.

"History that was not yours to steal," she said firmly, as if chastising a child.

She stared down at the ornate cane in her hand, its etched metal a match to the great rocks of the data farm. High Judge Titian had gifted her the cane all those years ago now. A design of ultimate strength, he had told her at the time. Minutely flexible so as to reduce jarring to the hand bones. Lightly weighted to aid momentum and sustain balance. "A precious and unique artefact for the Mother of our Holy Nation," her son had said. It was the equivalent of a blood diamond, Grizmare realised, overcome with agony and bitterness. Her son had made her carry a symbol of his grand dishonour and she had never thought to question it.

Now, there only seemed to be one appropriate response. 94 and Eva and the rest of the Resistance wanted her to infect the data farm with a tiny bug stored on a gel chip in her pocket. But Grizmare had never been good at subtle. Instead, she raised her cane as high as her age-crumbled shoulder would allow, then brought it hammering down between the stones. A great seismic pulse radiated out from the spot as the water stones cracked apart, surfaces ruptured. She stood back and watched as the gel ran between them like life's blood.

TWENTY-SEVEN

Hurrying to the medical suite, Groff thought about the other children in the camp, how their eyes were always bloodshot and syrupy. It wasn't enough to patch them up or sing them lullabies. None of that made any difference when doctors sliced them open. Abbandon's medical suite was an adventure playground for sadistic whitecoats and Groff was their golem.

But now there was a chance to change one child's fate. His own too.

The block chief was on guard duty. Seeing Groff, he put his hands on his hips and tugged on the smokestick between his lips. He spoke out a corner of his mouth.

"Afternoon, Suckgap."

"Chief." Groff put a hand on the door handle and was about to go inside when the man blocked his way with an arm.

"I thought you were at the factory in the pm this week."

"Mostly, but Doctor Harris instructed me to come back this afternoon. He is concerned about one of his subjects showing signs of septicaemia."

"I couldn't give a fuck if they were shitting gold." The block chief shook his head. His makeshift baton clinked against his knee, tack nails shining in the sunlight. "Shut the door after you. Doctor Harris has been complaining about the ground ash getting everywhere."

Groff opened the door just wide enough to squeeze through and left the block chief on the doorstep.

Inside, he made the pretence to scrub up at the stone sink as usual. Through the glass-sheet door, he saw the two doctors from earlier mulling around the children's ward. A pair of Gothendore Sisters led a riser cart between the beds, administering medicines – or toxins. The same pitiful children occupied the beds. Given more time, Groff would have made angels of them. And devils of their tormentors.

He rapped on the door and one of the sisters floated over.

She spoke through the glass. "Back so soon, Groff?"

Groff nodded. "There's a caustic leak in the holding bay. Officer in charge sent me back here until it is cleared up."

The sister peered through the glass-sheet. He half-expected her to bare a set of fangs.

She keyed the code into the gel pad and the door slid aside. The smell of iodine and soak rag flooded out. Groff walked through the ward, keeping his focus dead ahead. Out the corner of his eye, he saw the doctors glance up then look away again. Sometimes it paid to matter so little!

At the far end of the ward, he heard a child call out to him from the nearest bed. 'I don't know your name,' he thought, keeping on walking. 'I know only Shola Ricks.'

Shola Ricks was born two weeks early, to a young actress with a theatrical ensemble based out of the Eastern Rivers district of Nilreb. In the absence of the stone-wool trader who had provided his seed, Shola's mother attempted to raise her daughter amongst the scenery flats and pan stick. For the first two years of her life, Shola hadn't even guessed there was a world outside of those noisy streets, especially not one as barren as the desert surrounding Abbandon. Instead, there were sunrises and sunsets, rabbles and market squares, fireworks and silhouettes, and seats filled with strangers. Occasionally, Shola's mother cooked a grey-beak stew. Mostly, though, the pair tucked into grit biscuits and gravy from a tin can attached to one of the market carts.

Groff knew none of this, only that Shola Ricks had got to him. The mule boy kicked up his hooves but Groff took no notice. The child lizard splayed her claws against the glass-sheet and licked her eyeball with her tongue. Groff ignored her. If Mama Sunstar was on his side, he might just rescue Shola. He could manage no more. Besides which, he couldn't imagine putting such children out into the world. One little fox girl?

Maybe he could tuck her away.

"You come now, Shola Ricks," he said at the glass-sheet door to her cell. He flicked on the lamp. Shola lay in a foetal position on the cot. Her hair was shorn. One distended ear was visible, crisscrossed with infected stitches. Groff tongued the new gap between his teeth. Harris's operations were little more than a death sentence.

"I am feeling none too well, Mister Groff," said Shola in the familiar way which had got to him in the first place. She sounded so tired. Tired and resigned.

Groff entered the memorised keycode and the door slid open. He was hit by the sour smell of festering wounds and stale air. Hurrying over to the cot, he scooped Shola up into his arms. "Better to die trying than wait for death here," he told her as the other hybrids knocked on the glass-sheet walls of their cells and begged him to let them out in their catcall of howls and hissing. "Hush!" he demanded with the angry tone the doctors used daily. The children fell silent.

"Be patient. We will liberate you too," he said at the doorway to the lockup and, in some small way, believed it.

Kali tore off her shirt, revealing the dalma plates strapped to her body. If there had ever been a need for modesty, she had long forgotten it.

"Unstrap me!" She turned her back on Mohab and held her arms out.

Lieutenant Kali Titian exposed and asking for help? In another lifetime, Mohab would have taken up the mantle for his people and driven a makeshift blade into her spine. But horrors had a way of evolving. In some cases, and in some places, they could shift sides entirely, even if it went against the laws of nature like light through a solid.

He ripped through the woven stone-wool. Kali handed over the stones and tugged her shirt back over her head.

"Now what?" His voice cracked. She'd shown him the bridge

and the theoretical placement of the dalma plates, but what did any of it really mean next to the complex reality of manning a gunner?

Kali clearly noted Mohab's apprehension. He found a hand squeezing his upper arm. "We can do this, Speaker's son. A gunner needs a crew to function as a weapon of war. But as a spacecraft, it only needs one pilot. Plug in the dalma plates. We'll get clear of the hanger, by which time the others should be free so we can open the doors. Then we can arm the weapons and take out the National Guard."

It should have agitated Mohab to take instruction from a Bleek. Except he no longer thought of Kali that way. She could never atone for her sins, but she had been cleansed by other means – the heat of the furnace as they pushed his father's body onto the slab; the drips off the slop trough which caught her legs as she squatted over it each morning; the mingling of her breath and blood with that of the Vary.

He lined up the dalma plates over the twin brackets, slid them in, and let go. Thin steel rods buckled in either side of the stones. There was a faint ticking of internal workings and a burning, salty smell that reminded Mohab of the stench of the delousing showers. There was a more hopeful reminder too, of ozone-scented air after an electric storm. A deep green glow emitted from the blocks, lighting up the symbols. Fluid dripped from the topmost edge of each stone, lengthening out and down in tendrils, flooding the carved surfaces.

Kali nodded at Mohab. "Good luck with the rest of the men. Strap back in as soon as you can."

Mohab struggled to speak. He had an excruciating pain in the tender spot below his ribs – a mix of lactic acid and adrenaline. There was every likelihood that he was going to die before the hour was out. The thought turned his insides to liquid. But there was fire too, low down in the pit of his belly.

"I'll see you on the other side of this," he called over the roar of the waking engines.

Shola Ricks looked so much more alien in the daylight. Her stitches were raw and lurid, her skin gone grey. Groff saw beauty too. The fur of her fantastically long ears shone under the natural light. He saw the quick flick of exotic eyes, so utterly un-Vary. The tail wormed behind her.

"Stay close, Shola," he told her. Sun shining down. Fur so soft and yellow.

He pushed away the laundry trolley that he had used to smuggle her out, and gathered her to him. She smelt of dung and dry grass, shivering at his touch like a wild thing unused to contact.

"Suckgap?"

The block chief stepped out from the shadows of the building's generator. He screwed up his eyes, smokestick between his lips.

Groff struggled to breathe. The block chief bumped his makeshift beater against a thigh.

"Doctor Harris asked me to move this subject to the infirmary." Groff swallowed.

"That so, Suckgap?" The block chief swaggered closer. He'd earnt his position as head of the blockers on account of his height and muscle. He reminded Groff of a bull. The man's skin was deep red leather. His square head sat on folds.

"Thing is, I've never known the good doctor remove any of his specimens from this lab unless the abomination is on a furnace slab." Showing his teeth, the block chief rested his beater on Groff's shoulder. He glanced at Shola, tucked up into the nook of Groff's arm, and he winked. "Did Suckgap here decided to take you under his wing?" His nasty gaze slid back to the nurse. "Is that it, Groff? Did you take pity on the wretch and decide to hide her under your bed? Or were your intentions less pure?" He rested the tip of his beater against Groff's chest.

Groff forced his dry lips apart. "Block chief. I am telling the truth. I have no reason to lie. Where could I hide the girl? What would be the point of running with her? We are caged in."

"Caged in like the dirty beast that you are." The block chief poked the makeshift beater into Groff's chest, hard enough to hurt. "Tell me the truth now, Suckgap. Before I beat it out."

Groff laid Shola down in the ash. "Doctor Harris asked me..."

The beater struck Groff hard on one side of his collar bone. The block chief repeated the blow to the stomach as the nurse choked and doubled over.

"The truth, Suckgap." The man stood over him, blocking out the sun.

More blows connected at Groff's hip, his arm, his breastbone. He whined and fell sideways.

Shola Ricks was a blur of movement, crouching, re-angling and powering forward. The block chief staggered under the weight of the golden girl as her teeth ruptured his throat. Groff struggled to his feet under a shower of warm blood. The taste of it caught his lips.

The block chief collapsed forward and Shola sprang from his back. Only now did Groff notice the exaggerated width to her jaw. Fresh-grown muscle rippled under the skin of her thighs. Blood smeared her neck and chin like war paint.

She hunkered down beside Groff, ears twitching and turning slightly as they tuned in to each new sound.

"Thank you, Shola Ricks," he said softly. "Thank you."

TWENTY- EIGHT

The huge doors to the hanger drew apart, the hot desert air and blazing sunlight flooding in. Up on the balcony, the poison had dissipated; the National Guard slept on, their staring eyes engorged and glazing over. Below, others lay broken – guards mainly but also Vary. Those prisoners who had endured ran into the yard outside the factory. With every passing second, the likelihood of their nicks being activated increased. It only needed one guard to activate his wrist cuff and select to take out every Vary inside a five-metre radius. And so the Vary fought with blind mania, chopping and smashing with the tools they used as weapons.

One guard got lucky. Holding up his arm, he activated his wrist cuff's group setting, taking out the nearest vary in a wave of blood spray. Seeing their brothers writhing in the dirt and ashes, others attacked the guard responsible. A sledgehammer dislodged the man's jaw. A jack handle crushed his throat.

Up in the winch pit of the gunner, Mohab was struggling to open the doors. In theory, he needed to manually re-renter the keycode at the lock pad at the same instant that Kali flew the ship over the quarry. Hovering the belly of the craft in the mined-out dip, its lower doors would be accessable from ground level. With no one to help, Mohab knew the keycode was time-sensitive, but that he was also required to activate the door rig on his own – no easy task since it was a giant coil of motion mechanics with safeguard sensors. It took extra, precious seconds to contact Kali on the bridge and have her talk him through the manual override. Her voice carried through the comms unit, calm and reassuring. Mohab pictured her in charge of the legions of National Guard once at her command. Had she addressed them with the same measured tone and inexorable strength of conviction? Of course she had.

The vast ship responded to Kali's expert handling. After an initial lurch as it uncoupled in the holding bay, the gunner maintained a slow advance, its movement barely perceptible. Mohab was only fully aware of its flight once he cracked the hull doors enough to let in a sliver of sunlight. As he forced them fully open, rapid gunfire began to ricochet off the craft's exterior.

Kali needed to arm the gunner's weaponry, but without a skeleton crew to man the defence unit, she was forced to take fire without returning it. Titian's warcraft were specifically designed to withstand an assault by any of Bleekland's enemies, but that was with the hull doors secured. Honing her concentration, Kali poured her own energy into moving the huge ship over the quarry.

Spectroimages flitted across the walls, reflecting the scene below. She saw Vary workers, hundreds of them, scattering in every direction below the craft. Some were punished on the spot and twisted in pools of blood, their nicks activated by the panicking National Guard. There were instances of rebellion. She saw groups of Vary fighting to overcome the guards and stealing nick keys. Despite their emaciation, the workers found strength in sheer numbers. It was a strange, nihilistic sight and one she felt utterly removed from.

"You've got to set the ship down!" The voice came cracking through the comms unit. She heard rapid gunfire too. The National Guard were firing from all directions – the quarry, the walkway between the fences, and from the watchtowers where the guns were large and ammunition plentiful.

Mohab's voice came through again, squeezed high with desperation. "Kali! We need to get the others on board! We need to take out the watchtowers. You need to deliver us from this pit." There was a sob of maddened emotion, and then, "You owe us, Lieutenant."

She did, didn't she? For a fleeting moment, all sound closed off and her whole world refracted to a single pinpoint of light.

There was only her, floating in a warm ether of nothingness.

The ship lurched as a magnetic grenade attached and fired; Kali recognised the bloom of soft grey smoke off the gunner's helm. The wall screens showed more fire coming in from the watchtowers. Grenades slid through the air like birds. Explosions echoed in the distance, triggering light alarms across the length of the controls on the bridge.

"Bringing her down now," she said into the comms unit. Her chest tightened. It was time to land the craft and fill the hull with a people she had once known as beasts. Time to give the Vary a fighting chance at razing Abbandon to the ground.

Sister Eva was the next on board. "We've got the bastards on the run!" she cried, turning to stretch out a hand and help others up into the hull. Mohab recognised most, but not all.

"We take those we can!" he shouted, doing his best to process the scores of wild and bloody faces. "We must close the doors. We need to man the weapons."

There would be no chance of accessing the rest of the ship while the hull doors were still open. Kali had warned Mohab that much. In the black heat of the barracks, it had all sounded so feasible. 'Load up with able bodied prisoners, close the doors to seal the hull, gain access to the gunner's interior, then man the ship and activate its weaponry.' The reality, though, was crushingly different. Gunfire pinged off the exterior of the hull, taking out whole rows of men who would never make it inside. A lucky few dodged the rock-shot, making it on board before any guards could get close enough to trip the prisoners' nicks. Once hauled up inside, the diamantine skin of the craft disrupted the signal. Grown men cried in relief, even as the bullets whistled through the hull.

Mohab wanted to pull Sister Eva out from under the stampede. She deserved that much. But there was no time. He'd no idea how many men were on board. The initial plan had focused around volunteers from his barracks, but that hadn't accounted for the riot they had sparked. The quarry was an amphitheatre, the clash of guards and Vary playing out below like blood sport.

Kali's voice filled the hull, the sound distorted and disembodied. "I need those doors closed. Make sure Groff is in!"

"Groff! Groff?" Mohab pushed past the sweating bodies, checking faces and shouting at the men to fall back. He found Sister Eva; she held her arm to her chest where it had been crushed, but she was at least breathing still.

"Tuck yourself up at the back of the hull, out of the way," he told her, and scrambled on. He couldn't find the nurse or the hybrid child Groff had talked of rescuing. There were only the wild eyes of other men and the teeth-shattering hum of the hovering gunner.

"Oh, Shola Ricks. Oh, baby girl." Groff fell to his knees and cupped her bloodied face. "Only, not such much of a girl now. Not so much. More a wild thing. More a hunter."

Next to them, the block chief continued to bleed out from his shredded throat. He had stopped twitching and lay in the dust, red spit foaming at the corners of his mouth.

The camp sirens wailed. Mohab half-expected Shola Ricks to throw back her head and join in the howling. He stared at the fox girl in the stark sunlight and there was so much less of the girl he had known in the beast he had set free. She stank of alien, crawling things. Crouched at his side, her thin limbs jutting at strong angles, her breath, fast and shallow.

A roach skittered in front of them in the dirt and she leaned forward on all paws, cocked her head and sniffed at it. There was no recognition of the murderous act she had just committed, only this sniffing of a bug and tasting its carapace with her tongue.

"This place breeds monsters," Groff said softly.

There was nothing for it but to run and keep on running. In the distance, he could see the gunner over the quarry, the vast discs oscillating and leaving their film in the air.

"We've got to go, Shola." He tugged her arm and she snapped at him instinctually.

"Don't you even…" He tried again, squashing the roach under his foot to break her fascination with it.

This time she hissed.

"Shola… fucking… Ricks! I promised I'd deliver you from this hellhole and I intend to keep that promise." Grabbing the fox girl by the scruff of the neck, he dragged her away from the blood scent of the block chief's body and into the shadows of the generator and the barracks beyond.

Everywhere, Vary struggled to find weapons against the blockers' makeshift batons and the guards' beaters and lethal wrist cuffs. Those prisoners unfortunate enough to find themselves in range of the cuffs had no method to fight back; they collapsed in fits of rabid ecstasy and bled out. The sight made Groff sweat in terror. He'd no choice, though. He had to press on, whether Shola intended to come willingly or not.

The reflector walls showed different angles of the camp. Kali was most interested in events at the far side. Behind a second wall of slice wire, Vary women and children had been herded into the yard outside their barracks and were being processed for work detail.

Time was running out. Having steered her father's troops for so long, she had a keen understanding of procedure and protocol. Insurrection would be met with violence – short, brutal and meaningful. 'Cut out a man's heart and he will be made weak by blood loss.' Her father's rhetoric. Kali appreciated the sentiment. There had also been times aplenty when she and her fellow guards had taken the words literally.

"The sins of the father will be exacted on his children," she said aloud. The comms unit was still active and she imagined her voice echoing through the hull. She meant the words as much for herself as for the Vary.

"I am closing the doors," she shouted at the comms box,

trying not to think too hard about the chaos inside the hull or the camp at large. Instead, she unhooked the locking gear to the hull doors. A warning flash on the console told her that the doors had been damaged by the rapid fire from the watchtowers. Or jarred open by something. Either way, she hadn't time to worry. They needed to leave the nest of the quarry and fire up the gunner's weaponry. Else every man, woman and child would die in the ashes.

Groff beckoned Shola after him. Together, they crossed the patch of ground between the infirmary and the National Guard quarters. The quarry road stretched into the middle distance where the gunner squatted. The ship might have been birthed of the ruptured earth below, a scintillating blur.

The air cracked with gunfire. Voices, everywhere – screaming, pleading, demanding. Men lay dead or dying, a great bleeding spread of them. Vary with their nicks activated. Guards with their skulls caved in. Prisoners who lived, like him, in daily pain and terror, had found strength to fight back. Swathes of them had been taken out by the firepower from the watchtowers, but the Vary struggled on, pouring like termites from the dark crevices of the barracks, the factory, the quarry, and the assembly yard.

"We head for the ship," he told Shola Ricks, and hoped she understood. Seeing her rip out the block chief's throat had left him uncertain whether she had any semblance of herself remaining.

She stared at him with unnatural eyes.

I am a fool to have thought I could ever save you, Groff thought. I wanted to break you free, but now I see the cage is welded to you. He had committed to her rescue though, sacrificed easy passage on board the gunner to run and fetch her. And so he led the way, flattening against the wall of a barrack building, pressing her back with his hand when guards ran past. They hid often, in the shadows and in doorways. All the while, the gunner hovered at the quarry, its reverberant hum underpinning the atmosphere. Occasionally, Shola would give a short, sharp bark of alarm. Groff did his best to soothe and to quiet her.

At last they were on the quarry road. Groff found an abandoned riser wagon and he scooped Shola up and made her lie, belly down, on the wagon base.

"Don't peep over." He punched the drive unit to activate the board. Tucking in at the rear of the wagon, he guided it forward, in and out the fallen and the mayhem of battle. There were Vary running towards the barracks and Vary running towards the quarry, a great exodus who left a trail of wounded and dead in their wake. Groff felt a wave of hope. He and Shola had a chance now. Together, they would find ways to undo her animalistic behaviour and to right the wrong in her nature. First though, they needed to make it to the hull doors.

Groff counted down. His heart swelled with possibility and the franticness and hurt beneath his ribs. Breath burned in his throat. His limbs felt molten.

He could see Mohab waiting in the doorway, searching the battle below. Mohab's eyes fixed on Groff and he started yelling.

"We're going to make it, Shola Ricks." Groff believed it too. The pain fell away. He was lighter than air. He would save Shola Ricks where he had failed to save Ju all those years earlier. He would repair the girl, as he had failed to repair so many in the infirmary and the secret cells inside the zoo of the medical suite. He would watch her grow and laugh and live, somewhere rain fell.

At his wrists, there was a tiny click of twisting metal. Groff felt a cold rush of dread. He was a few short steps from the open mouth of the gunner. Giving the riser wagon a last, tremendous push, he felt it leave his grip just as the twin gel cylinders at either wrist bit in. He plunged face-first into the dust and skidded forward. Gravel pocked his cheek. Blood trickled over his hands, the pain and the terror of what was happening threatening to block out his world. Groff fought through, clinging on for a few more precious seconds. *I'm on my way back to that nightclub in Nilreb,* he thought. *I'll hear Ju sing and I'll catch his eye, as I did before, and together we'll share the sunset.*

Tears slipped down his cheeks as he measured out each slowing heartbeat. His eyes strained against the vivid blue until a shadow blocked his view, arm raised and revealing the shape of a beater in sharp silhouette.

I'm coming home to you, Ju, thought Groff with his last breath. *At last, I'm coming home.*

TWENTY- NINE

Mohab and a few brave others risked the gunfire to shoulder the riser wagon. It had rammed tight between the doors as they were sliding shut and now was wedged in the entrance, doors reverberating as they repeatedly attempted to close. Alarms pulsed all around as the Vary dodged rock shot and struggled to prise the wagon free. Trapped with its mechanism still in motion, the wagon juddered and roared, egesting smoke and filmy gas.

It was Mohab who clambered up into the wagon and found the girl. Or what had been a girl once. Her ears were stitched and distended, alongside which her pointed chin, orange eyes, and reengineered limbs told Mohab that she was one of Doctor Harris's experiments. Groff had tried to save her.

Mohab had been shouting encouragement at the nurse when the guard stepped out from his crouch position alongside a gravel pile. It was the officer who had beaten him so savagely on his very first day. The man's face had been carved into his mind, as deeply wounding as the nicks that had bled Groff dry. Mohab had seen the truth of what had happened though; the final blow came from the officer's beater.

The wagon pitched and growled under him. "Jump out!" he shouted to the hybrid girl. "This wagon will be crushed between these doors or pushed back out at any moment."

The girl stared up at him with wild, glittering eyes. He saw rage in the twist of her savage mouth. Sorrow too in the knead of her paws against her belly.

He reached out to her, but she skittered backwards to the far corner of the wagon. Either side, the doors inched apart and slammed back in. The hybrid child powered down on her limbs and sprang forward and up, causing Mohab to fall backwards in case her fangs were meant for him. She landed on the rim of the wagon, glanced down at Mohab and then launched herself back out into the sunshine.

Mohab made a swipe for her and missed. He wriggled round to see her hit the ground in a crouch and start running. In six strides, she covered the ground between the gunner and Groff's body, kicking up ash like a sandstorm. Mohab saw the officer turn, beater raised and tipped with brain matter. The man didn't get the chance to bring the beater down on the hybrid; with her new-made fangs exposed, the girl sprang at the guard. Her claws sank into his face while her jaws ripped into his arm. The guard tried to defend himself, but his arm was partially severed. The hybrid's claws tore the officer's eyes out before slicing up his breastbone.

Looking down on the scene, Mohab lurched between joy and nausea. The doors buffeted either side of the wagon, pulling him back into the present. "Push this wagon free if you want to see your wives and children again!" he shouted, clambering back into the hull. So many men had already succumbed to the bullet fire. He hoped the remainder were enough to man the gunner's weaponry. First though, they had to get the doors shut, and quickly. More National Guard vehicles were approaching from the main camp. The artillery fire from the watchtowers was relentless.

"You need to take us up, Kali!" he cried at the top of his lungs. He didn't get a reply. Had the comms unit taken fire? "You need to take us up!" He ran at the inside door, banged on it with the flat of his hand, tried to force the handle. The door didn't budge.

Staring wildly about, Mohab's eyes fixed on a large crank wrench in the hand of a dead prisoner. He grabbed the wrench and fired up the crank teeth until the power bar in the handle buzzed green.

"Open up you bastard!" He rammed the wrench into the door seal.

Lieutenant Kali Titian had witnessed the blind prejudice and rabid violence against the Vary. She had witnessed and taken part in it, and never once had she questioned doing so because her father was High Judge Titian and his word was law. More than that, she was Bleek and the National Guard had fought long and hard to bring the Vary vermin under control.

Only, her day at the Killing Fields had changed everything. Seeing oceans of bodies rotting in the sun had peeled her soul back from her centre. There was light above, fire and darkness below, and air between, and, everywhere, there was death. The world had shifted on its axis for her that day. Standing on the precipice. Sweat dribbling down her back like blood.

A similar sensation took hold of Kali now. Staring at the reflection walls on the bridge, she saw the women and children assembled in their yard and knew why.

"What's blocking the doors?" she cried into the comms unit. "I have to take us up. I need the weapons manned. I need the weapons manned!" A screen showed her the interior of the hull where a large object blocked the double doors and men scrambled to free it. Without weapons, the gunner was a floating refuge for a lucky few, but otherwise useless.

Kali slammed a fist against the control console. She only had one option and that was to watch. Watch as she had done two years before in the Killing Fields. Watch and feel her lungs and heart and gut liquefy.

Out at the wide-open space of the yard, guards assembled behind the women and children. Seconds stretched. The guards held up their arms, brandishing wrist cuffs. *Do something!* Kali demanded of herself. Tears flowed down her cheeks and burned like molten lava. *Do something!*

She chose to create a new option. She chose to fly the ship. Revolving the thrusters, she forced the entire framework to contract and buck against the tide of its momentum. The gunner roared as the rings reversed, its tessellated skin crashing into and over itself. Out the corner of her eye, she saw the interior of the hull in the monitor. The riser wagon wedged in the doors pitched forward and upended. The doors ratcheted closer by a foot. Men tumbled in free motion under the whistling pressure of the open hull. Kali winced but kept the gunner at a tilt while driving forward. Spectroimages showed her all that was occurring a few hundred metres below, where the watchtowers sparkled with bursts of rapid fire. Kali ignored the assault, even as the console pulsed with warning lights. The gunner, so recently repaired, was being stoned to death. Ammo tore up and under the skin of the ship. But Kali stayed true to one aim: *Stop the Guard. Halt the bloodshed.*

The gunner ripped and yawed around her, eating up the space between the quarry and the yard. In the reflection walls, she saw the factory – huge and grey and wreathed in the smoke of the dead. She saw the infirmary where the bodies of the Sisterhood were spread amongst those of the guards and prisoners. She saw the sweat cans of the barracks and the dome of the Officers' Quarters and the gravel pits and the remnant bunkers where shorn hair and shoes were stored. She saw the two rows of slice-wire with the walkway in-between; from that height, the fences looked like scars upon the land. She saw the ash covered ground and bone stacks and, at the far edge of the desert, the glass-sheet towers of Geno. If she hadn't grown up there under the care of her grandmother, she might have mistaken the city for a mirage. To see civilisation so close to the camp's barbarity almost broke her on the inside. The need to save the lives of the same Vary she had once despised lifted her above the sadness. There, above the twin watchtowers at the gates, the two antennae jutted towards the sky. Between passed the invisible current which controlled the prisoners' nicks.

On the assembly yard, stood front of centre, was Commandant Superintendent Joltu; Kali recognised his silhouette. If she'd had access to the gun system, she would have floored him. Wasn't that meant to be her final revenge? To penetrate him, as he had her, with terrible, inevitable violence?

She saw a first wave of Vary women and children sink to the ground, writhing in a bloodbath. A second wave fell, and a third. Kali fixed her gaze on the dalma plates. She drove the gunner at Abbandon's twin towers and prayed the enslaved had strength enough left to break down walls.

THIRTY

Twice in his life, Mohab had sensed the knife's edge between death and consciousness. The first instance had been the guard's assault on him when he stepped off the wagon outside the gates of Abbandon. The second instance was struggling to work the crank wrench as the gunner pitched and jolted. He was thrown hard against the inner door, the great hull echoing around him, inky and booming. Men screamed. The wagon upended between the groaning outer doors. For a split second, it was the single most terrifying experience of Mohab's life. The air itself seemed to splinter. Beneath him, the crank wrench wormed its way into the seal and the inner door opened very slightly. The sudden switch in pressure sent him tumbling away, vacuumed towards the outer doors and the upended wagon. His spine slammed hard against the riser steel at the base. The gunner rose and fell on a tidal rush; Mohab felt the wagon shunt free of the outer doors and then he was falling, away from the dark into the blinding blue. Wind buffeted around him, hot and hard like slaps from a hand. The great bowl of the gunner soared away and left him clinging, helpless and petrified, to the sides of the falling wagon.

He thought: *This is my end. I am the space between words.*

With gut-curling, manic desperation, Mohab located the power latch between his two stretching fingers. He punched a fist against the latch, felt the filmy blast of heat beneath the riser steel, and jarred every bone in his body as the wagon slowed and righted just short of the ground.

Damp with horror, his eyes followed the path of the gunner overhead. He would never make it back on board, never man those colossal guns and burst the camp's banks... A creeping inertia spread through him as he set the wagon down. The gunner travelled on a steep trajectory, heading straight for the watchtowers and their rapid firepower. No halting, no retaliation, only a strong and steady course as the ship itself became a weapon.

Was it in him to regret the choice foisted on Kali? Was it in him to feel sorrow for the men to be lost or Sister Eva, tucked into a corner? The gunner hummed on its eternal pivot, careered into the first watchtower and then, by proxy, took out the second. The noise was catastrophic. Stone turned to dust. Metal bowed and ripped. Fire tore up the broken ship, which slid sideways and rammed the ground, carving up a great wave of ash.

In its wake, the remains of the watchtowers crumbled.

All of his life, Commandant Superintendent Joltu had excelled, first as a student and later in the Bleekland National Guard. He and Kali Titian had shared that much in common. Now, as the towers fell and the Vary were no longer constrained by their wrist nicks, he excelled once more. This time, in making it to a solar jeep and out the camp gates before Kali brought the gunner crashing down. Because who else could have manned the craft, no matter how unsuccessfully? He had seen the hull doors left wide open, and maybe he and Kali alone had understood the consequences. Perhaps, in the end, the Vary had sent Kali to her death after all.

At his back, the gates and fallen towers of Abbandon were aflame, the remains of the gunner sprawled half in, half out of the camp like a slain beast. With the vast expanse of the desert spreading out ahead of him, Joltu had no idea if he was saving himself by fleeing the camp or delivering himself into Demonia's bowels. Through the thin stonewool taupe stretched over the roof bars of the jeep, he could already feel the sun's heat razing down. Flames at his back, flames above. And now, as he drew away from Abbandon, it became a blot on a smooth grey landscape, receding to a distant drift of smoke.

His eye became distracted by something running parallel to his vehicle, fifty or so feet away. At first he took it to be a young tiger dog – stripes yet to form and plunging along on its powerful limbs. But then the creature turned its head aside while running and he was forced to confront the godless truth. A child's face, corroded by re-stitched flesh. A fur pelt welded to her prepubescent body. And ears – tall, twitching, their tips feathered. Rotating to home in on every sound.

The fox girl steered east to Joltu's north – heading out to the true wildness of Bleekland's splinter zones and lava rivers. Joltu blinked against the tears which threatened.

"I'm sorry," he said to the abhorrent silhouette bounding away.

He wished he could have voiced something similar to Kali. But she was gone and Joltu realised he was utterly alone. In that moment, his single wish was that Doctor Tristan Harris might learn how it felt to be strapped to the gurney and dissected that evening, curtesy of the liberated Vary.

Hoping the pair of canteens he had taken from the body of a water boy would last, Commandant Superintendent Joltu maintained a course for the horizon.

THIRTY-ONE

A gorge had opened the length of the lawn. Against the verdant green, it looked like a rotting scar. Once, Grizmare might have felt dismay at the fact. Today she felt very little, except, perhaps, a quiet arrogance because the lawn no longer mattered. In fact she had gone so far as to demand the sprinklers be turned off. The gardeners didn't listen, of course. Hers was a Titian residence; the upkeep of house and gardens was a matter of state pride. There was also the matter of her being under house arrest and not a soul listening to a word she said any more. Even her medication was prescribed for her without consultation. The tiny green pills pressed upon her morning and night kept her in a fog. At their strongest, they transported her back into a room where she was surrounded by huge lettered blocks spilling words, and where the spark of her cane against the keystone destroyed the world around her.

"I have always been a disruptive influence," she muttered, mostly to herself as the new paid companion, another nun, spoon-fed her pills. "My son believes he is all powerful, but he is a leech. A parasitic worm!"

"Not a traitor, though," said the nun. Lips dry as leather. A flick of spit at her chin. "Grandmother like granddaughter. A vicious betrayal. Lord Gothendore will shear your soul in two, mark my words."

Words… They were meaningless. And also lethal… The fresh dose of meds kicked in and Grizmare felt as if she were floating away from herself, a faintly nauseating sensation. "I wish Kali was here now," she said softly. Her hands felt like mechanical pieces in a puzzle.

She had been dozing when the nun woke her with a firm shake of her shoulder. Grizmare took a moment to come around, struggling

222

to part her eyelids and find the saliva to lubricate her mouth.

"A visitor," said the nun. She left the room as quickly as a fleeting shadow.

A few moments later, a new figure entered the room. Grizmare blinked in the effort to focus her eyes; the medication had eased off to a slight, dull headache now she had slept. She was surprised to see Harriot Zoorbiah. It felt like a lifetime ago that she had endured the woman's idiotic prattle on the steaming rooftop of the Red Orchid Hotel.

Harriot still dressed like an oversized sagging infant in ribbons and bows. Her hair was royal blue today and she brought with her the smell of red cherries and apricots – at least Grizmare thought she did. Or was it a hangover from the drugs?

"Grizmare! Oh, my dear, you look as pale as Demonia's own corpse! Have you been eating? Should I order you quail? Or perhaps a rack of stock ribs? You may be in need of the marrow to restore your ailing constitution."

"I am well enough, Harriot. Enough with the fussing. Take a seat or show yourself out, I don't mind which."

"Now then, Grizmare. I know you don't mean that. Well, you can't mean that, can you? It's not as if you were overrun with visitors even before you committed treason. Now..? Well, I doubt you entertain more than once a week!"

"You are my first visitor," said Grizmare choppily. Better to get the admission out in a rush!

"Is that so?"

Harriot gingerly sat down on the chair opposite – the one Sister Eva had once occupied. Grizmare experienced a pang of loss. What had happened to the young woman, she wondered?

Out loud, she said, "How is Morantha?"

"The countessa has been confined to her apartments ever since your arrest." Harriot played with the lacy hem of her sleeve. "The authorities believe you and she may have been in league."

"Fucking imbeciles! Morantha was always more inclined to sell her soul for a chance at sharing company with High Judge

Titian than turning against him. It's the only reason she and I were friends." It was untrue. Moratha had, at times, been a genuine support to her, including when Kali was arrested. Grizmare sighed and rubbed her temples. "I'm sorry to hear of Morantha's troubles. I would protest her innocence, but who would listen?"

Harriot appeared to be staring through the wall of smoked glass-sheet at the ruptured lawn. "The horrors bubbling underneath finally broke through, I see." She shifted uncomfortably in her seat.

Grizmare nodded towards the blackened rift. "You are safe in here, Harriot. This property was designed to absorb tremors. The floors are reinforced against heat surges."

Harriot stayed on the edge of her seat and patted at her curls.

Running low on patience, Grizmare pitched forward in her chair. "Why are you here, Harriot?"

She was taken aback when the other woman lent towards her in a rush of sweet-smelling powder and perfume. "I wanted to look you in the eye, Grizmare. I wanted to understand how your son created this exemplary country and you did your best to destroy it."

"And did I destroy it? The datastacks, I mean. No one here will tell me a word."

Harriot sat back with a simpering smile. "I always thought your criticisms of me were unfair. You have treated me as a fool repeatedly over the years. And now I find it is you who cannot function in respectable society. You who does not value the teachings of your own son! You who has no love for this holy nation!" The woman's faintly moist cheeks beat in and out. "Of course you didn't destroy the datastacks. What a ludicrous idea!" She got to her feet abruptly and put her nose in the air. "You should have been nicer to me, Grizmare. I am not without connections. I could have helped you."

Grizmare stayed seated and watched the wrinkled doll of a woman tottering on ribboned heels. "Thank you for stopping by,

Harriot." She bared her gums. "I haven't been feeling myself
lately. But you, Harriot, you have reminded me exactly why this
false regime is destined to die. It thinks it is so beautiful, but
really it's just a pig wearing lipstick!"

She kept up her gummy grin while Harriot retreated, as if
scared to turn her back on the mad woman. At the door, Harriot
blinked her painted eyes rapidly then fled.

Grizmare's gaze returned to the garden and the lawn cleaved
in two.

Over recent days, Grizmare had seen various transport wagons
come and go, and been forced to watch as the animals in her zoo
were shipped off in boxes, crates and cages. It had broken the last
fragile pieces of her heart.

Only one beast remained. Too temperamental to be
rehomed, too old to survive out in the wild.

Doing her best to battle against the lingering haze from the
little green pills, Grizmare requested a walk through the gardens.
"To aid the push and pull of my bowels," she told the nun,
enjoying how the woman wrinkled her nose in disgust. Grizmare
had chortled to herself and found a broom to use as a walking
aid. Her cane was long gone.

Outside, the air had a taste of fire. Taste of dust too. The lava
flows were running just below the bedrock, so she had overheard.
The heat felt tight and dangerous around her. It was difficult to
walk, but she pressed on, digging one end of the broom into the
gravel path. To either side, the flowerbeds were wilting. Up close,
the welt of hot rock and soil across the lawn gave off a
sulphurous smell and steamed slightly.

"I wonder what my son would make of his grand design
now," she muttered grimly. Speaking aloud helped distract from
the dry rub of her hips and knee joints, and the fog inside her
head. It took her several minutes, but eventually she made it to
the far end of the grounds, where she found that the zoo was
unlocked. There was nothing left to steal – nothing anyone would

want, anyway. Grizmare clomped her way inside, and, with the help of the broom, managed to force the door shut. Under her feet was the familiar, comforting bed of sawdust. The sweltering heat immediately gave way to the dark, dank atmosphere of the hall. Her nostrils filled with the earthy smells of dung and rotting fruit.

The pens rose high about the walls, reminding her of another dark room where obelises towered. That time, she had felt divided about what lay ahead. Today, despite the drugs in her system, she felt clearer in her intent. There was a depth of resolution and, alongside an acknowledgement of dread, a degree of peace.

In shuffling steps, she made her way to the one pen that remained occupied. The urine-soaked bedding inside hadn't been changed in weeks, not since the last keeper was sent away.

"Hello, old friend."

The tiger dog came curling out of the shadows. Its fur was mangy and dull, its ribs prominent beneath. There was still a muscular bulk to the creature's shoulders and flanks. Grizmare saw herself newly reflected in those amber eyes, as she had years before when Kali let the beasts loose.

This time around, the tiger dog was old, like her. But when the mouth fell slack it still revealed huge razor fangs. The beast looked ravenous.

Hands on the gate, Grizmare just had time to hear the door to the zoo slide open. It was the nun, tasked with keeping her caged.

"Ah, good," said Grizmare. "I always did like an audience."

With the nun's shrieks echoing through the silenced zoo, Grizmare opened the gate and stepped into the pen.

THIRTY- TWO

The desert stretched away like an ocean of smoked glass. Overhead, the moon was huge, as if Mama Sunstar herself had nudged it closer to the Earth. Mohab and the rest of the scouts he had assembled were a mile, no more, from camp and it was already apparent that the combination of the cold night air and their starved bodies would prove lethal. Geno lay fifty kilometres east, with not a single settlement in between. The geological activity below ground had sent the bulk of Bleekland's populace to the cities where buildings were designed to stay standing and there was comfort in numbers; Sister Eva had confided that much when she was alive. But, somehow, locked up and lost to the horrors of Abbandon, Mohab had dared to dream of an oasis sprung up beyond its walls. At the very least, he had hoped to find a clear plan evolving in his mind, telling him just what to do to lead his people across the desert. Geno would surely swallow them up. All folk had to do was tread lightly and avoid detection. Then they might make it through without being picked off again by the National Guard and imprisoned once more.

The desert stretched, the air sharp as knives. It made his face ache.

Now they were away from Abbandon, he could smell its atrocities. Living in camp, the nose became immune. But now he was experiencing the great sweep of the outside world, he was newly aware. The smell reminded him of what it was – a waste dump, an abattoir.

"We cannot cross the desert," he said, hating the words. "I didn't imagine the depth of cold outside the barracks. I didn't expect the dust to sit so high."

They all knew what it was that had added to the depths of sand underfoot. Rather than taking their weight the ground gave way, the dust coming halfway up their shins. It was the ashes from the furnaces, emptied out of the gates over the months.

"We could attempt to repair the walls. Barricade ourselves in…" It was a pitiful suggestion. A slew of bounce bombs from a single gunner would obliterate their defences and raze the camp to the ground. He cleared his throat. "We must return to camp, take more than our fair share from the larders in the guards' quarters. Build up enough strength to survive the journey."

Even as he said it, the memories of those first wild hours of freedom came flooding back. There had been no methodical assembly of food supplies and careful allocation of rations. There had been no rush to escape the slice-wire, or hunt down family members, or bury the deceased. There had only been the savage rush of hunger. Men fought over one another to gain access to the guards' mess hall. Cans were emptied over ravenous mouths, packets ripped open, their contents swallowed whole. Fruit was tipped and sucked and clawed over. Like wild beasts, they snarled and fought over butter sticks, dried beans, jerky… By the time the women and children made it through the winding corridor of the guard dome, the larders were three quarters devoured.

Mohab had tried to feast, but the contents of a bread satchel made his mouth ache and his stomach hurt. He made himself tear off the tiniest of pieces and suck until the bread became a palatable mash in his mouth. Others were less restrained. Everywhere, starving men gorged themselves sick. Within 12 hours, five new corpses in Abbandon belonged to men who had shocked their starving bodies into death by the mere act of eating.

Time had seen the inmates of the camp start to nose in at other locked rooms. All too many stayed inert in the same corner of a stinking bunk or patch of ashy ground out in the yard where they had fallen, exhausted after battle.

Mohab had barely the energy left to drag himself into action. Standing in the freezing desert, he knew it had taken every last trace of strength to hold his head up and tell the rest what to do. And now he was tired and feverish and cold, his limbs threatening to dissolve out from under him.

"What now?" said the men and women around him. "What now?"

"There's a haulage train at the horizon!" The lookout came falling over himself into camp – one of the younger, fitter men who still had meat on his bones. Mohab had set the man as a sentry. And now here he was, tumbling over his own feet with news and fear-widened eyes.

"You think it's a fresh deportation batch? Or a battalion of National Guard sent to burn the lot of us?" A woman with sharp eyebrows, like two birds in flight, stepped forward. Her name was Ebolyn and the first night they had been free, she had kissed the tears from Mohab's face.

Mohab had his arms folded as he nodded. "We knew this would happen." It was five days since their failed attempt to set out across the desert. Mohab had hoped for longer to recover before setting out again. He had no idea what level of reporting existed between Joltu and his superiors, and he realised it would not take long for a grand assault. But somehow he hadn't thought to consider the arrival of more prisoners.

"We arm ourselves with the rock ammo and pistols we recovered. Lay low north of the quarry. Take out the guards as they go to unlock the wagons."

"And what about the Vary inside?" Ebolyn slung her knitted fingers around the back of her neck. She sighed. "We cannot feed ourselves. The infirmary is empty, the factory stripped of anything worth having. We cannot support more livestock."

"*Livestock?*" Mohab repeated the word to himself. It had edges.

Ten minutes later, lying alongside the others in the rock dust and ashes above the quarry, Mohab was still contemplating their next move. They would take out the guards and then what? Send the wagons back the way they came? Unload the new prisoners and attempt to commandeer the wagons for their own escape?

Welcome the prisoners in and attempt a poor mimicry of the Vary slums in any one of the big cities – deprived of food or sanitation, and with the threat of a raid by the National Guard at any moment?

'You stitched me up, father!' he thought, feeling a throb inside his throat. 'I thought this job was all about telling stories, but apparently now I am meant to lead our people out of exile.'

He stayed low in the ashes. Rifle at his shoulder.

The caravan arrived at the battered gates, sending up great waves of dust on braking. Mohab struggled to breathe quietly. Blood pummelled inside his ears as the doors rolled back on one side of the first wagon. Figures emerged, holding their own rifles.

Mohab squinted against the blinding sunlight.

"We come in the name of the Resistance and by the grace of Mama Sunstar!" The shout rebounded off the desert. "We're here to help! Don't shoot, don't shoot. We're here to offer aid!"

Cautiously, like a creature coaxed from its shelter, Mohab was the first to rise.

A figure strode towards him, materialising into a woman. Well fed. Tall. Authoritative.

She stuck out a hand. "My name is 94. You must be the Speaker."

THIRTY-THREE

"The world is ending," said Ebolyn. Mohab saw a subtle beauty behind her sadness.

"This version, yes." Mohab watched out the open doors of the moving wagon. One gunner had already fallen out the sky and lay beached and broken a kilometre or so to the east. Overhead, another of the colossal craft came scudding through the atmosphere at speed, trailing filthy smoke. When the ship struck the ground, the whole wagon shook and jilted in the slipstream. The noise, even from a distance, was a sickening crunch of bio matter and moaning girders.

94 nodded towards the desert as warcraft continued to rain down. "The United Dominions found a way to attack the central energy stem of every gunner. They extricated the information during a very precious window of opportunity when the datastacks went dark." She glanced over at Mohab. "It was a script written by Lieutenant Kali Titian many years ago, after she located a core weakness in the stem as a bio-engineer recruit. It had never been made public, even when she released her manifesto." 94 grimaced. "I guess High Judge Titian's daughter couldn't quite decide which side she was really on after all! Luckily, her grandmother didn't think twice."

"Grizmare Titian?" Ebolyn shuddered. "I always thought she was as bad as her son."

94 stared out at the latest gunner streaking through the purpled dusk on its descent. "History will judge Grizmare and her granddaughter. For now, what I can tell you is that they mattered when it counted."

"The dust is getting up." Ebolyn narrowed her eyes against the grit. "We should close the doors."

Mohab nodded and, together, he and Ebolyn pulled the

doors shut on the downfall of an empire.

The wagon buffeted and settled once more. Mohab rested back against one of the long perches which ran along each wall. All around, his fellow Vary sat on the floor in groups, huddled close for warmth but mainly comfort. This time around, there was no slow gas to force the journey to pass in a haze of fear and nausea. Instead, they had time to sink down into fathomless dreams and to sleep at last.

94 came and stood alongside Mohab. She held up a pair of nick keys. "Why are you still wearing those?" She nodded towards Mohab's wrists where the ugly bands still dug in at his skin.

It was a good question. He had been quick to help the majority of the living out of those lethal manacles. But he hadn't got around to unlocking his own, which, when he thought about it now, struck him as a perverse kind of clinging on to the life he had been forced to live. "In the end, my father and I were linked by these, by what they came to represent for our people and how we spoke out against the suffering." He clasped his hands together in a sort of prayer and held them up, so the inside of each nick rested against the other, right over his pulse points. "I suppose I've been loath to take them off because then he will be gone, just another character in a story, and I will carry on."

94 nodded towards Ebolyn. "And are there reasons to carry on, Speaker? I'd hate to think any of us were solely defined by the abominations of our past. There can be so much judgement, so much terrible, terrible suffering, and that can be all there is to us. Or we can choose to move forward." She held out the nick key. "May I?"

Mohab nodded. 94 slotted the key into each nick in turn, released the hinge and opened up the band. She tossed the nicks down by their feet, leaving Mohab aware of the newly expose flesh of his wrists. He held his wrists up to the fire lamp overhead and, where the nicks had rested against his veins, marks had been left behind. Each was in the shape of a star.

"So what happens now?" He rubbed at the skin to bring the

circulation back.

"High Judge Titian has gone into hiding. The war is lost. The battle is won." 94 leaned against the perch, put her head back and closed her eyes. "Now you let the world know what happened here. You speak up and tell our story."

Beyond the wagon, Mohab could hear Bleekland's warcraft falling from the skies, while inside there was the low murmur of voices and a soft whistle of slipstreaming air, and, from somewhere, a man's gentle baritone singing, "Varber iubită, Louanne, Louanne…"

THIRTY-FOUR

Kali Titian was visited in the court jail once by her grandmother. With the irrefutable evidence against her presented, the defence argued a temporary insanity plea that she herself refuted, and the twelve judges and her father retired to discuss her sentence. Because, in reality, there was no debate over her guilt. She had admitted her crimes the instant her father came bellowing into his office and found her at his dataframe. She expected her father to have her executed on the spot; at the very least, for him to strike her down in a violent fit of rage. Instead, he stayed at the doorway, barring her attempt to flee the scene should she be so inclined, and called out for his personal guard. She was arrested on the spot and when she was led past her father, he refused to even look at her.

With the evidence in her trial laid bare, the judges were relishing their hour in the spotlight. There would be no swift sentencing, not when they could make her sweat it out while milking more interviews on the nation's data reels.

Kali, meanwhile, sat on her narrow bed in the cell, legs crossed, a plate of grey chuck leg and bean stew in her lap. She was lost in thought and pushing the chunks of meat around the plate with a fork when the main door to the cell block rolled aside and a guard entered. He walked stiffly ahead of a second, smaller figure. Kali immediately recognised her grandmother's shuffling gait and the distinctive rap-rap of her cane over the floor tiles.

Her stomach knotted. She hadn't seen Grizmare Titian in six months. Even before her arrest, her posting at Capital Hall in Nilreb had kept her from casual visits back to Geno. She hadn't been entirely sorry; her grandmother was a cantankerous old shrew with too much time on her hands, and who wanted for nothing and despised the fact.

But as Grizmare took a seat outside the cell, the cracking of her dry bones echoing off the cold walls, Kali found that she was almost moved to see a familiar face amongst so many strangers.

Grizmare picked at one nostril. "Well, girl. Aren't you the idiot?" Her rheumy eyes fastened on Kali through the glass-sheet.

"Hello, Granny. This is a long way for you to come. Was it a trip you made specially to insult me?"

Grizmare leaned back in the chair the guard had provided and showed her gums, laughing with the wild abandon Kali had always envied. "Oh, I haven't even the energy for real insults, Kali. You make it all far too easy, sitting there on your sad sack, eating slop and waiting on a death sentence."

"Well, take a good long look, Granny. I am here for your amusement." Kali forked the stew up into her mouth, cramming it in as if she had never tasted anything so good. Anything to keep from showing Grizmare true emotion!

"So that's how it is with you, hmm?" Grizmare rested the tip of her cane on the floor between her open legs and leaned her hands and chin on the handle. "Shall we not talk about what a fuck up you have made of things? Corrupting the datastacks and using High Judge Titian's own datafeed? Leaving your sticky DNA all over the office? Even having the audacity to just sit and wait around to be found out? What were you thinking, Kali? Were you even thinking?"

Kali forced down the mouthful. "I believe I was thinking clearer than at any other time in my life." She downed the water from a tin cup that made it taste faintly metallic. "I have seen you in the public gallery. You've heard all the evidence, listened to my version of events and the reason why I acted." She scooted off the bed and came to stand directly opposite Grizmare the other side of the glass-sheet. "The craziest thing, Granny, is that you have always abided the Vary far more than anyone else I know. You have always argued for their fair treatment. It's just that your voice has never counted, has it? Neither me nor your son ever heard a word you said, not really. You have always been ever so slightly irritating in your opinions, but nothing to take seriously."

"So you're going down that route? Attack me first before I can properly attack you. How very Bleek of you!" Grizmare shuffled in her seat and gave a couple of taps with her cane. "Very wise, Kali. Except you misunderstand my visit. I am not here to gloat. I am here to listen."

"To what? I have nothing new to say."

"To how you are feeling. To how you really are." Grizmare took a deep inhale and shuffled again, slightly restless and a little uncomfortable, like an old dog. "What can I do for you, Kali? Really."

Kali peered through the glass-sheet. Grizmare had always taken pains to raise Kali to be as independent as possible. Her favourite response whenever Kali asked for help or assistance was 'Learn to stand on your own two feet, child.'

"Am I standing on my own two feet now, Granny?" She held out her arms to the walls of her cell. "I thought I was being reasonable in my personal manifesto. Not confrontational, or anarchic. But just encouraging a little more political wrangling when it came to the Vary. Just encouraging of a little less death."

"But you have always loved death, Kali. Anytime a thing got in your way in life, you took it out. Remember old Jimney, my favourite maw cat when you were growing up? I know you poisoned him on purpose. And all those swallows shot from your bedroom window? Innocent little things. You loved to string them up on the fence opposite Mister Thatchett's house. I'd find them all pegged out, wing to wing. Left to rot in the sun."

Kali couldn't disagree. She had taken great pleasure in exercising her superior domain over weaker creatures. Ever since she was small, there had been something undeniably pleasurable about holding the power of life and death in her hands. It had made her feel uniquely invincible.

"God-like," she murmured.

"What's that?"

She cleared her throat and said louder, "To say whether a

person lives or dies, or even whether they are treated humanely and with dignity, or beaten down and broken – it's a god-like power. It makes you feel as if sunlight itself is flowing through your veins. Like you've power over air to breathe, water to drink, even whether another person gets to speak. It's addictive."

She heard a small hack of breath in the background behind her grandmother. For the first time, she noticed the eerie figure of a nun, head to toe in black and standing very still and statuesque.

"Granny! You've brought your own little piece of religion with you. Are you hoping I'll atone for my sins? Or do you want me to join the holy order and dedicate my wanton life to Lord Gothendore? Beg him to take me as his bride?"

"Nothing so trite! The nun is with me. She is my paid companion, because none of the rest of you fuckers chose to stick around!"

Kali nodded at the nun. The young woman nodded stiffly in return. She had the most intense, crystalline green eyes, in which Kali caught the slight flare of revulsion. It wasn't entirely surprising. Kali understood that she was the perfect embodiment of betrayal.

She brought her focus back to Grizmare. "I did enjoy sharing in my father's vision of a strong and holy Bleekland. But sometimes a person can see something they can never un-see and it can change them. I think, if you will indulge me, Granny, there is a very great difference between hunting sparrows and witnessing mile on mile of trenches filled with the putrefying remains of executed Vary. That, Granny, is a leap too far from humanity, even for a murderer like me. The choice was to stand by and do nothing, or open my eyes and ears and mouth to the suffering. Sometimes, if you want to go on calling yourself a human being, you must stand up and say 'This Must Stop!' We are not beasts, we are not monsters, but right this instant, we are behaving like them!"

She waited for Grizmare to offer some quip or fresh attack

against her sanity. Only, her grandmother just sat and stared through the glass-sheet. Grizmare's wrinkled eyes misted.

"I am sorry I cannot help you more, Kali, but I have already used up any influence I might have with my son begging for clemency. You are guilty, of course, mainly of stupidity, but you are still our flesh and blood. For the sake of your mother, I have written and asked your father to take the death sentence off the table. My ideal would be that you are placed under house arrest back with me in Geno. But your father is as stubborn as cat shit on a silk blouse!"

Grizmare might have said more, but the door to the cells opened once more and the guard returned.

"Who says time's up?" Grizmare had snapped, turning to the guard and holding up her cane to her line of sight like a rock rifle.

Kali would have liked to watch the guard squirm, but she was exhausted after a day in court and decided to let him off the hook.

"Granny, leave the man be. Our time is done." She leaned closer to the glass. She hadn't expected to feel any particular emotion towards the woman who had raised her. They had been apart for so many years now, and, before that, Grizmare Titian had seemed less of a mother substitute than a miniature dictator. Only now Grizmare struggled to her feet and, hooking her cane over an elbow, pressed her trembling old hands against the glass-sheet.

"You were my favourite thing," Grizmare said, her unexpected sweetness threatening to make Kali's legs buckle out from under her.

The old woman turned and, counting out each step with her cane, went out the door. The nun followed like a shadow. But then the young woman stopped at the last moment and, turning to Kali, pressed a hand to her chest, thumb and forefinger joined. Sign of Mama Sunstar.

"Thank you," mouthed the nun.

And then they were gone. The guard stepped out and there

was the sound of a key jangling in the lock again, and then silence.

Kali slouched back onto the bed. She mustn't feel, she told herself.

I mustn't feel...

She couldn't keep the pain at arms' length any longer. Smashing the plate of leftover stew aside, she sent its contents slamming into the wall of glass-sheet. The thin mattress and blanket – she tore at those too, slammed her fists into walls and kicked at the bed, which was bolted to the floor.

She collapsed then on the cold hard floor of the cell, sobbing and clutching her chest for breath. Tears fell, like long forgotten rain. She needed the whole fucking sacrifice to be worth something! All this emptying out of everything she had known and stood for. All this loss of the love she never needed until now. There had to be a purpose to it all! She had to have a purpose.

Two days later, Kali was brought before her father and the other twelve judges and sentenced to end her days in the Vary labour camp, Abanddon. As the words were spoken, Kali half-expected to hear a commotion from the public gallery and to hear her grandmother hollering for her release. In the end, though, the court room remained silent and Kali stayed facing forward with her back to the past.

ABOUT THE AUTHOR

Kim Lakin-Smith is a UK writer living in Stroud, Gloucestershire. Her science fiction, dark fantasy and horror short stories have appeared in various anthologies and magazines, including *Interzone, Black Static, The Mammoth Book of Ghost Stories by Women, Celebration: 50 Years of the BSFA, Solaris Rising, Hauntings,* the forthcoming *Once Upon A Parsec* anthology, and others. Her novel, *Cyber Circus*, was shortlisted for the British Fantasy Society Best Novel award and the British Science Fiction Association Best Novel award and she is a previous British Science Fiction Association Best Short Story nominee. Kim's non-fiction centres on issues of gender, sexuality and otherness.

AUTHOR'S THANKS

To Ian Whates – editor, publisher, and dear friend – for bearing with me through all of the incarnations of *Rise*. To Donna Scott, for helping me shape the story I wanted to tell. To Farah Mendlesohn, for her wise words. To Ren Warom, for keeping me going when I just wasn't sure. To Daniele Serra for his fabulous cover image. And to Del, my harshest critic and greatest fan, for boundless love and support.

More New Titles from NewCon Press

Once Upon a Parsec – Edited by David Gullen

Ever wondered what the fairy tales of alien cultures are like? For hundreds of years scholars and writers have collected and retold folk and fairy stories from around our world. They are not alone. On distant planets alien chroniclers have done the same. For just as our world is steeped in legends and half-remembered truths of the mystic and the magical, so are theirs. Now, for the first time, we can share some of these tales with you…

Maura McHugh – The Boughs Withered

Kim Newman provides the introduction for this, the debut collection from accomplished Irish author Maura McHugh. Twenty tales – four of them original to the volume – which represent the best strange visions from an award-winning writer of fiction, non-fiction, comic books and plays. A series of contemporary revelations and murky pasts that draw upon the author's Irish heritage and so much more.

Simon Morden – Bright Morning Star

A ground-breaking take on first contact from scientist and novelist Simon Morden. Sent to Earth to explore, survey, collect samples and report back to its makers, an alien probe arrives in the middle of a warzone. Witnessing both the best and worst of humanity, the AI probe faces situations that go far beyond the parameters of its programming, and is forced to improvise, making decisions that may well reshape the future of a world.

Soot and Steel – edited by Ian Whates

Stories that explore London's dark underbelly but also celebrate the city's character and charm; stories that beat to the rhythm of the capital's heart. Sinister tales, ghost stories, menacing thrillers and revealing vignettes; stories of the streets, the alleyways, the sewers, the rooftops and the underground, all steeped in the essence of London's urban community, its industrial heritage, the docks, Victoriana, the Blitz, and beyond.

www.newconpress.co.uk

Immanion Press
Purveyors of Speculative Fiction

Love in a Time of Dragons & Other Rare Tales by Tanith Lee

'A time of dragons' might conjure the image of a fantastical medieval world, with knights dark and light, clever sorcerers and witches, doomed kings and charmed innocents. Love might seem to be very much a part of such a world, where passions rage and honour fires the blood. But the truth is that dragons come in many guises, even into modern times. As does love. In this volume of rare and uncollected tales, Tanith Lee takes up her sword to face the dragons – not only to slay them, but to see their stories reflected in the blade. For be sure they each have one to tell... ISBN: 978-1-912815-02-9 £11.99, $15.99 pbk

The Lord of the Looking Glass by Fiona McGavin

The author has an extraordinary talent for taking genre tropes and turning them around into something completely new, playing deftly with topsy-turvy relationships between supernatural creatures and people of the real world. 'Post Garden Centre Blues' reveals an unusual relationship between taker and taken in a twist of the changeling myth. 'A Tale from the End of the World' takes the reader into her developing mythos of a post-apocalyptic world, which is bizarre, Gothic and steampunk all at once. Following in the tradition of exemplary short story writers like Tanith Lee and Liz Williams, Fiona has a vivid style of writing that brings intriguing new visions to fantasy, horror and science fiction. ISBN: 978-1-907737-99-2, £11.99, $17.50 pbk

Songs to Earth and Sky by Storm Constantine and others

Some of the best Wraeththu Mythos writers explore the seasonal festivals of the year, dreaming up new customs, new myths, new dehara – the gods of Wraeththu. From the silent, snow-heavy forests of Megalithican mountains, through the lush summer fields of Alba Sulh, into the hot, shimmering continent of Olathe, this book brings powerful spirits and landscapes to vivid life. Nine new tales, including a novella, a novelette and a short story from Storm herself, and stories from *Wendy Darling, Nerine Dorman, Suzanne Gabriel, Fiona Lane* and *E. S. Wynn*. ISBN 978-1-907737-84-8 £11.99 $15.50 pbk

www.immanion-press.com
info@immanion-press.com